From Megan Maitland's Diary

Dear Diary,

I can't believe Mother's Day is right around the corner. Obviously we cherish the holiday at Maitland Maternity, but Mother's Day holds special meaning for me this year. My firstborn son is alive! As a mother, I'm overjoyed that Connor is here in Austin, but I tremble to think of the ramifications for my family and Maitland Maternity when the truth comes out.

Still, I'm a lucky woman to be able to enjoy all my children. Some aren't as lucky. My heart still aches for Mary-Jane Potter. She was so excited to be the surrogate mother for her best friend's baby, and now that woman will never see her child. What a tragedy!

News like that reminds me to count my blessings. Even my darling Jake is back in town, although in typical Jake fashion, he's come bearing trouble. I suppose he wouldn't be Jake otherwise. The fact is, I wouldn't change a thing about any of my children. They weren't put on this earth to make my life easy, but every day they fill my heart with love.

Dear Reader,

There's never a dull moment at Maitland Maternity! This unique and now world-renowned clinic was founded twenty-five years ago by Megan Maitland, widow of William Maitland, of the prominent Austin, Texas, Maitlands. Megan is also matriarch of an impressive family of seven children, many of whom are active participants in the everyday miracles that bring children into the world.

When our series began, the family was stunned by the unexpected arrival of an unidentified baby at the clinic—unidentified, except for the claim that the child is a Maitland. Who are the parents of this child? Is the claim legitimate? Will the media's tenacious grip on this news damage the clinic's reputation? Suddenly, rumors and counterclaims abound. Women claiming to be the child's mother materialize out of the woodwork! How will Megan get at the truth? And how will the media circus affect the lives and loves of the Maitland children—Abby, the head of gynecology, Ellie, the hospital administrator, her twin sister, Beth, who runs the day care center, Mitchell, the fertility specialist, R.J., the vice president of operations—even Anna, who has nothing to do with the clinic, and Jake, the black sheep of the family?

Please join us each month as the mystery of the Maitland baby unravels, bit by enticing bit, and book by captivating book!

Marsha Zinberg,
Senior Editor and Editorial Co-ordinator, Special Projects

VICKI LEWIS THOMPSON

Her Best Friend's Baby

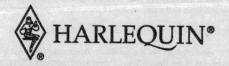

HARLEQUIN®

TORONTO • NEW YORK • LONDON
AMSTERDAM • PARIS • SYDNEY • HAMBURG
STOCKHOLM • ATHENS • TOKYO • MILAN • MADRID
PRAGUE • WARSAW • BUDAPEST • AUCKLAND

HARLEQUIN BOOKS
225 Duncan Mill Road, Don Mills,
Ontario, Canada M3B 3K9

ISBN 0-373-65070-1

HER BEST FRIEND'S BABY

A Note From The Author

I remember my first pregnancy as a time of great anticipation. My husband and I painted the nursery, bought baby furniture, debated names. My changing body was a source of wonder to us both.

Mary-Jane Potter has none of that, because she's carrying a baby for her best friend. No nursery plans, no name discussions and worst of all, no sweet man to rub her aching back. I found myself becoming very emotionally involved with Mary-Jane's plight. I was immensely relieved when it looked as if she might have the support of a wonderful man, after all.

Morgan Tate's that special kind of guy—a man who loves children. Plus, he's a pediatrician, so Mary-Jane's in good hands. *Very* good hands. Add to that deep brown eyes and great buns, and you have the perfect antidote to pregnancy doldrums. Yes, Mary-Jane will be just fine....

Vicki Lewis Thompson

To every waiter or waitress who has ever warmed up my coffee, made sure the food was cooked right, cautioned me about a hot plate and smiled no matter what. Please know that along with my tip, I leave my gratitude for a job well done in a world that doesn't always notice.

CHAPTER ONE

TWO WHOLE DAYS OFF.

"Freedom!" Mary Jane Potter closed the door of her rented town house and danced a little jig in the foyer. "You and me, babe." She gave her tummy a pat. "We're gonna pamper ourselves, that's what we're gonna do."

Pulling off the scrunchy that held her hair, she toed off her sneakers as she walked toward the answering machine on her writing desk. "Sleeping in, reading trashy magazines, and then, if the urge moves us, we'll row around Town Lake, or maybe drive out in the country to see what's left of the bluebonnets."

She punched the message button to rewind the tape on the answering machine. "One thing we're definitely *not* doing is anything that involves standing, or catering to people who think they're God's gift. Not that a lot of folks do that at the diner," she added, not wanting the baby to absorb a poor impression of Austin Eats. No telling how much information got through to the kidlet, but lately she'd started playing classical music when she was home. Couldn't hurt.

Right at the moment, though, she was in the mood for the Smashing Pumpkins. The doctor had warned her that she'd have some mood swings, and lately she'd been a wee bit depressed. She didn't do depressed, which was why she intended to have some fun in the next couple of days. Careful fun, of course. Nothing to jeopardize this baby girl she was carrying next to her heart.

The answering machine finally stopped rewinding and clicked to play.

Hey, girlfriend.

Mary Jane smiled. The sound of her good buddy Lana's voice could always lift her spirits.

We just got a new shipment of baby duds at the shop. I know you're scheduled for some days off. Come on by and take a look. You'll positively drool. If it's not too crazy around here, maybe we can do lunch.

Lunch sounded great to Mary Jane. She'd turned into a regular chowhound now that the morning sickness was gone. But looking at baby clothes…that might add to her depression.

As the machine beeped through several hang-up calls, she thought about whether she should have accepted Arielle and Morgan's offer to pay for a couple of counseling sessions. Mary Jane had laughed and said she didn't need no stinkin' shrink. And she hadn't needed one. Then.

When she'd agreed to be a surrogate mom, she'd been so sure nothing would make her happier than to carry this baby for Arielle, the woman who had been a big sister, mother substitute and best friend in the entire world. Mary Jane owed Arielle, big time. Doing something this major was the only way she'd ever settle that debt. She'd felt honored to have the chance.

But now, five months into the program, some other inconvenient emotions were getting her in trouble. Sometime after that first ultrasound, when she'd learned the baby was a girl, she'd begun having conversations with her. That had probably been a big mistake. Talking to the baby had started her thinking about how this little sweetheart would live in New York once she was born, and Mary Jane had no intention of ever leaving Austin.

That depressed her. Of course she had only herself to blame. She'd known from the beginning that once she turned the baby over to Arielle and Morgan, that was the end except for visits. Even if she flew to New York three or four times a year, which would be a lot, really, she'd still have only a tiny slice of this baby's life to enjoy. She'd be pretty much a stranger to the kid for the first couple of years, considering how fast young babies could forget people between visits.

She wanted more than that. And wanting more made her feel darned ungrateful.

As if Arielle and Morgan could read her traitorous thoughts long-distance from New York, Morgan's voice came on her answering machine.

Mary Jane.

He sounded hoarse. Probably a head cold, Mary Jane thought. The weather wasn't so good there, and as a pediatrician Morgan had his share of germy kids breathing on him. Plus he worked long hours. Both he and Arielle seemed consumed with work.

Mary Jane liked Morgan Tate, but he sure was anal. In spite of his hectic schedule he'd found time to make constant phone calls in the past five months to remind her to exercise, take her vitamins, watch her diet, get her rest, yada, yada, yada.

Once after a particularly lengthy session, Arielle had come on the line. With a chuckle in her voice, she'd begged Mary Jane to be tolerant of her dear husband. Being a prospective daddy *and* a pediatrician had kicked Morgan into overdrive.

So here he was again, ready to give her another tip even if he was sick as a dog. There was a long pause on the tape, during which Mary Jane pictured Morgan covering the mouthpiece of the phone and sneezing his head off. Good thing germs couldn't get through the phone lines.

Mary Jane, he finally said again, and he was in no better shape than the first time. *I have something—*

Well, he certainly did have something. The flu bug from hell, apparently. She listened for him to finish his message. Instead she heard a funny noise. It could have been Morgan clearing his throat, but it almost sounded like…a sob?

Then came a click, as if he'd hung up. There were no more messages.

A chill went down Mary Jane's spine. She refused to acknowledge it as being more than her funky state of mind.

There was a perfectly logical explanation for that weird message. Probably Morgan had called in the middle of a busy day to tell her he was sending a truckload of the latest mega-super-colossal prenatal vitamins he'd just discovered.

She could picture the whole scene, having paid one quick visit to Morgan's bustling office when she was in New York. Right in the middle of trying to call her he'd had a bad coughing fit and had decided to hang up and try later. Then Mrs. Very Pregnant had suddenly decided to deliver triplets, and he'd been called to the hospital to attend to the babies.

Glancing at the clock, she figured the time difference. Morgan and Arielle wouldn't be home yet. She'd put a message on their machine, anyway, so one of them could call her tonight and tell her what Morgan had wanted. Although Mary Jane complained to Lana about his fussing, she kind of liked it. Arielle and Morgan were the only people who had ever fussed over her.

It wasn't only because of the pregnancy, either. Arielle had always treated her as a precious and unique human being, and Morgan had picked up on that same behavior in no time. Mary Jane wished they could see their way clear to live in Austin, but Morgan had his practice in New York, and Arielle had made it clear that she loved the excitement of living in the heart of Manhattan.

Mary Jane punched in their number and sure enough got Arielle's voice on the welcome message.

Hi. You've reached Arielle and Morgan Tate. Please leave a message and we'll get back to you as soon as possible. If this is an emergency, you can reach us at our pager numbers.

Mary Jane listened to the pager numbers, which she also knew by heart, and wondered if she should try Arielle's. Morgan obviously wasn't free or he would have called again. But she hesitated. Arielle had said something about getting ready for a huge show for a big-name artist. Mary Jane didn't want to interrupt her in the middle of that.

Besides, a call on the pager might make Arielle think

something was wrong with the baby. So instead she left a cheery message on the machine, asked them to call her when they got a chance and hung up.

Then she turned on her CD player and headed for the kitchen to grab some eats. She'd call Lana later, after she'd decided whether or not looking at baby clothes would make her want to cry.

For the next two hours she tried to forget about Morgan's phone call, but she couldn't settle down to anything. The tabloids she'd bought to amuse herself didn't seem as exciting as they had on the rack, and she couldn't find the right music to suit her mood, either.

She prowled around upstairs looking for projects, but didn't feel moved to give herself a manicure or sew on a button. Even her favorite hobby, crocheting, didn't intrigue her tonight. She went downstairs again, watered all her plants and picked off any yellow leaves, but that didn't take long. Finally she plopped down on the living room sofa with the remote. She then proceeded to channel surf and make way too many trips into the kitchen for more snacks.

Good thing Morgan couldn't see what she was eating, she thought as she popped a cherry Jolly Rancher into her mouth. Once that was gone, she chewed on a carrot stick to ease her conscience.

The phone remained silent, and her restlessness grew. She walked to the small table that held the phone and answering machine to replay Morgan's message. Then she ran it again and turned up the volume, trying to decide what that last noise had been. The more she played it, the more it *did* sound like a sob.

Damn, now she was getting paranoid. If only she knew someone connected to Morgan and Arielle, someone she could call on a very casual basis to make sure everything was okay. She could think of no one. Arielle's parents had died when she was a teenager, which was one of the reasons she'd taken the job as nanny to Mary Jane all those years ago. As for Morgan's parents, Mary Jane had never met them and doubted she ever would. Arielle had admitted her in-laws weren't in favor of the surrogate mother project.

Against her better judgment, Mary Jane called the New York apartment again and left another message, this one even cheerier than the first, so they wouldn't think something was wrong.

An hour later she finally gave in and put a message on each of their pagers, but she began by assuring them nothing was wrong with either her or the baby. She made a joke that her hormones were to blame for all these calls. But she emphasized that she wanted a return call, no matter how late the hour.

Until she found out that all was well in New York, she wasn't going to have a very good night. She'd postponed calling Lana, postponed going to the store to stock up on food, postponed a long soak in the tub. No doubt she was making herself crazy for nothing, but the sick feeling in her stomach wouldn't go away no matter how she tried to distract herself.

And still the phone didn't ring.

Finally she decided to get ready for bed. Damn Morgan for calling her like that, anyway. If she didn't hear from one of them, she was going to have a tough time sleeping, which wasn't good for the baby. She'd probably mention that to Morgan next time she talked to him. *Hey, Morgan, you know all those lectures about getting enough sleep? Then stop leaving me weird messages with no follow-up call. I didn't sleep a wink that night!*

That should get him. He hated any hint that she wasn't in peak pregnancy mode. Stripping off all her clothes, she posed sideways in front of the mirror. Yep. Definitely preggers now.

She spread her hands over her stomach. "How're you doing in there, sweetie? Which did you prefer, the Jolly Ranchers or the carrot sticks? Like I don't know, you bad girl. Just like your moth—" She caught herself. Not a good thing to say. Arielle would be her mother, and Arielle didn't eat candy.

Mary Jane cupped her smallish breasts and decided they were bigger these days, too. Of course, how her breasts reacted was of no consequence, since she'd never breast-feed this kid. That was another thing that had started bothering her. Well, she'd have to get over it.

With a sigh she pulled on the oversize pink T-shirt that had the arrow pointing down to the words Baby Girl. Until a couple of weeks ago, the arrow hadn't had much to point out. But she was finally bulging, and because she was small-framed and on the skinny side to begin with, she'd soon look like a watermelon smuggler.

As she brushed her teeth, she decided to ask Lana to take a few more Polaroids of what they'd begun calling The Belly to send to Arielle. Come to think of it, maybe she should organize a girls' night out instead of meeting Lana for lunch. They could all catch a movie, like old times.

That was assuming she and Lana could pry Beth and Ellie away from their love nests with their new hubbies. Mary Jane had always known that she and her three friends wouldn't be bachelor girls hanging out together forever, but she hadn't expected to lose two out of four to the holy bonds of matrimony so quickly—Ellie over the New Year and Beth just last month. But then, Beth and Ellie were twins, so having them get married so close together made a kind of crazy sense.

Mary Jane wasn't sure if she counted as a bachelor girl anymore, either, now that she was PG. For one thing, she'd taken herself out of the dating scene for the duration. No point in trying to explain the situation to some guy. As luck would have it, she'd never felt more interested in sex than she did now, right when she'd decided to forgo the pleasure. From her reading she'd discovered that was common for pregnant ladies, and apparently she was a textbook case.

So. Ready for bed and still no phone call. She padded downstairs barefoot and toured the house, making sure that she'd turned off lights and appliances. In her distracted state, she might have forgotten something.

She stared at the answering machine and picked the phone

up to check the dial tone. "I tell you, baby, we're giving those people a piece of our minds when they finally—"

The doorbell rang.

Her heartbeat quickened as she glanced at the digital clock on the TV. Nearly midnight. Hardly anyone she knew would show up unannounced at midnight. Maybe Lana. Lana might be silly enough to ring her doorbell at midnight, but that was the only person she could imagine standing on her small front porch. Damn, were her friends out to scare her to death today?

She snapped on a light before walking to the door. Then she stood on tiptoe to peer through the peephole.

Morgan.

The breath went out of her as she twisted the dead bolt latch. She was nearly crying by the time she pulled the door open. Gasping, she stared at him.

Unshaven. Eyes red. Clothes wrinkled. Trench coat hanging open as if he didn't have the energy to button it.

She wanted to slam the door. Whatever he'd come to her door to tell her, she didn't want to hear it. She never wanted to hear it. *Mary Jane. I have something—* She began to shake.

His mouth opened, but no words came out.

Don't say it, she wanted to scream, but she couldn't speak. No. No. This was a nightmare. She'd gone to bed, and now she was having a bad, bad dream. The worst kind of dream. *Wake up, Mary Jane.*

His mouth opened. His words slurred. "She's de—"

"No!" Mary Jane hurled herself at him, beating her fists against his chest. "Don't you say that!" she screamed. "Don't you ever say that!"

Tears pouring down his face, Morgan took the blows as if he couldn't feel them. Then he wrapped his arms around her, pulling her tight against him as she screamed, and screamed, and screamed some more.

She struggled, trying to get away from him, away from what he was trying to tell her. He wrestled her inside the house and still he wouldn't let her go.

"Listen to me," he shouted, his voice raw as he kicked the door shut. "Arielle—"

"No!" She fought him. If she could get away and go upstairs to her bedroom, this nightmare would be over. She would wake up, and tomorrow Lana would take Polaroids of The Belly, and they'd send them to—

"...a wreck," he said, gasping as he crushed her against him. "Oh, God, Mary Jane. Don't do this." He began to sob. "Don't do this, Mary Jane. Please." He sank to his knees, pulling her down with him. "Help me."

She stopped struggling. With a wild, keening cry she wrapped her arms around him, pressing his head to her chest as if his tears could somehow stop the pain that burned there. She rocked back and forth, clutching his head with one hand and his heaving shoulders with the other.

"It's a mistake," she whispered. "Somebody made a mistake."

He shook his head and continued to sob.

"A mistake," she insisted again. "A m-mistake. A—" Then her throat closed and she bowed her head over his, pressing her open mouth against his hair to stifle her cries.

"The baby...is all...I have." He gulped for breath and held her tighter. "All I have left."

This couldn't be happening. She tried to escape to some faraway place, but his words kept coming, dragging her back to the pain.

His voice was toneless, muffled against her breast. "She was on her way...to the airport. To get...that artist. Raining...slick...she...skidded. It was instant."

The blood roaring in her ears was loud but not loud enough. She heard what he said. She ached all over. "I don't believe you."

"I don't believe me, either. But it's true." He clutched her tighter. "It's true."

"No."

"It happened yesterday. No. The day before. I...don't know anymore."

Arielle. She started to get up. "We need to go."

"Why?" He held her in place. "She's gone." He broke down again. "Oh, God. G-gone."

"No!" She tried to pry herself out of his grip. "We have to do something. She needs…" She searched for the words, couldn't make herself say them. "A…tribute."

He lifted his head, his face twisted with anguish. "She didn't want that," he whispered hoarsely. "She told me…after we got married. If she died, she wanted no funeral. Nothing."

And then Mary Jane knew this horrible moment was real. A steel band of grief tightened around her chest. Arielle *had* always said that she didn't believe in any of that. A person should be allowed to slip quietly out of this life, she'd said, without making such an embarrassingly big deal out of it. Mary Jane had thought that very sophisticated, very evolved. Now it made her furious.

"How could she?" she cried. "How could she leave and not let us…not give us a chance to…"

"She didn't think how it would be." Morgan reached up and brushed his knuckles over her wet cheeks. His voice rasped in the stillness. "How it would be for us."

Mary Jane stared at him for a long time. Her mind didn't seem to want to work. "What should we do now?"

"I don't know."

She'd never felt so empty in her life, or so chilled and weary, as if she'd been forcing her way through a violent storm. He looked as if he felt the same way, as if he hadn't slept since… She still couldn't say it to herself. Maybe tomorrow she could say it. Or the next day. When she wasn't so battered.

"You need to rest," she said finally.

"I've tried. Can't sleep."

But he would collapse soon. She could see that. "Come upstairs and lie down. I'll stay with you. Maybe then you'll sleep."

"You need your sleep, too. For the baby."

She couldn't imagine going to sleep now, but she

wouldn't tell him that and upset him even more. "I'll try to sleep, too."

"Good."

"Tomorrow we'll think about what to do next."

He nodded. Slowly he stood and helped her to her feet. Supporting each other like war casualties, they made their way up the stairs.

In her bedroom, Morgan stripped down to his T-shirt and shorts with mechanical detachment and climbed into bed. She left the light on as she crawled in beside him. For the first time since she'd been four years old she was afraid of the dark.

He pulled the covers to his chin. "I can't seem to stop shaking."

"Me, either."

As if by mutual agreement they turned and scooted into each other's arms, holding each other close.

Fine tremors ran through him, as if he had a fever, and his bristly chin scraped her cheek. "I tried to call," he said.

"I know." Not minding his scratchy beard, she snuggled closer, needing the body contact while she tried to keep her own shakes under control, tried to get warm.

"That was stupid. Trying to tell you on the machine. I wasn't thinking."

"It's okay." She wanted to rewind the day and go back to that golden moment before she'd played her messages. That moment when she'd been excited about two days off. She would work every day of her life if she could make this not be true.

"It's not okay. What if...what if the shock of hearing it on the phone...what if something had happened to the baby?"

She squeezed her eyes shut and clenched her teeth against the wail of despair that strained at her throat. *Arielle's baby.* And the little girl was Arielle's, in every sense except that she would develop in Mary Jane's womb. And now Arielle would never see her daughter.

A heavy steel door seemed to have slammed, separating

Mary Jane from the woman she loved, the woman she would do anything for. Now she could do nothing. Nothing. "Oh, Morgan." Her voice was thick with tears. "I wanted so much to give her this baby."

"I know," he said roughly. "The baby is all that's kept me going."

"Oh, Morgan." She began to cry again, and so did he. They held each other desperately, shuddering with anguish.

He choked out the word *baby* and put his hand over her stomach.

"The baby... Arielle's still here," she said, crying.

"Thank God." He kissed her hair, her wet cheek. "Thank God, we still have the baby."

She hugged him close as tears streamed down. "Yes."

"The baby." He kissed her throat between choked sobs.

"It's okay." She needed to comfort him, needed it more than anything in the world. She pressed his head to her breast. "It's okay, Morgan. Everything will be okay."

"Oh, God." He rubbed his damp, bearded face against her breasts, almost as a baby might. "I need to feel...." He slipped his hand under the hem of her T-shirt and flattened it against her belly. His howl of misery echoed in the small room. *"Arielle!"*

Her heart broke into a million pieces. And she understood what she'd never wanted to know, that death and birth are spokes of the same wheel. Instincts older than time moved within her. Laying her hand over his, she guided it down between her thighs.

"She's here," she murmured.

He lifted his head and looked into her eyes.

"Here." A wisdom handed down through the ages urged her to open her thighs. A wound this deep could only be healed with the ultimate bonding of man and woman. "Come to me."

Moving like a sleepwalker, he held her gaze as he discarded his shorts and moved over her.

They came together smoothly, as if they'd been making love to each other for years. He said nothing as he thrust again and again into her, his teeth clenched against the sobs racking his body.

Concentrating on his face, she clutched his shoulders and rode the crest of the wave carrying her toward the only salvation they could find tonight. He seemed to understand it, too. As they neared the crest, the despair in his eyes gave way to a new light. At the moment before they climaxed, she drew strength from that light. Then she tumbled with him into chaos, bearing with her the faint yet steady glow of hope.

CHAPTER TWO

MORGAN AWOKE with a sense of well-being. He loved waking up with Arielle tucked in close beside him like this, especially after a night of—

Nausea washed over him, and he scrambled out of bed as if it were full of a million snakes. Snatching up his pants, he held them over his nakedness as he fought the gorge rising in his throat. What had he done?

Mary Jane turned toward him, a smile on her lips, her eyes still dazed with sleep. Then she focused on him.

He watched in horrified fascination as reality replaced fantasy in her blue eyes. He knew exactly what she was going through.

"I'm sorry," he said, his voice rusty and coarse. What an asinine thing to say. Sorry didn't begin to cover it. He couldn't imagine how he could ever make up for what he'd done last night.

She swallowed and kept staring at him, her gaze bleak.

"Say something," he pleaded. "Call me names. Tell me I'm the worst sort of slime ball you've ever come across. I deserve whatever rotten things you want to say about me."

She squeezed her eyes shut. "Why? I'm the one who threw myself at you like some—"

"No! It is *not* your fault. You were upset! I hit you with the news, and then I..." He couldn't bear to think of what he'd done. Unforgivable.

She opened her eyes and sat up, still wearing the pink sleep shirt he hadn't bothered to remove before he took advantage of her. Arielle had sent her that to wear once they'd seen the pictures from the first ultrasound. And now he had profaned that cute, silly T-shirt.

God, she was so young. He'd never seen her like this, flushed with sleep, her hair a tousled riot of curls falling to her shoulders. Arielle once said Mary Jane's hair was the color of maple syrup, which was appropriate, because Mary Jane was so incredibly sweet. Morgan closed his eyes, awash with pain and shame. And damn his soul to hell, he wanted her. Still. Stirring like a dark secret, desire taunted him with his worthlessness.

"I knew what I was doing," she said in a not-quite-steady voice.

His eyes flew open. "You most certainly did not! You were carried away by the news and your fluctuating hormones, which is perfectly understandable, especially at your age. But there's no excuse for me, a thirty-one-year-old man who's supposed to be in control of himself."

Her back stiffened. "What do you mean by that crack about my age? You sound as if I'm a mere child!"

"I consider twenty-two pretty damn young!" He wasn't going to tell her that this morning she looked younger than that, which made the heat within him even more reprehensible. "That was one thing that bothered me about this whole pregnancy. Physically you're a perfect age for bearing a child, but mentally—"

"What a crock! You don't know a damn thing about my mental age. I have to say, Morgan Tate, you are a real pr— uh, prude."

"Go ahead and use the first word you thought of," he said. "It fits." He'd much rather have her anger than the bleakness he'd seen in her eyes when she first woke up. He'd probably shattered her illusions forever, but she was trying to pretend she was worldly enough to handle it. He'd never loathed himself more than he did at this moment.

She whipped out of bed. "Go ahead and beat yourself up about last night if you want. I don't intend to do that, because I knew exactly what I was doing, and it seemed like the best thing for both of us at the time. Maybe it was wrong." She sent him a challenging look. "But it's done. Now I'm going to go take a shower."

"Mary Jane, it will never, ever happen again."

"I wouldn't expect it to." She drew herself up a little taller, which still wasn't very big. She couldn't be more than five-three, max. "Especially since you consider me such an infant. There's a half bath downstairs if you want to use it." Then she marched into her bathroom like royalty and shut the door.

He wanted her so much he nearly groaned aloud. He was a pig, not worth someone putting a bullet through his head. His wife had been dead two days. Until Mary Jane had taken him into her warm body, he'd been as good as dead, too. She had saved him, pulled him from the black pit of hell, and he yearned for her with an unholy fierceness.

But she would never know.

MARY JANE STOOD under the shower and let the hot water pour over her head. She wondered if a person could drown in the shower if they breathed in the water. It was a tempting thought, but it probably wouldn't work. You had to be pretty determined to drown yourself, like the guy who walked into the ocean in that old movie *A Star is Born*.

Besides, even if she started to drown, there was a doctor in the house. He'd revive her. Yes, there was a doctor in the house. An embarrassed doctor who thought he'd forced himself on an innocent young woman. He'd turned a thing of beauty into something ugly.

It was right, what she'd done last night. She clenched her fists and raised her face to the hard spray. The right thing. If he couldn't understand that, then to hell with him.

Except that she wanted him to understand it. She wanted him to see that last night had been her last gift to Arielle, her attempt to take care of the man Arielle had loved so much. Arielle would have understood. Mary Jane would never have allowed last night to happen that way if she hadn't believed, deep inside, that Arielle would have been okay with it.

Well, if she didn't intend to drown herself in the shower,

which she would never do anyway because she had the baby to consider, then she might as well stop stalling and wash up.

As she moved the washcloth over her body, her nerve endings hummed in response. Her heart might feel like a hunk of lead, but her body was saying thank-you for the favor of a little loving. She'd only had two serious boyfriends in her life. One had been a good lover but a terrible conversationalist, and she'd discovered how important it was to her to be able to talk to a man when they'd stopped kissing for a little while. So the second relationship had started with lots of conversation. Great conversation. And he'd turned out to be a dud in bed.

According to Lana, finding the combo of a good talker and a good lover was definitely the old story of looking for a needle in a haystack. And Lana, being twenty-six, had four more years of experience than Mary Jane, so she knew all about needles and haystacks. Lana said some women finally settled on which was more important, the body connection or the brain connection, and went with that.

Mary Jane had never had the guts to ask Arielle if she got both when she married Morgan. Arielle had been so enthusiastic about what a great *person* Morgan was, not mentioning his body, that Mary Jane had concluded the brain connection was the main thing. And yet...*powerful, smooth strokes... feeling complete...rising, reaching together.*

Shaking her head, Mary Jane put the image out of her mind. It could have been a lucky accident that she and Morgan had been so in tune last night. One time didn't count. Morgan and Arielle had likely connected primarily on the mental level. After all, Arielle was extremely smart, and she'd once said sex wasn't the most important consideration in a husband. Mary Jane remembered how she'd laughed and argued with Arielle about that. But Arielle had stuck to her guns. She...

She was gone.

Stuffing a washcloth over her mouth to hide the noise, Mary Jane cried under the shower until the water turned cold.

WHILE GETTING DRESSED, she could hear noise downstairs in the kitchen—the faucet going on and off, the refrigerator door closing and cabinet doors banging shut. She could guess what Morgan was up to. He was checking to see what she'd been eating. Wonderful. She'd planned to stock up on fresh veggies today. Her supply was pretty much gone.

She wondered if he'd found the brownie mix in the cupboard or noticed the box of doughnuts sitting on top of the refrigerator with one stale raised glazed left in it. She'd left the bag of Jolly Ranchers right out on the counter.

Well, too bad. She would not be treated like a wayward child in her own house. Glancing at herself in denim overalls and a T-shirt as she passed the dresser mirror, she realized that's exactly what she looked like. Damn.

Quickly she rummaged through her drawers and pawed through the clothes in her closet, looking for something more sophisticated. Finally she gave up. Unless she planned to parade downstairs in the silky silver number she'd worn on New Year's, she was SOL. The silver dress wouldn't fit anymore, anyway.

She should probably do something with her hair. Freshly washed, it curled and cavorted everywhere. But she had to tame her hair for work, and after six days of that she was sick of tying it back. Screw it.

She should put on shoes. Otherwise she'd appear in the kitchen barefoot and pregnant. Smiling grimly, she slipped her feet into a pair of leather mules, took a deep breath and went downstairs.

Morgan sat in her sunny little kitchen nook making a list on the back of a paper sack. With the dark stubble on his chin and the sleeves of his white dress shirt rolled back, he looked like a gangster, or maybe a pirate. He sure didn't look like a respectable New York City pediatrician.

He glanced up when she walked into the kitchen. "We need to go to the store, but first I'll take you to breakfast. There's nothing decent to eat here."

She wasn't hungry, but she'd deal with that question later. "I was going to—" She caught herself as the words came out sounding more belligerent and defensive than she wanted them to. Clearing her throat, she started again. "I was planning to shop today," she said quietly. "I just got off six straight days at work."

"Six days straight?" He looked scandalized. "You're still at the diner, right?"

"Yes."

"We have to do something about that. Six days straight is criminal. Who's your boss? I want to talk to—"

"Hold it!" So she sounded belligerent. She couldn't help it. He wasn't going to waltz in here and take over her life. "You are so not going to talk to Shelby Lord! She asked me to work an extra day as a special favor, and she's *very* concerned about my health, if you must know. I told her I would be fine with it, and I *am* fine with it." She'd never admit that the last day had been more tiring than she'd expected.

He tossed the pen he'd been using on the table and pushed back his chair. Standing, he ran his fingers through his hair and glanced at her. "You may be fine with it, but hours and hours on your feet are not the best thing for the baby. Why do you insist on continuing to work there, when we've offered to subsidize you so that you could quit?"

Pain shot through her and she stared at him, wondering if he realized he'd just used the word *we*. There was no *we* anymore. She saw the exact moment his mistake registered. His brown eyes clouded and he looked away, swallowing several times.

Watching him struggle with his grief, she quickly lost her anger. "I keep my job because I like it," she said softly. "I know waitressing doesn't seem like a career to you, but I have a good time helping customers, at least most of the time. All of us weren't meant to be white-collar workers."

He shook his head, but he didn't look at her. Instead he pretended great interest in birds gathered at the feeder in her tiny back patio. "I didn't mean that," he murmured. "You may think I'm some sort of elitist snob, but I'm not."

"The truth is I don't know you very well, Morgan." She thought of the way they'd come together last night, the knowing that had taken place on an elemental level, and wondered if she knew him better than anyone else on earth.

He cleared his throat and glanced at her, his eyes moist. "I guess you don't know me. There were those few days before the wedding, and then the last visit, for the procedure."

She nodded. "Arielle kept saying the two of you would visit Austin, but you never came."

"No. She really liked New York."

"I know." She looked into his eyes and knew they had to get out of this house or they would both break down again. "You said something about shopping."

He nodded. "Your food supply leaves much to be desired."

She decided to ignore the insult. At least he hadn't specifically started in on her about the sweets. "Do you want to go out looking like that?"

"Like—" He looked startled, and then he rubbed a hand over his chin. "Maybe I should shave."

"Unless you want to frighten old ladies and small children."

The ghost of a smile flitted across his mouth. "I'd rather not."

She'd forgotten that he had a wonderful smile. This wasn't a real version of it, but it reminded her why she'd taken a liking to Morgan when she'd first met him. When he smiled, really smiled, he put his whole heart into it. His whole heart wasn't in it now, but she could hardly blame him for that.

"Come on upstairs and I'll find you a new razor," she said. "You'll have to lather up with soap instead of shaving cream, though. And the razor will be pink. I hope that doesn't offend you." She started out of the kitchen.

"Nothing could offend me more than I've offended myself."

Whirling, she threw out both hands in exasperation. "Good Lord, will you *stop?*" She'd never been a patient person under the best of circumstances, and he was sorely trying what little patience she could find this morning. "We were both under a hideous strain, and we comforted each other! I thank God you were here to tell me in person! Don't you thank God that you had someone to run to, someone who loved Arielle as much as you did?''

His throat worked. His dark eyes filled. ''Yes. I thank God for you, Mary Jane. I will thank God for you for the rest of my life.''

She looked into his eyes and something happened to her heart, making it go all squishy and warm and tender. Wow. The guy packed a wallop. She needed to get him moving or she was liable to do something really embarrassing, like move closer and kiss him. Like suggest they go upstairs for something besides that razor...

''Shaving,'' she said. ''We can get through this, Morgan, if we just put one foot in front of the other.''

''Maybe you should get the razor and bring it down. I can shave in the half bath.''

''You can, but the light's no good in there. And the mirror distorts a little. Believe me, I know these things, having stared into both mirrors more times than I should probably admit. Come on.'' She started up the stairs.

''That's okay. I'll use the half bath.''

One hand on the railing, she turned and gazed at him. She wondered if he was one of those stubborn men who turned everything into a power struggle. If so, the sooner he left Austin, the better. ''I hate to say this, Morgan, but you are being a pain in the ass. I'll bring the razor down if you insist, but what damned difference does it make where you shave?''

He cleared his throat and looked away. ''I just think... it would be better if I stayed down here. And out of the...bedroom.''

Oh. As she gripped the railing and considered the implications of what he'd said, she couldn't hold back a small feeling of triumph. He'd liked his experience with her last night. He'd liked it so much that he wanted more. Maybe Morgan wasn't all brain, after all.

''I'll get the razor,'' she said, her step much lighter as she went upstairs.

AT MARY JANE'S suggestion, they'd driven across town to an area she seldom visited to have breakfast and shop for groceries. Morgan thought it was a smart move. Mary Jane didn't want to run into anyone she knew until she had herself more emotionally together, and he didn't want to run into anyone who had known Arielle. After all, his wife had spent the first twenty-two years of her life in this town.

Taking another sip of his coffee, he sat across the table from Mary Jane in the booth of a small neighborhood restaurant and watched her not eat. She made a show of it, cutting her omelette into bite-size pieces, sipping her juice, putting a little pepper on her food. His plate looked as untouched as hers, but he wasn't pregnant. She needed to eat.

"Look, I know you're not hungry," he said at last. "But you need to try."

She glanced at him. "Couldn't I swallow twice as many of those prenatal magic bullets you've prescribed for me?"

He shook his head and felt a smile trying to work its way through his pain. "They don't work very well if you don't have food in there, too."

She sighed and took a bite of omelette into her mouth. Chewing and swallowing, she made a face. "It's cold and the cheese has congealed."

"Then I'll order you another one." He lifted his hand to signal the waitress.

"You most certainly will not!" She shoveled in another bite. "I'm eating. See? Eating."

"That's silly. They can throw that away and get—"

"Put your hand down." She reached across the table and grabbed his wrist, smacking his hand on the table. "We are not going to put the waitress and the cook to more trouble because I dawdled over my food and let it get cold. They'll think something was wrong with it. It's not good karma to send your food back uneaten."

"But you weren't eating it." The back of his hand stung where she'd whacked it against the table, but it was the warm grip of her fingers around his wrist that really bothered him. Her fingers against his skin reminded him of how she'd clutched his shoulders last night while he buried himself in her. He forced himself to stay focused. "The food would have gone back to the kitchen eventually, anyway."

"Nope." Her blue gaze held his earnestly. "I would have asked for a doggy bag. Nobody's insulted if you ask for a doggy bag." She looked at his hand on the table. "Can I trust you not to try to get the waitress over here?"

"Guess so."

"All right, then." She released her hold and went back to eating her cold omelette. "It's a matter of professional courtesy."

"I can see that."

She paused and glanced pointedly at his plate. "Eat up."

"But I'm not—"

"Hungry? I don't think that's the issue. You need your strength."

He pushed his plate aside. "I'll ask for a doggy bag."

"Oh, no, you don't. If you're going to force me to eat this cold food, you can do the exact same thing. Start chewing."

"We're not in the same boat."

She shoved his plate in front of him. "We're in exactly the same boat. I may be physically carrying this baby, but you are the father."

And the only parent. He went still, bracing himself for the blow if she decided to point that out. She didn't. She was incredibly sensitive. He hadn't known that about her. There were lots of things he hadn't known about her, like the silken welcome she provided for a man in bed. That was one thing he'd be better off not knowing, and the one thing he'd never forget.

"Let's say you let yourself get run down," she said. "You weaken your immune system, and there you are, a sitting duck for every bug that cruises by. So you have one illness after another, getting even more run down, and then, when this little girl is born, you're too full of germs to be in the delivery room, let alone ready to function as her father." She pointed her fork at him. "What do you say to that, Mr. Pediatrician? Is that fair to anybody?"

"No. No, it's not." He picked up his fork. Eating food

when you'd rather not had never seemed like an act of courage to him before. But he realized that in Mary Jane's case, that's exactly what it was. He could do no less.

"Attaboy."

He couldn't help it. He grinned. Yesterday he'd been absolutely sure that smiles and laughter were a thing of the past. But here was irrepressible Mary Jane Potter, valiantly shoving down food she didn't want and cheering him on to do the same. A person would have to be made of stone not to respond to that.

She grinned back. "But I gotta warn you, it tastes like crap."

His grin turned to a chuckle.

"You look great when you do that."

"I never thought I would again."

Her blue eyes grew warm with compassion. "She wouldn't want you to stop smiling, Morgan."

His fork clattered to the plate and his throat closed. He fumbled for his napkin as his grief came flooding back.

"Damn," she said softly, bolting out of her seat.

He tried to choke out an apology and couldn't. Through his tears he saw her throw a bill on the table.

"Come on." She grabbed his hand and led him, stumbling, out of the restaurant.

Bright sunlight gave way to cool shade as she pushed him into an alley. Then she wrapped her arms around him and he clung to her and cried. He felt her shaking in his arms and was ashamed that he'd caused her to lose control, too. But he couldn't do anything except curl his body over hers, bury his face in her glorious hair and hold on for dear life.

Eventually he managed to stop crying, but he couldn't let go of her. He lifted his damp face, straightened a little and laid his cheek on the top of her head. "I was going to leave today," he said. "Go back to New York."

Her arms tightened around him.

"I won't," he said. "Not yet."

Her grip slackened. Then she sighed, and when she spoke, her voice was hoarse from weeping. "Good."

CHAPTER THREE

MARY JANE got behind the wheel of her neon-green Super Beetle while Morgan leaned down and moved the passenger seat back to accommodate his long legs. She'd sold her old junker and found a smokin' deal on this slightly used buggy. It had been love at first sight the minute she'd seen the bud vase set into the dash. Sure, she had monthly payments, but she also had a silk daisy smiling at her every time she climbed into the car.

Before starting the engine, she turned to Morgan. "How long do you think you can stay?"

"A few days, maybe. But I'll need to call the office and tell them where I am. My partner can probably take care of—"

"You didn't tell your office you were coming here?"

He looked surprised by the question. "I didn't tell anyone."

"Morgan!"

"I haven't been in the most organized state of mind recently."

"Well, I know, but people must be frantic! Your office is one thing, but what about your friends, your parents? All sorts of people."

He regarded her steadily. "I called my parents right after the accident. As I talked to them and felt no empathy at all, I was brutally reminded that they try to avoid anything messy and cruel. When I told them there would be no funeral, so they weren't required to do anything, they sounded relieved. They told me to call if there was anything they could do. But I knew they didn't really want me to call."

Her heart ached for him, but she knew exactly what he was talking about. Her father had been like that after her mother died. He'd promptly hired Arielle as Mary Jane's nanny and then had proceeded to distance himself from his daughter, who was a constant reminder of harsh realities like death. Arielle had been her family from that moment on, Arielle and the good friends she'd made here in Austin.

"As for friends," Morgan went on, "I have to confess we weren't all that close to anyone. We were both busy with our careers, and we didn't take much time to socialize other than business dinners, meet-and-greet kinds of things. I can't think of anyone who would be all that concerned as to my whereabouts."

"I'm sure you're wrong about that, but you should at least call your office."

He nodded. "Yeah, I will."

"Do you have a calling card?"

"Of course."

She pointed to a pay phone a few feet from the restaurant. "I'll wait."

His eyebrows rose. "Are you giving me an order?"

"As a matter of fact, I am. I don't know how they do things in New York, but out here in Texas we give people a shout when it's necessary. I would say running off to Austin and leaving your medical practice high and dry qualifies."

"My God, you're lecturing me!" He seemed ready to give her an argument.

She met his gaze. "I may be a mere child in your eyes, and an uneducated waitress on top of that, but it's possible I know more about some things than you do, in spite of the fact you've gone to college for about a million years and probably graduated magna cum incredible."

He blinked. "I don't think of you as an uneducated waitress."

"That's what I am," she said quietly. She noticed he hadn't contradicted her statement that she was a mere child. He still thought she was too young—*too young for him.* "I finished high school," she said, "but I was sick to death of sitting in stuffy classrooms by that time. Waitressing is the only thing I know how to do." She paused. "Well, that's not quite true. I know how to—"

"Never mind!" he shouted.

Her eyes widened. "I was going to say crochet. What did you think I was going to say?"

"I'll make that call." He was out of the car in an amazingly short time, considering that he had to unwind his body to get through the low-slung door.

But he didn't get out quickly enough to keep Mary Jane from seeing that he'd blushed red as a stop sign.

While he made his call, she studied him without fear she'd be caught gawking. She needed to look at him more closely and decide what she thought about all this. For one thing, she wanted to make sure that she wasn't rising to the bait. If she wasn't careful, she'd take his assumption that she was only a kid as a challenge to prove she was every inch a woman. That would be bad.

Once he'd made his connection to New York, he leaned a shoulder against the curved cubicle surrounding the telephone. Now that she'd begun to see him as a man instead of a pediatrician and her best friend's husband, she allowed herself to notice the wide set of his shoulders, his narrow waist circled with a black leather dress belt, the pleated trousers that didn't totally hide his nice butt. He shifted his weight. Definitely a nice butt.

He wore his wavy brown hair short, and she found herself gazing at the nape of his neck with the urge to kiss him there. They'd never really kissed at all, come to think of it. What had happened between them last night hadn't been a romantic interlude, more like a bid for survival. She wondered how it would feel to be truly kissed on the mouth by Morgan. For some reason she figured he'd know how to use his tongue.

She imagined him without those rumpled clothes and felt the stirrings of lust. He had strong-looking legs. She remembered that much from this morning, before he'd started getting all guilt-ridden and she'd stopped noticing his body.

No doubt it wasn't kosher to be sitting here checking him

out, considering their circumstances, but she couldn't seem to help it. Maybe she was using curiosity as a distraction from the scary grief that hovered over her like King Kong. If so, it worked pretty well.

Yeah, she was damn curious about what kind of lover Morgan was. Arielle wasn't the type to drop coy little hints, like some wives did, about her husband being a stud. Mary Jane had assumed Morgan was a nice guy but not particularly exciting in the bedroom.

Last night notwithstanding, and she couldn't really count that, he might still be a ho-hum Romeo. But if Morgan was no fun in bed, then her radar was way off. She was picking up signals like crazy from this man. He was starting to make her drool, to tell the truth. She didn't feel particularly noble admitting that to herself, but it was true.

She might be able to blame the pregnancy for her sexual interest in Morgan. In a way, that made the lust all his fault, his and Arielle's. She liked the idea of pointing the guilty finger at her hormones. Those rambunctious little dudes were the villains, getting her all worked up.

But if she followed that line of reasoning, she should be drooling over anything in pants. Plenty of male customers came through the door at the diner, and she hadn't felt inclined to jump their bones. She'd felt generally deprived sexually, but it hadn't affected her discrimination.

Morgan hung up the phone and turned. As he walked to her, her heart did a little dance of welcome. He was only staying a few days, she reminded herself. They obviously needed each other to make it through the first shock and come to grips with their tremendous loss. When they'd recovered their balance, he would go back to New York and continue with his life there while she would stay in Austin and continue hers. She'd probably better cool it.

He climbed into the car and shut the door. "Calling was the right thing to do." He looked at her. "Thanks."

"So they can manage without you for a little while?"

He nodded. "Chuck told me to take whatever time I needed. I said I'd check in with him in a couple of days."

Mary Jane had another sudden thought. "You didn't get any pets since I was there last, did you?"

"Nope, no pets. And only fake plants. A weekly cleaning service." He stared out the window. "The apartment could go on forever just fine without anybody being there. We planned it that way so we could have more freedom." He shook his head, bemused. "We planned everything carefully. We had a smooth, neat life. No wrinkles."

"Then why in the world did you want a baby?" The question came out before she even knew she was going to ask it.

He turned and looked at her for a long time. "The truth?"

"No better time than now."

"I wanted the baby. Arielle wasn't sure a baby was a good idea. I often wondered if there was some sort of mind-body thing going on that kept her from getting pregnant. I was the one who suggested finding a surrogate mother. I may even have been the one who thought of you."

Mary Jane realized she'd known all along that Arielle wasn't absolutely gung-ho about having a kid, although her friend had never said anything to give herself away. She'd tried to be a good sport. But looking back on it, Mary Jane recognized that most of the enthusiasm had come from Morgan and herself. She'd been so excited about doing this huge favor, a favor that would prove her undying love for Arielle, that she'd told herself Arielle wanted the baby more than anything in the world.

But she hadn't. She'd gone along with the idea for Morgan's sake.

"I think on some level I knew she wasn't wild about the idea," Mary Jane said. And then a disloyal thought came to her. If Arielle hadn't wanted this baby more than anything in the world, what kind of mother would she have been?

"She would have loved that little kid, though, once she got used to motherhood," Morgan said. "Once the baby was here."

Mary Jane glanced at him and wondered if he'd been thinking the same thing she had. "She would have been a wonderful mother," she agreed quickly, not wanting to admit a chink in her loyalty, even to herself. "And I should know. She practically raised me."

"I know. She told me all about that. She was very proud of her job."

"She should have been." But disloyal thoughts seemed to be the order of the day, because Mary Jane was thinking another one. She wondered why she felt so obligated to Arielle for taking her on. Arielle had needed a job as much as Mary Jane had needed a nanny. And yet the way the story always came out, Arielle had rescued Mary Jane. Which was kind of true, but it hadn't been exactly a one-way street.

"I guess this is a pointless discussion," Morgan said.

"Not really." She leaned her head back against the seat. "I'm looking for any way I can to deal with what's happened, and I have to admit it helps to know that she wasn't as excited about the baby as I...thought she was."

"She would have been, once the baby was born," he insisted.

"Of course she would have." Mary Jane didn't think either of them totally believed that. She took a deep breath and glanced at him. "I figure besides a phone card you also have a gold card."

"Yeah."

She switched on the engine. "That's good, because unless you were planning to fit into some of my outfits, you need to do some clothes shopping."

"Oh." He looked at his wrinkled shirt. "Good plan. Any major department store will be fine. I'll just get a few shirts and a couple of pairs of slacks, some underwear."

She backed the car out of the parking space. "You mean more stuff like what you already have hanging in the closet at home?"

"Pretty much. Why?"

"Because you're in Texas, my friend. Why not go native?"

"You mean buy Western clothes?"

She gave him a quick once-over. "Why not? You have the build for it. Come on, now, haven't you ever wanted to be a cowboy?"

"No."

"Never? Not even when you were five? You never galloped through the back yard shooting bad guys?"

He shrugged. "Sure, maybe, but that doesn't mean that I want to parade around in those kind of clothes now."

"Betcha do."

He sighed and settled back against the seat. "You're going to take me to a Western store, aren't you?"

"When was the last time you tried on a cowboy hat?"

"*A cowboy hat?* You think I'm going to put out my hard-earned money for a damned *hat?* I might need some shirts and pants, but I do not need a hat."

MORGAN nearly knocked the Stetson off his head when he climbed in the Beetle two hours later. "See? It gets in the way," he complained to Mary Jane, who looked incredibly smug about the entire shopping expedition. "I'll probably lose this very expensive hat in no time."

"No, you won't. Not if you took a good look at yourself in that full-length mirror. The hat is essential." She closed her door and gave him a triumphant glance. "Did you or did you not have more fun buying those duds than you have ever had shopping for boring suits and ties?"

Well, he had, but he felt guilty about it. The fact was, he'd never had so much fun shopping for clothes in his life. And fun wasn't what he was supposed to be having right now. "At least I have something to cover my body with that doesn't look as if it went through the trash compactor."

"There you go." She seemed satisfied with his response, as if she could tell from his tone that he'd enjoyed himself. "Now let's hit the grocery store and then we'll go home."

Home. They needed to talk about their living arrangements. "Look, if I'll be staying a little while, then I think sleeping on the couch downstairs is the best—"

"I'd absolutely planned on that." She gunned the engine and made it through a yellow light.

He wondered if she'd planned on that. During the shopping spree she'd had many excuses to touch him while she'd checked the fit of a shirt or the length of his jeans. She'd taken those opportunities. And to his shame, he'd liked that part of the expedition most of all.

But a few casual touches were one thing. They weren't going to share a bed again. Sharing her town house might be risky, but moving into a hotel would defeat the whole purpose of his staying. He needed to stay clear on his purpose. He and Mary Jane were the two people most affected by Arielle's death, and it was only logical that they'd ride out the storm together, at least during these first few days. They were a safe haven for each other. They could trust each other with their tears.

On top of that, he needed to consider the health of his baby. If Mary Jane went into a depression because she'd lost Arielle, then she wouldn't eat right or exercise. She might forget to take her vitamins. The pregnancy could be compromised. He wanted to make sure that she was in good mental health before he went back to New York.

Come to think of it, he'd probably have to make a few trips to Texas in the next four months to check on her. She'd had a sweet tooth before this tragedy, judging from the evidence he'd found in her kitchen. That was a problem that could quickly get out of hand. Yes, he definitely needed to monitor her progress closely.

"You're smiling." She whipped the little car into the parking lot of a large grocery store. "I knew those clothes would cheer you up."

Startled, he glanced at her. He hadn't been aware of smiling and he hadn't been thinking about his new clothes. He'd been thinking of spending time with her.

"I'll bet wearing those jeans and boots reminds you of the fun you used to have playing when you were a little kid," she said.

"Maybe." He wasn't about to admit the real reason he'd been smiling. She was liable to read something into it.

"Something else I've always wondered." She slipped the car neatly into a parking spot and cut the engine.

"What's that?"

"How come you decided to be a pediatrician? I mean, once you made a decision to be a doctor, why didn't you go, Hey, I think I'll be a brain surgeon, or maybe a heart surgeon."

He recognized familiar territory. Not particularly attractive territory, but familiar. "You mean because it might pay better?"

"Yeah, I guess."

"Funny, but Arielle tried to convince me to switch over to one of those specialties while I was still in med school. Did you guys talk about that or something?"

"No, no, we didn't. She seemed pretty happy about your job."

"Well, yeah, she was." But she hadn't always been. He'd shoved that terrible fight under a stack of happier memories. She'd nearly broken their engagement when he wouldn't consider restructuring his classes so he'd be qualified for a more glamorous specialty.

"I feel comfortable with kids," he said. "Always have. In high school I did one of those shadowing things where you spend time with people in professions you'd like to enter. I shadowed an older woman who'd been in pediatrics for thirty years. I knew I'd found what I wanted to do."

Her blue eyes shone. "That's so wonderful. Not very many people find their calling in life so early. You're very lucky."

"Lucky? That's kind of a strange thing to say right now, Mary Jane."

Her expressive eyes clouded and she laid a hand on his arm. "I didn't mean it like that. I meant—"

"I know what you meant," he said gently. There was her touch again, making him yearn for things he couldn't have. "And you're right. In some ways, I've been very lucky. I wonder if it's true, that life has a way of evening out. Strike it rich in one area and you're liable to strike out somewhere else."

"I refuse to believe that." Her grip on his arm tightened. "I refuse to believe that just because something good comes along, something bad is right on its heels."

He watched her mouth and realized he'd never even kissed

her. He knew what it was like to sink deep inside her and feel her powerful contractions, but he had no idea how her lips tasted. And he would never know. "Or just because something bad comes along, something good is right on its heels?"

"That's more reasonable," she said. "Now, let's shop." She opened her door and got out of the car.

He chuckled. It was hard not to with Mary Jane around. It was hard not to feel alive and hopeful, although the positive emotions she inspired carried a certain amount of guilt. "I like your way of looking at things," he said as they walked together toward the store's entrance.

"And my taste in men's clothing?" she prompted, giving him the once-over.

"It's different. I would never have picked a shirt with blue lightning streaks across the shoulders."

"It looks good. You should probably stay close to me and pretend we're a couple or somebody's liable to hit on you."

"I seriously doubt that."

"Then wander by yourself down the aisles and see what happens, if you don't believe me. Thanks to my suggestions, you're now a genuine piece of eye candy."

He laughed out loud and was sure his face was red. No woman, not even Arielle, had ever paid him such an outrageous compliment. He'd made points with women by being an all-around good guy, but he'd never considered himself sexy-looking. Having a twenty-two-year-old tossing out comments like that was likely to go to his head.

And become addicting.

GOOD THING she'd dressed Morgan in snug jeans and a hat that made him look like John Michael Montgomery. If he hadn't looked so damned good, she would have killed him in the bakery aisle, Mary Jane decided.

The man was determined to stuff her full of everything green and deprive her of the finer things of life, like the Black Forest cake that had been on sale for half price. She might even have paid full price for a beauty like that, with whipped cream and chocolate sprinkles and bright red cherries sitting on top like beacons of delight. About the only thing she could say about this load of veggies was that they weren't all that expensive, so if they went bad she wouldn't have wasted much money on them. Maybe the birds would like some of this stuff.

"I could have frozen half of that cake," she grumbled as he positioned the cart next to the checkout counter and began unloading enough produce to make Peter Rabbit jump for joy. "Then it would have been spread out longer. It's not like I planned to eat it all at once, you know."

"That thing was made from white flour and white sugar, and I'll bet it was loaded with preservatives. We picked up lots of fruit. That's about a thousand times better for your system."

"So you're one of those misguided people who thinks fruit constitutes dessert?"

"Sure. Fruit and cheese." He kept putting things on the conveyor belt.

Mary Jane eyed them, thinking that most of that kind of food had never been in her house, let alone in her stomach. "Fruit and cheese is a snack," she said. "It's fine in its place, but don't try to tell me that it could ever, in a zillion years, take the place of cherry pie à la mode. Ask any of my customers which they consider dessert. And to make my point, we don't have fruit and cheese as one of the selections for dessert at Austin Eats Diner. So there."

He gave her a tolerant smile. "Some people go without dessert altogether."

"And those people have no idea how to enjoy life." She started digging in her purse for her wallet. "There's not much in this world that can't be fixed with a decent hot fudge sundae. I've seen it a million times in my line of work." She opened her wallet and noticed that she needed to go to the bank, but she should be able to cover the groceries.

"Mary Jane, I don't—"

"You might not believe me, but it's true." She searched through the receipts and coupons she'd stuffed in her bill section and managed to locate two twenties. "Somebody comes in down in the dumps, and I make them a sundae, swirl the whipped cream up real perky, load on lots of nuts and pop that happy little cherry on top. You can't be down in the dumps when something like that is set in front of you.'' She glanced at him. ''Right?''

His gaze was gentle. ''Right. Now put your money away.''

''What?''

''I'm buying these groceries. And paying you back for breakfast.''

''Oh, no, you're not buying these groceries. We can talk about breakfast if you want, but not the groceries.'' She tried to work her way past him. ''Miss, I'm paying for these. Don't let him give you his money. These are mine, all mine.''

''No, Mary Jane, now stop it.'' He blocked her way. ''I'm buying these. There's my toothbrush and razor in there, for one thing.''

''Oh, like I can't afford to buy you a toothbrush and razor.''

''That's not the point. You shouldn't be paying for anything. I never could understand why you haven't taken more financial help for this.''

''Because.'' She gritted her teeth. ''Let me past so I can pay for the groceries.''

''Because why?''

''That'll be thirty-six forty-nine,'' the clerk said.

She took a deep breath. ''Because if you started paying for things besides my medical bills, then I wouldn't be doing you a favor. I'd be sort of like your employee, that's why.''

His jaw dropped. ''Employee? Since when did you get a ridiculous idea like that?''

''Thirty-six forty-nine,'' the clerk repeated.

''Some people hire women to have their baby,'' Mary Jane said. ''It's a business arrangement. It's like a job for them. But it's my pleasure to have your baby.'' She didn't realize that what she'd said might be embarrassing until he began to blush. But she could use that embarrassment to her advantage. ''Now let me by so I can pay.''

He did.

''Personally I think you should let him pay,'' the clerk said as she took the money Mary Jane held out. "I mean, the guy didn't even have enough foresight to bring a toothbrush and razor, for God's sake."

Mary Jane winked at her. "What he gives me is lots better than money," she said. Then she took her change and waltzed out of the store, leaving a red-faced Morgan to come sputtering along behind, pushing the cart full of veggies.

"You're impossible, you know that?" he said as he drew alongside her.

She glanced at him and smiled. "Maybe next time you'll let me have my cake and eat it, too."

CHAPTER FOUR

MARY JANE DID the best she could by the steamed vegetables Morgan so endearingly insisted on fixing for their lunch. She wasn't very hungry, but she didn't think he was, either, and yet he ate the veggies with such determination that she had to follow suit.

She used the time to find out a little more about his background and discovered that he had a younger brother named Scott who was traveling through Europe with his girlfriend and wouldn't be home for several months, although he called home every couple of weeks. Morgan's parents had said they wouldn't tell Scott about the accident until he returned home so his trip wouldn't be spoiled.

"But wouldn't he want to know?" Mary Jane thought his parents' attitude was a little callous and hated to think they were cutting off another source of emotional support for their eldest son.

"Maybe not." Morgan sighed and ran his fingers through his hair. "Scott tends to avoid unpleasant things, too. It was the way we were raised. Besides, I wouldn't want him to race home just to hold my hand. That would be pretty selfish. He's spent a long time saving for this trip."

And his only brother has suffered a devastating loss, she thought. She couldn't say that, though, because it wasn't her place to butt into their family dynamics. So she changed the subject, and they talked about what it had been like for him growing up in snowy New York compared with her childhood in sunny Texas.

But as they cleaned up the lunch dishes, her thoughts returned to Morgan's family members and how their remote behavior had left him so alone at this critical time in his life. She was beginning to feel very protective of him.

No wonder he'd come to Austin. No wonder he didn't want to leave. Not that she wanted him to, at least not right away. Once he was gone she could turn to Lana, Beth and Ellie, of course, and they'd help her get through the grieving.

But—and this was tough to admit—they'd never been crazy about Arielle. In fact, when Mary Jane had first told them she was planning to carry Arielle's baby, they'd wondered how Arielle could ask such a thing of her. She'd tried to explain that she *wanted* to do this for Arielle, but they'd made it clear they thought Arielle was not thinking of Mary Jane's best interests, considering she was only twenty-two and had never had a baby before.

Once the pregnancy had become a reality, though, her friends had come through like champs. She was positive they'd come through this time, too, and help her deal with her grief. But the fact that they hadn't been totally pro Arielle would make their sympathy less comforting than Morgan's.

Lana. Mary Jane remembered that Lana had expected her to call back. She needed to make that call, although she probably wouldn't tell Lana about Arielle over the phone. Lana would be over here in a shot, and Mary Jane wanted to protect Morgan's privacy a little longer. *Or keep him to myself?* Maybe that, too.

She finished wiping the kitchen counter and draped the dishrag over the faucet. "Thanks for fixing lunch."

"I take it you don't eat like that very often."

She smiled at him. "Would you believe never?"

He winced. "I'm afraid to ask what you usually eat."

"Diner food, if you're talking about lunch. I'd probably do burgers and fries most of the time, but you'll be happy to know that Shelby usually pushes a helping of green beans or a salad at me. Come to think of it, our cook Sara's been on me about my diet, too. So if you want to give me a lecture, you'll have to get in line."

"At least it's not fast food."

"Oh, I've been known to take a swing by those places on

occasion. But the diner's kind of spoiled me for fast food.''
She reached for the vitamins she kept on the counter and got
a glass of water. "And I'm very good about taking these.
Don't I get points for that?''

"Sure. You get a million points just for agreeing to carry
this baby." He sighed heavily. "But in case you hadn't noticed, I have a slight tendency to try and control things.''

"No, really?" She gazed at him with some fondness. It
was perfectly natural for him to want to control things after
a freak accident had taken away the person he loved most. If
it made him feel better to force veggies on her for a few days,
it was no big deal. He'd be going home soon.

She closed the vitamins and put them on the counter. "I
need to make a quick phone call," she said. "A friend left a
message on my machine yesterday." It seemed impossible it
had only been yesterday. She felt as if five years had gone by
since then.

His warm brown eyes clouded with uncertainty. "A guy?''

"No, a woman. Lana Lord. She's an old friend.''

"Oh." He looked relieved.

She wondered at his reaction. He'd acted as if he'd been
afraid she was about to tell him she had a boyfriend. Could
he possibly imagine she would have allowed last night to
happen if she did have a man in her life? "I decided not to
date for the duration," she said. "To simplify things.''

He studied her for a long time. "I don't think I had a clue
how this pregnancy would turn your life upside down. This
is the time when you should be dating, going to parties.
You're only twenty-two, for God's sake.''

She grimaced. "I do know that, and if I had any doubt,
you've reminded me about a hundred times in the past twelve
hours.''

"Maybe I have to remind myself, because obviously I
wasn't thinking much about it when we came up with this
plan. I was so focused on what I wanted that I've been guilty
of...well, using you. That's inexcusable.''

"You make it sound as if I had no say in the matter. As I
keep telling you, I wanted to do this as a special gift for

Arielle, who's done so much for me. I've never once felt used or taken advantage of.''

"Well, maybe you should have."

"But I didn't." She rested her hand against the gentle swell of her belly. "And it's a little late to worry about that now, isn't it?"

His gaze fell to where her hand rested. Warmth gradually replaced the concern in his brown eyes. "I confess that I love looking at you and knowing you're carrying this baby," he murmured, glancing into her eyes. "I may be having a real attack of conscience about the sacrifices you're making, but I don't wish that baby away. Not for a minute."

She had the feeling that if he'd trusted himself to do it, he'd have come closer and put his hand on her stomach. The yearning was there in his eyes. She wanted him to touch her there, too, but she didn't think the touching would end with that, so she'd be better off not encouraging him.

"I guess you should make your call," he said.

"Okay. I'll call her from upstairs." She started to leave the kitchen.

"Are you going to tell her?"

She turned to him. "Not yet."

"I don't mean to cut you off from your friends at a time like this. If you want to tell her, if you want to go over and see her, it's fine with me."

She was touched that he'd say that when she doubted he'd really want her to desert him today. "There's time for that after you leave," she said.

He looked into her eyes. "Thanks."

"You're welcome." She wanted to go over and hug him, because he sure looked as if he could use a hug. If last night hadn't happened, she'd probably be able to get away with doing that. But last night had happened, and a hug was too risky now. Eventually maybe they could be casually affectionate, but it wouldn't happen today. "I'll be right back," she said, and hurried upstairs.

The phone conversation was tricky, and no doubt Lana suspected something was going on, but Mary Jane was able to stall her friend for a few days. From Lana's teasing reaction, she probably thought Mary Jane had met a guy and had reconsidered her self-imposed ban on dating. Lana had warned her she might be sorry if the right guy came along and she refused to give him the time of day.

Apparently Morgan felt she was making a terrible sacrifice to have given up dating. She thought about that as she combed her hair and put on fresh lipstick. The fact was, she'd been discouraged with the prospects recently. Compared with someone like Morgan, they were...uh-oh. Her lipstick only half applied, she paused and stared at herself in the mirror.

Comparing past boyfriends with Morgan was a bad sign. She could not allow herself to fantasize, even for a second, that there could ever be anything but a strong friendship between her and Morgan. They would always be linked by the baby, but this unusual intimacy they were experiencing was brought on by shared tragedy and wouldn't last. Besides, he'd been Arielle's husband. Getting involved with him beyond what had happened the night before would be just too weird. End of story.

Finishing with her lipstick, she headed downstairs, but she hesitated when she saw Morgan sitting on her flowered couch with his back to her. He held a framed picture in both hands, and although he blocked most of it, she could see a corner of the frame and knew exactly which one he had. She'd also have known by glancing at the top of her television cabinet where this particular photo was missing from the collection she had displayed there.

It was a professional portrait that Arielle had had taken when she was twenty-two, the same age as Mary Jane was now and a year before Arielle had met Morgan. The head shot showed Arielle gazing dreamily into the distance instead of looking at the camera. Not a blond hair was out of place. Mary Jane thought of it as Arielle's Mona Lisa picture because of the mysterious little smile on her face.

Morgan sat quietly, his shoulders still, so at least he wasn't weeping uncontrollably, but Mary Jane hated to intrude. Yet if she went upstairs, he might hear her retreating and be even more embarrassed. A lump in her throat, she sat quietly on the carpeted stairs and waited for him to put the picture back.

Instead he continued to stare at it. Tears filled Mary Jane's eyes and dripped silently down her cheeks and into her lap. She felt a raw, jagged hole in the place where Arielle had always been, but she hadn't lived with Arielle in years. What must it be like for Morgan, who had built his entire existence around this beautiful blond woman? Mary Jane couldn't comprehend what he must be going through.

Finally he stood, walked slowly to the television cabinet and replaced the picture, tilting it exactly the way it had been before.

Mary Jane had intended to stand immediately and pretend she'd just been coming downstairs, but she was crying too much to pull that off, so she continued to sit on the steps. A small whimper must have escaped her lips, because Morgan turned quickly.

She'd expected to see tears on his face, too. He looked devastated, but he was dry-eyed.

Catching sight of her sitting there, he hurried over and came up the stairs to crouch in front of her. "Poor Mary Jane," he crooned, cupping her face in his hands. "I'm so sorry."

"I'm so sorry for *you*," she cried, choking back a sob. "How can you bear it?"

"I can bear it," he said softly, brushing her damp cheeks with his thumbs. "It's you I'm worried about. You were closer to her than anyone."

"That's silly." She hiccuped and swallowed fresh sobs. "She was your w-wife."

"I know." His eyes searched hers. "And after six years, I still didn't feel that I really knew her. We shared a house, a marriage, a bed, but she never really let me get close to her."

She understood the gift he was giving her, to reveal something so stark and hurtful. Placing her hands over his, she mirrored his tenderness, cradling his hands against her face. Effortlessly she sank into the depths of his gaze, connecting with him on that same elemental level they'd reached the night before.

"I have to believe you knew her far better than I ever did," he said, his tone raw and vulnerable. "So you must be in worse shape than I am."

"Nobody really knew Arielle," she whispered. It was something she'd never admitted to herself, let alone said out loud.

Confusion shadowed his eyes. "But surely, in the years when she was like a mother to you, she—"

Mary Jane swallowed. "She was like the perfect china teacups she collected," she said in a hoarse voice. "No one ever saw a crack or a chip anywhere. I loved her, idolized her, wanted to be like her, but I knew I couldn't ever make it. I was too...too..."

"Human?"

"Yeah." She smiled sadly. "Way too human."

"I guess that makes two of us." The warmth in his eyes shifted subtly, taking on a different gleam. His grip tightened, and his attention drifted to her mouth.

She couldn't remember a time in her life when she'd wanted a kiss more. But if she let Morgan kiss her in her present state of mind, or in his, they'd make love right on these stairs. Then they'd continue making love until finally she had to go back to work day after tomorrow. Yes, it would take away the sharp pain they both struggled with, but afterward they might never be able to forgive themselves.

She reached up and pressed two fingers against his mouth. A wonderful velvet mouth that would feel like heaven against hers. "No," she said quietly.

He released her so fast she nearly tumbled forward into his arms. "Damn!" He steadied her quickly before letting go of her shoulders. Then he moved down a couple of steps and collapsed with his back against the railing. "I can't imagine the opinion you have of me now."

She took a shaky breath. "The same opinion I've always had. You're a good guy stuck with no one to comfort you except me. And I'm—well, I'm sort of a babe. Your urges are perfectly natural." She glanced at him. "And that's *babe*, not *baby*."

His mouth turned up. "You're a whole bunch of things, Mary Jane, including a babe."

"I wouldn't even care if you kissed me," she said. "Except I know where that would lead, and you'd hate yourself afterward."

"You've got that right." He closed his eyes. "Maybe you should take me to the airport this afternoon."

The thought of him leaving abruptly made her stomach tighten. "I'd rather take you rowing on Town Lake."

"And throw me overboard?"

"Not in those new clothes." She wiped at her eyes. "I'll go repair my makeup and then we'll see the sights."

He sighed. "Mary Jane, I don't think I should stay. I—"

"Please stay. We have to work out how we're going to be with each other, considering that I'll want to keep in touch with this baby in the years ahead. If you go running off before we figure it out, we might feel awkward about our relationship for a long time. That wouldn't be good for us or for the baby."

He glanced up at her. "You sure are smart."

"For a twenty-two-year-old?" She couldn't resist.

"For any age. Okay, I'll stay another day or two. And I promise to keep my hands off you. But you don't have to play tour guide."

"Look, you don't know the area," she said. "You didn't come here with any props. No books to read, no projects to do. I'm not crazy about having the TV on during the day."

"Good. Me, neither."

"Then unless you want me to teach you how to crochet, I think sight-seeing is the best option."

He smiled. "I'm no good at needlework. But how do you usually spend your days off? What would you be doing if I hadn't shown up?"

"You don't want to know."

"Sure, I do."

"I'd probably be lolling around upstairs in my jammies, reading tabloids and painting my toenails."

The poor guy's tongue was nearly hanging out before he

got himself under control. He cleared his throat. "Well, if that's your usual routine, don't mind me. I can—"

"Morgan, I'm not going to follow my usual routine. We're dealing with unusual circumstances. Besides, I like my city. I enjoy showing it off."

"Okay. But I'm beginning to feel like a leech, especially after you bought breakfast and groceries. Can I take you someplace really nice for dinner? Don't forget I'm the proud owner of a gold card. What's the most exclusive restaurant in Austin?"

He really was a sweetie. Arielle had talked about being ..ted like a queen, and Mary Jane could see how that was a real possibility with a guy like Morgan. Arielle had obviously loved all this wining and dining, but she hadn't worked in a restaurant five or six days out of every week, either.

"That's a nice thought," she said, "and I appreciate it. But to tell you the truth, I'd rather rent a movie and order a pizza tonight. I suppose that doesn't sound very exciting to someone from New York City, though."

His gaze, usually so open, became unreadable. "You might be surprised."

THE EMOTIONAL SHOCK of Arielle's death must have shaken something loose in his brain, Morgan decided a couple of hours later as he pulled on the oars of the boat he and Mary Jane had rented. He was supposed to be admiring the Austin skyline visible at the far end of the lake, but instead he was admiring Mary Jane in the bow of the boat, and wondering how he'd get through another night in her town house without hitting on her. He didn't remember being this obsessed with sex even as a sixteen-year-old.

She seemed unaware of his preoccupation, and he was sure she was making no effort to be provocative. Probably just the opposite. For the boat ride she'd changed into some light-weight drawstring pants, a faded, roomy T-shirt with the Texas Longhorns mascot on the front, and red sandals.

Maybe it was the sandals. Her exotically painted toenails peeked out from under the strap across her instep. Each chilipepper-red toenail had a silver star in the middle that winked at him. She'd been barefoot when she'd come to the door last night, and although he didn't remember paying any attention to her feet, part of his brain must have recorded those toenails and associated them with what went on later in her bed.

Or maybe it was the way she was leaning back against the end of the boat, her elbows on the rail, her knees slightly apart. Or his new black cowboy hat on her head. When he'd nearly lost it in the lake they'd decided that whoever wasn't rowing should wear the hat, so they could keep one hand on it if the wind picked up.

So they'd traded, and he now wore her wire-rimmed sunglasses to shade his eyes and she wore the hat, pulling it low over her brow the way a desperado might. She looked so damn cute in that hat. The breeze was tangling her hair, which she'd left loose around her shoulders, and the sun was reflecting off the curls that escaped from the shade of the hat.

She clapped a hand over the crown and tilted her head to let a little sun fall directly on her face. "I spend too much time under artificial light," she said. "It's the only thing I regret about my job."

"I know what you mean. I've often wished I could set up a booth in Central Park and see my patients there."

She glanced at him with a smile. "Wouldn't that be *cool?* I'll bet kids wouldn't mind coming to the doctor's office so much if they didn't have to sit in those scary little waiting rooms. You could call yourself the Doc in the Park. I think you should try it."

"I'm pretty sure my insurance agent would have a heart attack."

She waved a hand. "Minor detail. I'll bet you could revolutionize pediatrics with a gig like that." She sat up straighter. "Okay, my turn to row again."

He didn't want to give up the oars. For one thing, it kept his hands busy. "It can't be. I just got started."

"You've been rowing for at least fifteen minutes, and I admit you're better at it than I thought you'd be, considering you're such a city boy."

"I keep telling you I was on the rowing team in college."

"Yeah, yeah, but that doesn't give you special privileges. Come on. Trade places with me. The rowing's the fun part."

"Another five minutes. Then we'll switch." He'd quickly discovered that physical exercise was exactly what he needed. Besides, rowing the boat across a section of water gave him a sense of accomplishment and control. Apparently he'd needed that, too.

Of course, Mary Jane needed and wanted those rewards as much as he did. He'd figured out right away that she wasn't the type to sit in the boat and let the guy take the oars, no matter how many rowing medals he had stashed in his closet at home. She'd gone so far as to push back the sleeve of her T-shirt and flex her muscles for him to prove that she was capable of rowing them across the lake.

He'd never had a woman insist on doing her share of the manual labor, and he'd tried to talk her out of it, even using her pregnancy as a reason. She'd laughed and mentioned the heavy trays she carried at work every day. Finally he'd run out of arguments and had let her take the first turn at the oars, much to her delight.

Watching her row had proved to be its own special torture. Each time she'd pulled on the oars her breasts had thrust against the fabric of her T-shirt. By now he was pretty sure that Longhorns logo was burned permanently into his retina.

"Wasn't this the greatest idea?" she asked.

"Yes." He couldn't believe how something so simple was so cleansing. He wasn't really in shape for rowing, but the slight ache in his shoulders felt great. While he worked up a mild sweat and listened to the rhythm of the oars clunking against the oarlocks, he enjoyed the lush green of the trees surrounding the lake, the familiar dank scent of the water, the white clouds scudding across the sky and the sun warming his back. "It makes you feel glad to be a—" He brought the sentence to a screeching halt and stared at Mary Jane in horror at what he'd been about to say.

She leaned forward and put a hand on each of his knees. "We are alive," she said, looking hard at him as she gripped his knees. "And, Morgan, that's not our fault. We shouldn't feel guilty about that."

"I guess not." But he had plenty of other things to feel guilty about, and topping the list was the selfish, wild pleasure he felt whenever she touched him. They'd rowed into a fairly secluded inlet, and nobody seemed to be around on this week day. If he had no conscience... But he did have a conscience, and fortunately it still worked. "You can have the oars now," he said.

CHAPTER FIVE

IN SPITE OF what she'd told Morgan, Mary Jane found herself battling feelings of guilt as the afternoon continued to be more fun than two grieving people should be having. After the rowboat ride, she'd driven him outside the city, cruising past Garrett Lord's place because she remembered Lana telling her that the bluebonnets were still looking good on her brother's property. Sure enough, the wildflowers were doing their thing in an open meadow.

Morgan insisted on stopping the car so he could get out and look at a bluebonnet up close. The spot he chose was not too far from the turnoff to Garrett's place. If Lana's brother happened to be out riding and caught a glimpse of Mary Jane with a man, word would be all over in no time.

Crossing the road with Morgan to look at the field of wildflowers, Mary Jane hoped they wouldn't be seen. She still felt very protective of their privacy.

"I've heard of these things for ages," Morgan said. "Thanks for humoring me. I'm a scientist. I want to examine one up close."

"Just don't pick one," she warned as he started into a field. "Or we'll be arrested."

"Seriously?" He turned to her in surprise. "Arrested for picking wildflowers? Isn't that what you're supposed to do with them?"

"Not these. These are our state treasure. And they reseed themselves every year. If people went around gathering bouquets, they wouldn't reseed and we wouldn't have this." She spread her arm to encompass the lavender-blue carpet of flowers.

"Okay. Gotcha. No picking." He crouched next to a single plant and touched the delicate cluster of small blue flowers that covered the slender stalk. "I like to see the detail that goes into the big picture."

She stood by the edge of the road and watched him, fascinated by the way he could focus his attention like a laser. Although she'd been in his office, she'd never seen him dealing with one of his small patients. If he devoted this much careful attention to them, he must be one hell of a doctor. *And one hell of a lover.* She pushed the thought away.

"Incredible. I love the color." At the gentle brush of his fingers, one small bloom dropped from the stalk. "Oops." He drew his hand back. "What's the penalty for that? Fifty lashes?"

"You're out west now, pardner. We string up varmints like you from the nearest tree."

He stood and walked toward her. "Gonna turn me in?"

"Depends." She could swear he'd developed an amble in his walk now that he wore jeans and boots. And that hat was a killer. She wondered if he'd have the nerve to wear it in New York. "You being from back east and all, you might have strange customs, like thinking pizza should have anchovies on it. If you're going to make me eat anchovies on my pizza, I might have to report that bluebonnet crime of yours."

He grinned. "No anchovies."

"Then I'll cover for you on this deal." She glanced around. "Sun's going down. We'd better head on back before the video store rents out all the decent movies. I have a specific one in mind."

"Such as?" He fell into step with her as they crossed the road to the car.

"I was thinking *Toy Story.*"

"But isn't that a kids'—"

"I knew it! You've never seen it, have you? No point in asking if you've seen *Toy Story 2.*" She shook a finger at him. "And you call yourself a father-to-be. We are going to remedy this serious gap in your education right away. Climb in. We're making tracks for the video store.'' She started to get in the car.

"Wait!"

She paused with one foot in the car. "What?"

"Look at the hills. They're…they're *purple.*"

"Oh, yeah. They do that a lot when the sun goes down."

Morgan turned in a slow circle and took a deep breath. "Wow. A lot?"

"Yep. In fact, Austin is known as the City of the Violet Crown for that very reason." She got out of the car and stood looking at the hills that surrounded Austin like the rim of a bowl. Sure enough, the hills were putting on a show tonight. She was glad Morgan was able to see them at their best. "I guess I've started taking it for granted, which isn't a good thing."

"Arielle must have, too," he said. "She never told me about this."

Mary Jane noticed that the mention of Arielle's name was now possible without both of them getting weepy. "I don't think she would have made a very good member of the Chamber of Commerce. She once told me that after seeing New York City, she had no interest whatsoever in coming back to Austin to live."

"Well, New York has lots of things to recommend it, but the hills definitely don't turn purple at sunset." He stood with his hands shoved in the back pockets of his jeans as he continued to gaze at the color washing the hillsides. "I'm beginning to understand why you turned down the job of being the baby's nanny."

She took a deep breath. Rejecting Arielle's plea that she move to New York and be a nanny to the baby had been the most difficult decision she'd ever made. "I know Arielle was upset about that."

"Yeah, she was, but I guess she had a tough time understanding why you wouldn't want to move there. She probably figured if she loved it so much, you would, too."

"I would have loved being close to Arielle, because I missed her. But I know myself, and when I tried to picture being cooped up in your high-rise with all those artificial plants…oops." She gave him an apologetic glance. "Sorry. It's a gorgeous apartment."

"But sterile."

"Different strokes," she said. "And it's not only the living arrangements. I have a lot of good friends here, and I like my job at Austin Eats. Besides, I would miss…" She paused and smiled. "The Violet Crown, I guess, and the sunshine, and the wide-open sky, and the moonlight towers."

"Moonlight towers?" He glanced at her expectantly.

"Gigantic streetlights." She was glad to move away from an uncomfortable topic. Arielle's reaction to her refusal of the nanny position had caused an argument between them, and at first Mary Jane had been afraid her grand gesture of having the baby for Arielle would be ruined because she hadn't been willing to be a nanny, too. In fact, Mary Jane had figured that the topic had been set aside, not closed.

"Tell me about the moonlight towers," Morgan said.

"I'll show you one on the way to the video store. They were put up more than a hundred years ago, a whole bunch of them, to light the city. Before that I guess it was black as pitch once the sun went down. The type of light in the towers has changed, of course, but a lot of them are still up and working, even though they aren't really needed anymore. It's one of our claims to fame."

"I know another one."

"I'll bet you're going to say the National Wildflower Research Center. Lots of people have heard of that."

"Except me. You have such a thing?"

"You bet. Around here we take our wildflowers seriously."

"So I'm learning. But that isn't what I was going to say."

"Town Lake? The capitol building? UT?"

He shook his head. "I was going to say that one of Austin's biggest claims to fame is that Mary Jane Potter lives here," he said quietly.

The extravagant compliment caught her by surprise. Heat burned in her cheeks, and her heart started to race. "You only say that because I gave you an extra turn rowing the boat."

He gazed at her with the heart-melting smile that made mincemeat out of every defense she tried to throw up. "Yeah," he said, his voice husky. "That's what turned the trick, all right."

She swallowed. "Time to go get *Toy Story*." She hopped into the car and started the engine. She hoped he hadn't noticed that her hands were shaking.

Once he was buckled up, she headed off, concentrating on the road and not the very appealing man sitting in the seat next to her. Her determination not to glance in his direction might have been why she noticed the For Sale sign on the gate of the small ranch adjoining Garrett's place.

Apparently his neighbors, the Slatterys, had finally decided to move closer to their children in California. Lana had told her the house was a real gem, solidly constructed and nestled away from the road. The property included a pecan orchard, a small pond and plenty of room for horses. It was more than Mary Jane ever expected to be able to afford, but maybe she'd go if they had an open house, just to dream a little.

"You're upset with me," Morgan said.

"No." His gentle voice did things to her. Nice things. Dangerous things. She cleared her throat. "But you really shouldn't pay me compliments like that."

"I know," he said quietly. "But somebody should be saying them. You are a rare and wonderful woman, and somebody should be holding your hand, bringing you flowers, taking you dancing. When I think of how you've interrupted the natural flow of your life in order to have this baby, I'm humbled by your generosity and ashamed that I never saw it before as the incredible sacrifice that it is."

She shook her head. "You're making me out to be more noble than I am. When Arielle proposed the idea of me being a surrogate mom, I remember being incredibly relieved."

"Relieved?"

"I owed her so much. She got me through those years after my mom died and my dad became a zombie. But as a kid, even as a teenager, what could I ever do to pay her back? And then she handed me the one way I could. I knew that if

I could produce a healthy baby and give it to her, I'd finally have settled the score."

"I'm sure Arielle never expected you to settle any score."

"Of course she didn't," Mary Jane said quickly. "I didn't mean that she expected repayment. Far from it. Still, I was very aware of my debt."

"But now…"

"Arielle's death hasn't made me regret my decision about this pregnancy. I'm glad I'm doing this." She switched on the headlights. "Maybe more than ever."

"Because you still want to settle the debt? I've already told you she wasn't the one who really wanted this. I realize now the baby was my attempt to break through, to get to the real Arielle underneath the protective shell, to get some emotional depth into our marriage."

Mary Jane gripped the wheel. His honesty helped her be more honest with herself. "Maybe my reasons weren't so different from yours, now that you lay it out like that. Arielle never seemed to need anything from me, while I needed everything from her. She was like a goddess. But here, at last, was something I could do that she couldn't do. I thought it would make us…closer to equals, I guess, maybe even break down the wall that always existed between us. I never realized how much I longed for that."

He met her comment with a long moment of silence. "Okay. I'm probably the one person in the world who totally understands that reasoning. But that still leaves us both at the same place. The reason to have this baby is gone."

"No," Mary Jane said. "Not gone. Changed."

"What do you mean?"

"She's real, this baby. She's a person to me now. No matter what the reasons were before, she's become her own reason." She thought about the tiny life growing within her, and her chest grew tight with unspoken love. "Morgan, this is going to be one awesome kid."

MORGAN LOVED *TOY STORY*. Or maybe it wasn't the movie so much as sitting on the floor in front of the coffee table, eating pizza right out of the box while they watched the video. Maybe it was the fun of dribbling strings of cheese without worrying about an expensive Oriental carpet, and drinking cola straight from the can. Maybe it was glancing up to see cheerful prints of bright flowers on the walls instead of original abstract art.

Or maybe it was Mary Jane, sitting cross-legged beside him, scarfing up pizza and giggling like a little kid at the antics of Woody and Buzz Lightyear. She was completely relaxed with him, and he felt the knots inside his stomach loosen.

He didn't remember her being this open when she'd come to New York for the wedding, or more recently when she'd spent a few days to complete the medical procedure that had resulted in her pregnancy. She'd been much more hesitant then, as if waiting for cues from Arielle before she said or did anything, the way a child behaved around a powerful parent.

He sensed that the bubbly person sitting next to him on the floor was the real Mary Jane. Being around Arielle had sent that person into hiding. That explained why he'd never truly noticed her. It didn't excuse his willingness to throw a monkey wrench into her life with this baby, but he knew if he'd come to know her then as he was beginning to know her now, he would never have allowed Arielle to ask this favor.

By the time the movie ended, the pizza box was empty. And they'd ordered an extra large because that was what she'd had a coupon for. Morgan stared at the remaining crumbs with some surprise. "We ate it all."

"Yeah." She smiled at him. "It's a good sign that we could polish off a pizza. Did you taste it, or were you just eating to be polite?"

"I tasted it." He drank the last of his cola and set the empty can on the coffee table. "It was good."

"I thought so, too. Of course, this is a primo pizza parlor. The dough recipe is a well-kept secret, but if we were still in bad shape, we could have eaten this pizza and not tasted a thing.''

"That's pretty much the way I've been eating—just going through the motions. This is the first thing I've had that I actually tasted.''

She nodded. "Good. We're getting better, Morgan. I'm not saying we're not going to have bad spells, but maybe the worst is over.''

"Maybe." He couldn't say her eyes were exactly the color of the bluebonnets, but they had that shade in them, along with flecks of gray and gold. He'd been impressed with the bluebonnets, but he could imagine eventually getting bored gazing at them. He'd never get tired of looking into Mary Jane's eyes.

"Want to see the movie again?"

"No." He glanced at her mouth, hoping to find a crumb of pizza crust that he could reach over and brush off. But he could find no excuse to touch that wide, expressive mouth. And he wanted to.

"I have some movies that I've bought. But they're mostly...sentimental. I don't think we should watch *Titanic*, do you?''

He studied her expression to see if she was kidding, and bless her heart, she was completely serious. He didn't want to hurt her feelings or seem callous, but he felt the inappropriate urge to laugh. "No," he said as the laughter worked on him some more, making his lips twitch. "I think *Titanic* would be a bad choice.''

Her eyes began to sparkle, and her mouth turned up at the corners. "I guess *The English Patient* wouldn't be so good, either.''

"Nope." He grinned at her, relieved that she got the joke. "I don't think so.''

"Or *Braveheart*." She began to giggle. "I know! *Steel Magnolias!*''

Her giggles were all it took to set free the laughter rumbling in his chest. "The choices keep getting worse! What's next, *Bambi?*''

She burst into helpless laughter. "Yes! I have that!"

"God, woman!" He laughed until his sides ached. "For an optimist," he said, gasping, "you sure have a morbid...video collection."

"I do!" She giggled harder. "I never thought of it that way!" She struggled to get her breath. "I rent the funny ones, but I buy the sad ones."

"No kidding." He wiped his eyes and chuckled as he held up the case for *Toy Story*. "Now I know what to get you for your birthday." He paused and glanced at her. "I don't even know when that is. Arielle took care of it."

"Yes, she did." Her heart squeezed as she thought of the bouquet of flowers Arielle always sent on her birthday.

"I'll bet you know when mine is," he said. "In fact I know you do. You send me silly cards every year."

"And don't forget we deliberately calculated this pregnancy, hoping the baby would be born in September, close to the fifteenth, so now I'll probably always remember your birthday. But that's my thing. That doesn't mean you should feel an obligation to remember mine."

"I sure as heck should! We're practically like relatives, and when the baby gets older, I'll want her to send you cards on your birthday, and maybe even on Mother's Day. I think she—"

"Morgan." She put her hand on his arm. "That's going to be pretty weird for a little kid if you try to explain who I am in terms of how she was born. Maybe you'd better think this through some more."

He stared at her as the truth of her statement sank in. In less than four months he would become a father, but Mary Jane wouldn't become a mother, at least not in the strictest sense. Arielle's egg and his sperm grew within her. She was providing the environment, but the baby would be biologically Arielle's daughter.

In clinical terms he understood that. After all, he was a man of science. But his heart refused to understand it. His heart believed that there would always be a natural, unbreakable link between Mary Jane and this baby. He was doubly sure of that after getting to know the kind of person she was. She could no more give birth and turn her back on this child than fly.

Maybe there was a solution they could all live with, a compromise that would give everybody something they needed. "You're right," he said. "I should think about this. I guess we both should, now that things have...changed." He picked up his empty cola can and turned it between his fingers. "About the nanny thing. I could commute."

"From *Austin?*"

He glanced at her. "That might be a little far. No, I meant, if you would consider the nanny position, I'd be willing to buy a place outside the city. You could help me look." He warmed to the idea. "There are some wonderful little towns in the Hudson Valley. I could even keep an apartment in Manhattan, if the place you liked was too far for a daily commute. I could spend weekends there and weekdays in the city. And you could come back to Austin several times a year, so you could see your friends, and the Violet Crown." He paused, feeling more hopeful than he had in days. "What do you think?"

As she looked into his eyes, he could see her refusal. He rushed to stop her from speaking and making it official. "Don't decide yet," he said. "Give yourself some time to think about it."

"But—"

"I know. I'm asking you to uproot yourself from your home and travel into snow country, where you don't know anybody but me. Trust me, Mary Jane, you wouldn't be a stranger long. With your natural charm, you'll have more friends than you know what to do with inside of two weeks."

She smiled. "That's nice of you to say, but the thing is—"

"Please. Don't reject the idea yet." He had pretty much fallen in love with the picture he'd created in his mind of a cozy cottage in the Hudson Valley and Mary Jane tending the baby there. He'd like to find something close enough that he could commute daily, but if not, he'd make the sacrifice of only coming home on weekends.

Whatever Mary Jane wanted, he'd do. He'd noticed she had a bird feeder in the back yard. The new place would have as many bird feeders as she wanted, and he'd have the place decorated the way she liked. She could pick out the furniture, or he'd pay to have this furniture moved there.

"Really, Morgan, I don't think—"

"Give it a couple of days. That's all I ask."

"Okay."

He saw the compassion in her eyes and decided he'd trade on her good nature, if necessary, to get her there. She didn't really know what she was turning down. All she'd seen was the sleek, soulless apartment in Manhattan. The more he thought about that apartment, the more he wanted to move out of it. Maybe he'd try to break the lease. That apartment had been Arielle's dream, not his. He'd never felt comfortable there.

But he felt comfortable here, in Mary Jane's little town house, comfortable enough to sit on the floor and eat pizza out of the box.

"If you'd let me buy that cake I could offer you dessert," she said.

He had a horrible thought. "Don't tell me *today* is your birthday?"

"Maybe it is. Does that mean we can go out and buy a big ol' honkin' cake and make pigs of ourselves?"

"If it is, I'm going to feel like a complete jerk." He looked into her eyes and saw the amusement lurking there, although she was struggling to keep a straight face. "But it's not."

"No. My birthday's the twentieth of July. You have lots of time to prepare."

"What a relief." He counted ahead. She'd be well into her seventh month by then. And he wanted to be here for that birthday of hers. She would be, he reminded himself, only twenty-three. At his next birthday he'd be thirty-two.

''I'll bet you go for the whole deal, with silly hats and horns and balloons,'' he said.

''Yep. And cake.''

She'd be round as a balloon by the end of her seventh month, and he could hardly wait. ''You're not going to let me forget that cake business, are you?''

''Nope.''

''You realize that you're making me feel like some anal-retentive creep for denying you that cake.''

She grinned. ''That was the idea. Are we going shopping?''

It was either buy her that cake or lean over and kiss her, he decided. ''Yes, we're going shopping.''

CHAPTER SIX

MARY JANE didn't really care about the cake anymore, but she decided that focusing on getting one would take up more of the evening. And they needed to stay occupied. In high school she'd had to read a Greek story about a guy named Ulysses who'd sailed on a perilous voyage. At one point he'd had to go through a narrow passage, and bad things were on both sides.

As she drove across town to the same grocery store where they'd shopped that morning, she thought about Ulysses and his narrow passage. Constantly being with Morgan meant navigating between delicious temptation on one side and overwhelming grief on the other. She'd always had pretty good balance, which came in handy as a waitress. So far it was coming in handy in this situation, too. She wondered if Morgan appreciated how hard she was working to keep them both on an even keel.

Probably not. He'd been dumb enough to suggest that nanny thing. If he could imagine the two of them could live together in a cozy little house in the Hudson Valley and never, ever become sexually involved, then he wasn't thinking clearly about anything. Well, of course he wasn't, poor man. She'd give him the couple of days he'd asked of her and pretend to consider his dopey idea, and by then he'd probably come to his senses and realize it wouldn't work without her having to say a word against it.

The half-price cake was gone. Most of the cakes were gone, in fact, except for a sad-looking vanilla one, which wasn't what she had in mind.

"I guess you're out of luck," Morgan said.

"Not on your life. We'll bake one." She led him to another aisle and loaded him up with a chocolate cake mix, powdered sugar and cocoa. Baking the cake would take a good hour, she thought with some satisfaction. By the time they were ready for bed, they'd be so exhausted they'd sleep like logs.

Once they returned home, she taught Morgan how to use the electric hand mixer while she greased the cake pan. She treated him to the Smashing Pumpkins on the stereo while they worked. From the corner of her eye she could see the subtle movement of his hips keeping time to the music as he swirled the beaters through the chocolate batter. Interesting. Arousing. She stopped watching him.

They stayed very busy until the cake was in the oven. Then Mary Jane realized they had at least thirty minutes on their hands with nothing to do. And Morgan stood in her kitchen in those snug jeans, licking the chocolate batter off the beaters. Damn, but he looked good.

She searched her fevered brain for a distraction. "Gin!" she said at last.

Morgan glanced up from the beater and he transformed from yummy hunk to stern physician in no time. "Cake is one thing. But you're drinking liquor over my dead body."

"Cards," she said. "What sort of a person do you take me for?"

"Sorry." He looked contrite. "That was dumb on my part. I wasn't thinking."

She propped her hands on her hips. "I might not have the perfect diet, according to you, but I would never drink alcohol while I'm pregnant with this baby, Morgan. Or smoke cigarettes. I don't know if you noticed, but I was drinking caffeine-free cola with my pizza, even though I offered you the regular kind."

"I noticed." He set the beaters on the counter, and his gaze begged her forgiveness. "I realize you're very responsible and I'm sorry I implied otherwise."

She took a calming breath. "Apology accepted. I'm probably touchy on the subject, because I haven't been able to

forget what you said this morning, that you thought I was
mentally too young to handle a pregnancy.''

He winced. "I hurt your feelings with that one, didn't I?"

"Well, duh. Of course."

He started toward her, then seemed to think better of it and
ran his fingers through his hair instead. "I said a lot of stupid
things this morning, and that was one of the stupidest. I was
speaking out of total ignorance of your character. Maybe it's
because of the way Arielle talked about you that I had the
impression you were...immature. But that's no excuse. I
shouldn't have spouted off until I'd had time to form my own
opinion."

The way Arielle talked about you. Her mind snagged on
the words. "What do you mean? How did Arielle talk about
me?"

"Oh, you know. She thought of you like a little sister. She
used to say how sweet and loving you were. Too sweet,
maybe. She implied that you needed looking after because
you were..." He hesitated, as if realizing he might be headed
into a ditch.

"Spit it out. Because I was what?"

"Naive. But I think she was wrong," he added quickly.
"It's natural that she had a tough time accepting the fact that
you were growing up. She really liked the big sister routine."

"Yes, she did." Mary Jane struggled with her anger. How
could she be angry at someone who had just died? But she
was. She'd always suspected that Arielle liked keeping her
one down. Lana, Ellie and Beth had come close to saying that
themselves the night they'd told her she was nuts to get pregnant with Arielle's baby.

But it had felt like the right thing to do. It still did. "I
probably was a little naive," she said, more to herself than to
Morgan. "And I really didn't know what I was getting into,
having this baby."

"I'm sure. And I'm going to be there for you, Mary Jane.
I'm going to help you make it through this with a minimum
of problems so that you can get on with your life."

She met his gaze. "I appreciate that, but don't worry too

much about me. I don't know if I can explain this, but from the minute the pregnancy test was positive, I've felt this *power* inside me." She wondered if he'd smile indulgently, which would make her feel stupid about what she was trying to tell him.

Instead, his attention sharpened, as it had when he was examining the bluebonnet.

Being the focus of that attention was pretty cool, and she spoke with more confidence. "From then on I've known, deep down, that carrying this baby for nine months was going to change me. Recently I've been sort of resisting that change, but now...now I feel ready for it."

He continued to study her, and then he nodded. "I can see that. But it doesn't mean I don't want to help in any way I can."

She thought about the moment when he'd soothed his soul with the womanly gift she'd given him. She remembered the sense of purpose and courage that had flowed through her when he had accepted her offering. He'd validated her in a way no one ever had.

Later he regretted what he'd done, but for a brief moment, she'd understood what that glow of power within her was all about. "You already have helped me," she said.

"I hope so. I can't tell you how much you've helped me. Before I showed up here last night, I wondered if I'd survive. Now I'd say I have a fifty-fifty chance."

"A big piece of chocolate cake is gonna raise those odds."

He smiled. "No doubt."

She'd love to think that if they made love, she'd raise those odds even more. But maybe not. He had a conscience the size of Texas. And then she'd have to worry about whether she'd get hooked on him and do something dumb like go to New York as the baby's nanny. An employee.

No. Never. This baby was a gift of love. At first the gift had been meant for Arielle, but now Mary Jane knew the gift belonged, had probably always belonged, to the little girl she carried close to her heart. The minute she started taking money for what she was doing, she would destroy the beauty of that gift.

She glanced at the clock on the stove. "I still have time to beat your butt in gin." She crossed to a drawer, opened it, took out a well-worn pack of cards and motioned to the table in her kitchen nook. "Prepare to get annihilated."

"You're that good, huh?" He grinned and sat down at the table.

"Yep." She sat opposite him and shuffled the cards. "Ask Lana, Beth or Ellie, who have all fallen victim to my killer instincts." She slapped the deck on the table. "Cut."

"Okay." He flexed his fingers a couple of times and held them poised over the cards.

Naturally she found herself watching those fingers as they curved over the stack of cards and deftly separated them into two piles. Good hands. A doctor's hands. Gentle, caring, precise. And suddenly there she was, imagining those hands all over her, while the needle spun out of control on her lust-o-meter.

His knee bumped hers under the table. "Deal," he said.

She snapped out of her daze and blushed. "Right." She misdealt the cards, something she never did, and had to do it over.

"As an intimidation factor, misdealing leaves something to be desired," he said as he picked up his cards and fanned them.

Cards might not have been the best idea, she thought. Her table was smaller than she'd remembered, and their knees kept touching. Before they'd started the cake baking, he'd unsnapped the cuffs of his shirt and turned his sleeves back. She hadn't thought much about it until she was sitting across from the table staring at his muscular forearms and missed a critical card in the discard pile.

And his lashes. My God, the man had sinfully long lashes, which she noticed every time he looked at his cards. And the way he fingered those cards while he debated his discard was almost pornographic.

He won the first hand. After the point tally, he glanced at her. "Don't go easy on me, now."

"Well, you are a guest, after all. And I am very polite."

When he won the second hand, she vowed to buckle down and forget that little freckle on his cheekbone and the lock of hair that kept falling over his forehead, no matter how many times he combed it with his fingers. She had to ignore the way he caught his lower lip between his teeth as he studied his hand. Most of all she couldn't look forward to the glow of triumph in his eyes when he threw down his gin card. There was something almost sexual in that look, and she was in danger of losing the third game just so she could see that gleam of victory again.

She squeaked out a win. And another, making them tied at two all.

"And now for the championship of the world," she said, right as the kitchen timer buzzed. "While the cake cools." She gave him the cards and stood. "Go ahead and deal while I take it out of the oven."

"You trust me not to stack the deck?"

She laughed as she opened the oven door. "Honey, you invented the word trust."

She put the cake on the cooling rack and turned to the table to find him staring at her. "What?"

He blinked and shook his head. "Nothing. I just…when you called me honey, I—"

"Oh." She clenched the oven mitt in her fist. Arielle had probably called him that. Damn. "Sorry. It's a waitressing habit. I didn't mean to remind you of…"

"No, you didn't. She never called me that."

"Never?"

He shook his head. "She thought those little pet names were too common. I wasn't supposed to use them for her, either."

"Now that you mention it, I never did hear stuff like that when you talked to each other. Maybe that's why I thought—" She stopped and felt the heat rise to her cheeks.

"Thought what?"

"Never mind."

"No, I'd like to know."

She shrugged. "I got the impression that your relationship with each other wasn't very physical, that's all. And I'm sure I was wrong, and I'm *really* sure we shouldn't be talking about it."

"It wasn't very physical."

She took a step back. "Morgan, I think it would be a whole lot better if we dropped this subject."

He gazed into her eyes. "Yeah, maybe you're right."

"I'm sorry I called you that and started you thinking along those lines. I'll try to remember not to do it again."

"But that's the thing." He glanced at the deck of cards in his hand and began to shuffle with those supple fingers of his. Then he looked at her, his eyes soft and warm. "I liked it."

Oh, no. They were headed down that slippery slope again. She swallowed. "You know what? I haven't done my exercises yet today. While the cake cools I think I'll go upstairs and do some stretching. We can finish the card game when I'm done."

He put the cards down and sighed. "Don't run away. Please. I'm the one who has to watch what I say and how I say it. It's just that you're so damned appealing, and I find myself reacting to you as a man."

"A vulnerable man." He'd said she was damned appealing. She liked the sound of that. She still had to be careful, of course, but it was comforting to know that he found her damned appealing. "You're under a lot of stress."

"So are you. You're pretty vulnerable yourself." He looked at her with great tenderness. "And before you take exception to that, I don't mean because you're young. I'll admit that when I came here I expected to spend my time consoling someone who was little more than a kid. I was wrong. You've been the one consoling me, for the most part." His gaze traveled over her. "And I'm well aware you're no kid."

Heat washed over her. "You're not helping, Morgan. I thought you were going to watch what you said."

"I am. I promise." He gestured toward the chair opposite him. "Come on. We haven't settled the championship of the world yet."

She approached the table. "You do know that the cozy cottage in the Hudson Valley is a bad idea, right?"

Awareness of her flickered in his dark eyes. "Yeah, I know. You'd hate the snow."

"Right." She sat down and won the hand in no time flat. She had the definite impression that Morgan was no longer concentrating on the game.

HE SHOULD BE missing Arielle, Morgan told himself as he lay sleeplessly on Mary Jane's couch a couple of hours later. Instead he missed Mary Jane, who was upstairs in her bed. They hadn't been this far apart in the past twenty-four hours, and he felt bereft.

What a weakling he'd become. He should be on his way to New York instead of playing house with her. And that's exactly what this felt like, playing house. He hadn't realized how much he'd hungered for the homey activities of shopping for groceries, fixing lunch, going out in search of a blasted cake and then baking one of their own. The scent of chocolate still hung in the air.

He turned over, trying to get comfortable on the too-short couch. In hopes that it would help him sleep, he'd taken a hot shower while she'd cleaned up the dishes from the baking project. But showering in Mary Jane's bathroom had only succeeded in making him think of Mary Jane naked, which hadn't relaxed him for sleep, that was for sure. So he lay here in his new underwear and fought his sexual frustration.

Staring into the darkness, he was determined to think of something besides making love to Mary Jane. A night-light burned in the half bath, sending enough illumination so he wouldn't bump into the furniture if he had to get up during the night. He could see the *Toy Story* video on the coffee table, ready to be returned to the rental place tomorrow. He wanted to rent another crazy movie, buy another pizza and do the whole evening over again.

Who would have guessed he'd come to Austin and find something he hadn't known he was missing? Arielle had set the tone of their marriage from the beginning. She'd picked out and decorated the apartment, and he'd let her have free rein. After all, she'd majored in fine arts, and everyone had said she had beautiful taste. As a result, the apartment was a showplace.

Exactly. It was for show, not for living—a gallery for her art collection, a place to bring business acquaintances for cocktails, a spot to house an answering machine so they could keep track of each other, an address for the people who delivered a few groceries, although most of their meals were eaten out. In six years of living there he'd never felt as relaxed as he had sitting on Mary Jane's floor eating a pizza.

Yet he'd been proud of his beautiful, elegant wife. The setting she'd created had suited her, and he'd seen the admiration in the eyes of other men who had obviously envied him. That had been a heady feeling, but he was beginning to wonder if that's all the marriage had been about—showing off.

One thing was for sure, a baby wouldn't have fit into that environment very well. Maybe his determination to have at least one child had come from a need to shove something warm and unpredictable into that cold, changeless setting. That wasn't a very good reason for bringing a new human being into the world. If the parents of one of his small patients had admitted such a thing, he would have been horrified.

Whatever his misguided reasons for pushing the idea, he'd succeeded in helping create a baby girl. If he was the only one to deal with the consequences, that would be one thing. But he'd totally altered Mary Jane's existence by bringing her into this. And he was pretty sure it had been his idea, although Arielle had gone along with his suggestion to ask Mary Jane. As a doctor he'd pledged to do no harm, yet all pregnancies carried some risk. He felt sick with dread whenever he considered the potential danger Mary Jane faced when the hour of birth came.

He'd invaded her life five months ago, and he was doing

it again now. She'd be all right without him, at least until the delivery. He'd kidded himself that she needed him, both to get over the shock of Arielle's death and for support during the pregnancy. She didn't. He was the needy one around here.

His neediness might be the very thing that attracted her, because she was a caring person. Besides, there was a perfectly logical reason for her interest in him. Pregnant women often had an increased sexual appetite. Mary Jane had decided not to date, and he was happy about that, but the decision left her with no partner to help ease her frustration.

Fortunately both of them had been able to keep their senses today, but she had the whole day off tomorrow, too. The longer they stayed constantly in each other's company, the greater the danger they'd forget themselves.

He really should get on an airplane tomorrow, no matter if this cheerful, chocolate-scented house felt like a safe harbor. The longer he stayed here, the more trouble he was liable to bring down on Mary Jane's head. She had friends who would look out for her.

As he considered that, he realized he'd like to meet her friends and assure himself that she'd have a good support system when he went back to New York. Okay, that would be a good project for the next day and would break up this cozy twosome that threatened to become too cozy. He'd ask her if he could meet some of her friends.

Closing his eyes, he breathed in the chocolate fragrance and vowed to go to sleep. He didn't think he had, but he was definitely out when a sharp cry of agony woke him.

He threw back the blanket and leaped up so quickly he banged his shin on the coffee table. The pain didn't even make him pause as he took the stairs two at a time. Images of an emotional trauma causing Mary Jane to miscarry drove him frantically up the stairs. Before he reached the top, the light flicked on in her bedroom.

Dashing through the doorway, he found her sitting up in bed surrounded by about a million stuffed animals, her face white and her eyes wide. "What is it?" he asked, gasping for breath. "Are you hurting?"

"Oh, Morgan." She began to tremble and held out her arms.

He crossed quickly to the bed, shoved furry creatures aside and climbed in, gathering her close. She grabbed him around his waist and held on for dear life. His heart thundered with fear. If the shock of all this had caused something to go wrong, and she was going to lose the baby, he didn't know if he could live through it.

She whimpered and clutched him tighter.

"Just tell me what's wrong," he coaxed, rubbing her back. "Are you having cramps?" *Please, dear God, not cramps.*

It seemed like an eternity before she finally spoke, and her voice was high-pitched and young, so very young. "I dreamed...of the crash." She shuddered. "Oh, Morgan, it was so horrible."

His stomach twisted with a new kind of pain. He hoped she hadn't imagined anything close to the reality. The police had taken him to the scene just as they'd finally extricated Arielle's lifeless body from the wreckage. Morgan would carry that picture for the rest of his life, but he didn't want Mary Jane to envision it.

But of course she had. She'd worked so hard to be brave, to comfort him when he fell apart. She'd done a fine job of being strong until she was alone in the dark. He held her close and murmured reassurances while he continued to rub her back.

She had on a different sleep outfit tonight, a scoop-necked shirt and boxers made of some incredibly soft flannel. He hadn't had much of a chance to notice, but he vaguely remembered seeing Winnie-the-Pooh on the front of the shirt before she'd plastered herself against him. Her hair smelled like flowers and chocolate. He resisted the urge to bury his nose in it.

Gradually her trembling eased, but she didn't let go of him. "I should have known this would happen," she murmured. "I have this habit of pretending everything's fine during the day, and then at night, wham! All the scary stuff hits."

"Even when you have all your friends in bed with you?"

She sighed. "There goes my reputation as a grown-up, huh?"

"I have to admit that sitting there in the middle of all those stuffed animals, you looked about twelve." And he was trying to keep that image firmly in his mind. Now that her fear was subsiding and he knew she wasn't having contractions, he had time to think about other things, like her breasts, warm and cushiony against his chest. And the womanly scent of her, completely at odds with stuffed animals and Pooh sleep shirts.

He could feel her heartbeat. That steady rhythm was keeping his baby alive. A rush of emotion swamped his objectivity, and he wanted...everything.

"I keep my stuffed animals tucked away in the closet unless something really bad happens," she said. "Then I bring them all into the bed. And this is my cuddliest set of PJs. I wear them whenever I'm feeling sad. I was hoping the PJs and the animals would work. I thought they were working, because I went to sleep. But then..." She quivered again.

She still slept with stuffed animals, he told himself. She'd only been out of high school four years. For all he knew, she chewed bubble gum and loved MTV. And he wanted to make love to her more than he'd ever wanted to make love to any woman in his life.

"Can I get you something?" he asked. "Maybe some warm tea, or—"

"No." Her hold relaxed, but she didn't let go. "What I need is probably not a good idea."

His heartbeat kicked into overdrive. She was going to ask him to make love to her. And he would have to find the strength to refuse.

She kept her cheek pressed tight against his T-shirt and didn't look at him. "I want you to stay with me for the rest of the night," she said. "I want you to hold me."

"And?" He was trembling.

"And that's all," she said. "I realize that might be very difficult for you, and I do understand that we shouldn't become lovers. Believe me, after that nightmare, sex is the last thing on my mind. I just can't make it through the night without someone here. Maybe by tomorrow night I'll be okay.''

The way he saw it, he had no choice. Stress wasn't good for her and it definitely wasn't good for the baby. She needed her rest, and if sleeping in his arms would give her that rest, then he would provide that comfort.

Somehow.

CHAPTER SEVEN

FOR THE SECOND NIGHT in a row, Mary Jane went to sleep in Morgan's arms. The nightmare that still flashed through her mind had totaled any hot feelings she might have had under the circumstances, which seemed weird. As much as she'd lusted for him earlier, all she wanted at the moment was a strong, warm body to protect her from her bad dreams. She'd heard that if you were in enough pain, normally addictive painkillers wouldn't become habit-forming. Maybe that was why she could sleep tucked in close to Morgan without wanting to get sexual.

She couldn't speak for him, however. If he was suffering because of the situation, he hadn't let her know. He'd turned out the light, lain down next to her and cradled her gently against his chest. He hadn't suggested moving the rest of the stuffed animals. Gradually a feeling of peace settled over her, and she slept.

Light was peeking through the slats of her bedroom blinds when she awoke. This second morning was easier to face than the first one had been, although she had to go through the same painful process of remembering about Arielle. But now she had a whole day of Morgan memories to cushion the horror of that fact.

During the night she'd turned in his arms so that they lay spoon fashion, her back against his chest. His hand rested against her belly, and the gesture seemed perfectly right. If she scooted backward a few inches she'd know whether Morgan, like many men, had an erection first thing in the morning.

But the nightmare had lost its power during the night. As

her body heated at the thought of Morgan having an erection, she decided scooting backward wouldn't be a very good plan.

She lay quietly, enjoying the weight of his arm around her, his steady breathing, the warmth of his hand over the rounded place where she was growing his baby. She had something of Arielle inside her, but she also had something of Morgan. Being close to him like this was perfectly natural, considering that she carried his child. She couldn't imagine how a woman could agree to have a child for total strangers, although she knew it happened.

At the moment, the baby in question was causing fluttery feelings in her stomach. Mini moves, she called them, because no one but the baby and Mary Jane would even know anything was going on. The little twitches had begun a few weeks ago, and she was used to them.

The sweet baby girl did her delicate, girly thing, making Mary Jane smile. And then the baby hauled off and gave her a kick. *A kick!* Mary Jane gasped and instinctively put her hand over Morgan's.

He came instantly awake. "What? A pain?"

"No! She kicked me! Like she was going for a soccer ball! Feel!" She lifted his hand to shove the waistband of her boxers out of the way. "There she goes again!" She held his hand tight against her tummy, and the baby landed another kick. "Feel that? She's jammin'!"

"Oh...my...God." He flattened his hand, pressing gently. "There! She did it again! I felt it!"

"You go, girl," Mary Jane whispered as a feeling of awe surged through her.

"This is amazing. Completely amazing."

"Yeah. She's really real now." Mary Jane felt all sorts of warm fuzzies for this little kidlet. "It's almost like she's announcing herself."

"It sure is. There she goes again! Wow. I think we have a future gymnast on our hands!"

We. There was no *we* in this equation. Mary Jane's excitement faded. Finally she sighed, and the bubble of joy she'd carried inside went with it. "Yes, maybe you do," she said quietly.

He didn't say anything for a long time, although he didn't move his hand, and the baby kept kicking. "I can't imagine this baby without you being there, too," he said at last. He rubbed his hand across her belly. "Damn it, this is your baby, too, Mary Jane."

If she knew what was good for her, she'd discontinue this discussion and get out of bed, get away from his touch. All he had to do was move his hand down a little and he'd be in the danger zone—for both of them. "Not technically. You contributed the sperm and Arielle contributed the egg. I'm only the—"

"Most essential part," he finished. His voice grew husky. "Without you there would be...nothing." He caressed the curve of her stomach. "Nothing," he whispered, his breath warm against her ear.

She needed to get out of this bed right now. If she didn't, she knew what was going to happen. She could hear it in the tempo of his breathing as he stroked her round belly. Ah, but she needed something to happen. He had the power to heal this hurt, at least for a little while.

If she allowed it, though, there would be hell to pay. She needed to get out of this bed. He'd thank her later for having the strength to stop him from...

Too late. He murmured her name and slid his hand beneath the elastic.

She moaned softly as he slipped his fingers through her moist curls, his touch gentle and sure. If he'd doubted whether he'd be welcomed, he knew the truth as she parted her thighs in invitation. Her breath caught as he pushed his fingers inside. Oh, yes. She needed this. Nothing fancy. Just...right there.

He stroked her as if he knew all there was to know about how she wanted to be touched. He had great hands. So great. Oh, Lord. He'd reduced her to putty, and she was embarrassingly close to...

"Let go," he murmured.

And she did, gloriously, loudly, joyfully. Hallelujah and good morning. As the tremors slowed, she turned in his arms to look into his smiling eyes. She couldn't believe something so wonderful could be a mistake, and he didn't look as if he thought so, either.

But in turning toward him, she'd brushed against the firm length of his penis and realized he was in dire straits himself. A gift such as he'd given deserved something in return. But when she put her hand against his erection, he moved away.

"No?"

"No," he said with a slight shake of his head.

"Why?"

"I can justify it for you, but not for me."

She stared at him. "I don't get it. We're all entitled to life, liberty and the pursuit of satisfaction."

"Some of us are more entitled than others." He combed her hair from her face with great care and tenderness. "I'm a doctor, and I know full well that pregnant women often feel very sexual. In a more normal setting, you'd have a husband to help you out with that. That's another thing that's wrong with this setup."

"Wait a minute." She drew away from his caress. "You did that because as a doctor you felt I needed it? Like a clinical procedure?"

"No! There was nothing clinical about it!"

"I didn't think so, either, until you started talking like a guy standing over me in an examining room!" She scrambled out of bed. "I'm not your patient, Doc. And furthermore—"

The phone interrupted her, which was a good thing, she decided as she reached to the nightstand and picked up the receiver. She'd been about to tell Morgan where he could stick his stethoscope. She needed time to count to ten before she said something she'd regret.

"Mary Jane?" Shelby said her name in that apologetic way that told Mary Jane she was about to be asked to work. "I really hate to call you at the last minute like this, but Georgette has a family emergency. She said she'd fill in for you one day next week, if you could possibly—"

"I'll be there as soon as I can," Mary Jane said. She glanced at Morgan, who had flopped down on the pillow and was staring at the ceiling, his brown eyes stormy.

"You're a good sport, Mary Jane," Shelby said. "I hope you didn't have anything big planned for today."

"Actually, I was working on a project, but it didn't pan out, so I'm free."

That crack brought Morgan's gaze to hers. She stuck out her tongue at him. He'd consider that juvenile, but he didn't look so adult himself, lying there with a pink bunny by his elbow and a green frog sprawled on the pillow beside his head.

"That's my good luck, then," Shelby said. "See you soon."

"Right. Bye." Mary Jane hung up the phone. "They need me at work. If you want to drop me off, you can have the car for the day. I'm through a little after three, so you can pick me up around three-fifteen."

He held her gaze. "But if you took the car, I could call a cab to take me to the airport."

Impossible as he could sometimes be, like very recently, for example, she didn't want him to leave. But he'd have to go eventually. His partner couldn't handle both practices forever. And once she went back to work, she'd end up telling people about Arielle, and it would make the rounds. She and Morgan wouldn't have time to themselves anymore.

He sat up. "I think I'd better leave, Mary Jane."

"Probably." She felt as if someone had wrapped her in a very heavy, stifling blanket. She really didn't like this business of him leaving. But maybe it was for the best.

"Okay. It's settled then." He swung his legs out of bed and stood. "I'll fix you some breakfast while you get ready."

She couldn't help looking at the way his T-shirt molded itself against his chest. And he really did have outstanding legs—muscled thighs and nicely shaped calves. He'd be fun to touch. "I usually don't have much for breakfast."

His lips curved in a faint smile. "So I figured. But if I

scramble some eggs and pour you some juice, will you give it a shot?''

"Sure." She could force down one more meal to please him. The thought of not having him there to supervise her diet was extremely depressing. She couldn't be pleased, apparently. She resented his meddling, but she didn't want him to stop doing it.

He started out of the room. "How long before you'll be down?''

"Ten minutes." She allowed herself to enjoy what might be her last good view of his butt in those skimpy briefs he wore. Damn, but she'd love to get her hands on those tight cheeks.

"Ten minutes?" He turned in surprise and caught her ogling.

She raised the level of her gaze and looked boldly into his eyes, determined to brave it out. Unfortunately she couldn't control her blush.

"You were staring at my butt." He sounded astonished.

"What if I was? Is there a law against that?''

"No, it's just—''

"That you're offended because I'm treating you like a sex object? Well, I didn't mean for you to catch me at it, so I don't think that counts." She felt like staring at his crotch, because she had a sneaky suspicion something was going on down there, but she diligently held his gaze. "But if you're offended, then I apologize for offending you."

"I'm not offended. I'm...I guess I'm flattered. Nobody's ever—that is, I've never been aware that a woman was, uh, would want to..." He seemed at a total loss.

Her jaw dropped. "You don't *know* that you have a sexy tush?''

He shook his head.

"I can't believe nobody's ever told you that you have a nice butt." She couldn't believe Arielle had never told him, to be specific, but she decided not to bring his wife's name into this discussion. "But if they haven't, then I guess they weren't paying attention. You have a fabulous set of cheeks,

Morgan Tate. And that's why I wanted to sneak a peek before you hopped on a jet plane and I wouldn't get the chance anymore."

She might have struck him dumb, but his eyes were doing a lot of talking, and it was one hot conversation he was having with her. She couldn't resist letting her attention stray south, and sure enough, he was ready for action. "I guess you like hearing that," she said.

"I love hearing that. And I'm dangerously close to taking advantage of this situation. Advantage of you. That's why I need to go home today."

Looking into his eyes, she nodded. "Guess so," she said softly. Then, because she felt sorry for the poor guy, she turned, went into the bathroom and shut the door. He needed someone who truly appreciated what a hunk he was, but that person couldn't be her, obviously, so it was best if they parted ways.

MINUTES LATER, his fabulous cheeks covered in jeans, Morgan stood in the kitchen cracking eggs into a bowl while a skillet warmed on the stove. Fabulous cheeks. A sexy tush. He was still semiaroused thinking of Mary Jane standing in her nightshirt and boxers, her outrageous toenails winking at him as she talked about the merits of his backside. If he really had a great butt, then obviously he'd never dated the kind of woman who would tell him so.

He thought back to the two serious girlfriends he'd had before he'd met Arielle. They'd been a lot like Arielle, come to think of it. Elegant and brainy, with a cool sort of beauty, like marble statues. And they were distant.

The thought made him blink. Distant. Like his parents.

Standing with half a cracked eggshell in each hand, he stared out the kitchen window at the birds gathering around the feeder. It was low on seed. Before Mary Jane left he needed to ask her where she kept the birdseed.

He also needed to get a move on with breakfast if she made good on her boast to be down in ten minutes. After whipping the eggs with a fork, he dumped them in a pan and pushed down the handle on the toaster.

Ten minutes. He still couldn't get over it. Those cool, elegant women he'd known, including his mother, had never been able to get dressed and out the door in less than an hour. He hadn't timed Mary Jane yesterday; his mind had been on other things. She'd likely been stalling, anyway, after the confrontation they'd had about... He paused. He still had no adequate way to label what had happened between them that first night. It was far more significant than sex, yet he couldn't call it making love, either. The same thing went for this morning.

In his experience, making love involved so much more than they'd shared. He'd never even kissed her. Yet he'd brought her to orgasm twice, and each time had filled him with wonder and joy. She was so responsive, so warm, so lacking in any pretense at all.

"Is something burning?"

He glanced at the smoking skillet of eggs. "Damn!"

"Hey, no problem." She crossed to the toaster and pulled out the two pieces of whole wheat toast, which were perfectly browned, thanks to the wonders of automation.

He couldn't say the same for the blackened eggs he scooped down the garbage disposal. "Listen, I'm sorry. Do you have time for me to start over?"

"Not really. Shelby needs me there for the morning rush." She opened the refrigerator and took out a jar of grape jelly. She grabbed a knife from the silverware drawer, opened the jar and spread the jelly on the toast.

Considering that he'd burned the nutritious breakfast he'd meant to feed her, he didn't think he could say a word. Besides, he was too busy taking in the picture she made, her wild curls tamed into a ponytail, her rounded body filling out the short-skirted white uniform she wore.

"I know this is a little tight." She patted her tummy where the waistband of the dress was straining at the button. "I have a maternity version on order, but I haven't really needed it until just lately."

Now that she'd brought his attention to the waist of the dress he could see what she meant, but he'd been too engrossed in the swell of her breasts and the smoothness of her legs to notice. Her name tag was pinned over her heart, and he'd become mesmerized watching the plastic tag rise and fall with each breath she took.

"You look great," he said.

She swallowed a mouthful of toast. "Thanks. Would you please pour me some juice?"

He rolled his eyes. "I didn't even get the juice poured for you. If I were you, I'd fire me." He turned toward the cupboard to get her a glass.

"You had your mind on other things," she said with a hint of a tease in her voice.

"Birdseed," he said, taking down a large glass.

"Birdseed? Hey, not the giant size!" she protested when she saw the glass he'd chosen. "If I drink that much juice before I leave here, I'll have to wait tables with my legs crossed."

"You need fluids," he said, sounding every inch the stuffy doctor. It was a disguise. The earthy way she talked reminded him constantly that he was every inch a man. He'd never spent much time with women like Mary Jane, and he was discovering things he'd never known about himself. Mostly he was discovering that he was an earthy guy himself. Who would've guessed?

"I'll drink water at work," she said. "And pace myself."

He took down a medium-size glass.

"Much better. Now, what's this about birdseed?"

"Your feeder needs some. Where do you keep it?" He opened the refrigerator, took out the juice and poured the glass full.

"You would fill my bird feeder for me?"

He handed her the glass. "It beats watching those little suckers flying past the window carrying protest signs in their beaks."

She nearly choked on her juice.

"Hey, I'm sorry."

"No!" She swallowed and glanced up. "Don't apologize for making a cute little joke! We need those."

"We do?"

"Yeah." Her eyes turned a smoky shade of blue. "Jokes are good when you have to say goodbye to someone you care about."

Goodbye. He'd told himself that he had to leave, but he hadn't pictured this moment, when she would go off to work and they'd have to say goodbye. His stomach tensed.

"It's okay, you know." She drained her glass and set it on the counter. "We'll both be fine. We needed this time together, and now we can go our separate ways before things get sticky."

"I'm planning to come back when the baby's due."

"Well, of course. You don't think I'm going to put her in the overnight mail, do you?" She waited, a little smile on her face. "That was another cute little joke. You're supposed to laugh."

"I don't feel like laughing. This doesn't feel right, me leaving and then coming back in four months to take the baby away."

Sadness filled her eyes, but she kept that brave smile on her face. "You'll get used to it. We both will."

He had a hard time believing that, but he wasn't in the most objective frame of mind. "Maybe you're right," he said. He tried to think of it from her standpoint. In another four months she could go back to being a carefree young woman, ready to party and eventually find the right guy so she could start her own family. At that point she wouldn't want him and the baby hanging around. "This feeling between us is…temporary. Unreliable. We're under stress, that's all."

"You'd better believe it. Why else would a man like you find himself gaga over a girl like me?"

He stared at her in astonishment. "What in hell does that mean?"

She shrugged. "I'm a twenty-two-year-old waitress in Austin. You're an up-and-coming pediatrician in New York City.

I can see why this lust you're feeling is embarrassing to you. I'm not in your league."

"That's bullshit!" He grabbed her by the shoulders and gave her a little shake. "If we're talking about leagues, how about me not being in yours? You're the most selfless person I've ever met, and you're kind, and warm, and funny, and fantastic to look at. Any guy who got you should fall down on his knees and thank God that you'd have him."

She gazed at him with shining eyes. "You don't have to say that to make me feel better. But thanks."

"I'm not saying it to make you feel better!"

"Sure you are. And I appreciate it."

"I'm not trying to make you feel better, damn it." He could tell from her expression she didn't believe him, and that's when he finally lost it and kissed her.

Oh, God. She tasted like…the richest hot fudge sundae he'd ever had. He sort of went crazy—kissing her, and kissing her, and kissing her some more. He was afraid he also used his tongue quite liberally as he continued to enjoy her full, sexy, incredibly sweet mouth. His hands found their way to her bottom and pulled her in tight, and boy, oh, boy, did she fit.

She filled his arms in a way they'd never been filled before. He'd never held such energy, such excitement, such heat. Mary Jane's body pressed against his caused a spontaneous combustion that made him dizzy with wanting to have her, all of her, right now.

Then she put her hands against his chest and gently pushed him away.

He stood there panting like a freight engine, his eyes glazed. If she hadn't stopped him, no telling how long he would have kept that kiss going.

She was breathing so fast her name tag was jumping up and down. "Okay…so you weren't…trying to…make me…feel better," she said, gasping. She tucked a strand of hair into her ponytail with shaking fingers. "All things considered—" she gulped in another breath "—we'd better not kiss goodbye. I have to, uh, fix my lipstick. Then maybe I should slip out the door.''

He nodded, unable to think of anything to say besides *Stay here*. She couldn't do that. He didn't want her to. For her own good, he needed to get the hell out of her life. If she could find the strength to walk out that door, he'd find the strength to get on a plane.

She walked into the entryway, where she'd put her purse on the small table. He followed her like a puppy. A small mirror hung over the table, and she used it to apply the lipstick she dug out of her purse.

Her hands trembled, but she managed to get the lipstick on. She parted her lips to get it right and gazed at herself with a half-lidded stare of concentration. He'd never thought of this beauty ritual as erotic, but then he'd never watched it performed by Mary Jane.

He gazed at her lips like a starving man. The color hadn't mattered to him before, but he focused on the rich tone because it was on Mary Jane's mouth—a mouth he wanted more than he wanted to draw another breath.

Leaning toward the mirror, she pressed her lips together.

He groaned.

Without turning, she met his gaze in the mirror. "You have lipstick on your face."

Lifting the back of his hand, he started to wipe it off.

"Just lick it off," she said. "It tastes like fudge." Then she picked up her purse. "See ya around, cowboy."

As she unlocked the door and went outside, he clenched both hands to keep from running, grabbing her and hauling her inside. He was going insane over a woman who wore fudge-flavored lipstick and slept with stuffed animals when she got scared. This attraction made no sense for Morgan Tate, conservative pediatrician, but all his usual points of reference had deserted him.

Fudge lipstick. No wonder her mouth had tasted so good.

Maybe it was only the lipstick that had him turning into a madman.

But he knew it wasn't the lipstick. And in another minute it would hit him that she was truly gone.

CHAPTER EIGHT

THE SILK DAISY in the bud vase on her dashboard wasn't enough to cheer up Mary Jane as she drove to Austin Eats. She was very much afraid she was falling for Arielle's husband. And that was bad. He'd said their feelings couldn't be trusted when they were both so stressed, and she believed that—for him.

After all, he'd just lost the most important person in his life and he was about to become a father. Mary Jane would bet that some professor of psychology at some big university had written a paper about the sort of emotions Morgan was feeling. Deeply buried instincts were driving him to find a new mate quickly, and Mary Jane was in the line of fire.

That explained why Morgan would think he wanted someone like Mary Jane, who was clearly not the right person to fit into his personal and professional life in New York, even if she wanted to, which she didn't. But Mary Jane's feelings for Morgan couldn't be explained so neatly. She wasn't looking for anybody to fill a gap in her life. Come to think of it, she hadn't expected to get married for several more years.

But she wanted Morgan Tate. She wanted him on a gut level she'd learned to trust over the years. And the wanting went beyond sex. She had yearnings that involved white lace and promises. She wondered if it had to do with seeing him as husband material because he had *been* a husband, and a good one, from all the evidence. With Morgan, she wouldn't be buying a pig in a poke. Of course, that didn't matter, because he would never consider her as wife material.

But then there was the matter of the baby. If mating instincts drove her, they would be all about forming a bond with the father of this baby. The kidlet, prizewinning kicks included, did feel like her baby despite the complicated biology involved.

Possession was nine-tenths of the law. Ha.

Or maybe she wanted Morgan because he'd belonged to Arielle and secretly she coveted anything connected to Arielle. Damn, she hoped that wasn't it. She thought back to the wedding six years ago, when at the age of sixteen she'd been Arielle's maid of honor. Oh, she'd envied Arielle then, envied the fairy-tale ceremony, the honeymoon to Paris, the china, the silver and the lace tablecloths.

But she hadn't really envied Arielle for having Morgan. To Mary Jane's sixteen-year-old self, Morgan at twenty-five had seemed far too old, far too brainy and far too professional for anybody like her. At thirty-one, he still did, when she stopped to think about it. Unfortunately he had a way of short-circuiting her brain. And there was that gut-level feeling of rightness that had nothing to do with logical thinking, either.

She'd have plenty of logical thinking time coming up, though. Today he was going away. Sooner or later she'd have to face the fact that he wouldn't be there when she got home from work.

But not yet.

She whipped her little Beetle down the alley that ran behind Austin Eats and parked behind the diner. Between having to tell folks at the diner about Arielle and then going home to an empty house, today wasn't going to be much fun. Might as well get it over with.

LESS THAN AN HOUR later Morgan was in a cab headed for the airport, his few belongings in a small duffel bag he'd found in Mary Jane's closet. He'd left her a note telling her he'd borrowed the duffel and he'd mail it back to her.

He hadn't wasted much time once she'd left. After cleaning the kitchen and making the bed, he'd searched out the birdseed because she'd never told him where it was. But once he'd gone out to her little patio he'd found a colorful trash can that looked like the obvious place to store it. To eliminate all doubt, she'd used red nail polish to paint Birdseed on the lid.

The same nail polish she'd used on her toes, most likely.

Morgan sat in the back of the cab thinking about Mary Jane's toes. In another couple of months she'd have trouble painting her toenails. He wondered if she'd ask a friend to do it, or get a pedicure. She wouldn't let them go. Not Mary Jane. He pictured himself doing it for her and loved the idea, although he'd never painted a woman's toenails in his life.

He hadn't even reached the airport yet and he missed her so much his throat hurt. Instead of making a reservation on such short notice, he'd decided he'd be better off trying to grab a seat on standby. It had worked at JFK on the way here, so it should work again on the way home. No, not home. Not anymore.

But he didn't have a home with Mary Jane, either. She'd agreed to have a baby for him, and that was more than he should have asked of any human being other than his wife. He couldn't expect anything more from Mary Jane.

THE EARLY-MORNING crunch at Austin Eats prevented Mary Jane from exchanging anything but minor conversation with Shelby or the cook, Sara. Mary Jane was just as glad. She wanted to work up to breaking the news about Arielle, and falling into the regular routine helped steady her for the ordeal. Telling the news would no doubt put her through an emotional wringer all over again.

Because the diner was right next door to Maitland Maternity, it provided a handy alternative to the clinic's cafeteria. The medical staff ate there regularly, and people visiting patients often headed to Austin Eats for a quick bite or to celebrate the arrival of a new baby with towering hot fudge sundaes.

Originally founded to provide care for single pregnant women in difficult financial situations, Maitland Maternity had been adopted by the rich and famous as *the* place to have their children. Mary Jane had served food to her share of celebs. Hollywood types showing up unannounced definitely made her job more exciting, but she found most of her satisfaction in providing good food to the regulars—hardworking doctors and nurses, maintenance workers and clerical help.

Mary Jane put a smile on her face for the sake of her customers, who deserved to have a happy waitress bring their food. People who didn't know her might think she laughed and joked with her customers to get a better tip. Although it usually worked out that way, Mary Jane knew she'd treat people the same even if tips were abolished.

She was perfect for this job, and she knew it. Her personality fit right in with the snappy diner decor—a black and white checkered floor, sparkling red vinyl seats and a reconditioned jukebox in one corner that played CDs instead of forty-fives. Austin Eats served all the old favorites like burgers, shakes and a meat-loaf dinner special, but it also served a healthy helping of good cheer with each meal. Mary Jane took pride in contributing to that mood.

As a result of pretending to be upbeat for a couple of hours, she actually began to feel better. By mid-morning, when the flow of customers let up, she wished they'd have another rush so she could forget about Arielle for a little longer and imagine that Morgan was still in her town house instead of on a plane bound for New York.

But Shelby and Sara would be hurt if she kept something this important from them. After checking to make sure all the customers were settled for the time being, she asked Shelby to come in the kitchen with her.

"Is something wrong?" Shelby asked immediately, concern in her green eyes. One of the Lord triplets, she had the signature red hair, just like Lana. "Don't tell me you've had some complication with the baby."

"In a way."

"Oh, no." Shelby followed her into the kitchen. "I should never have asked you to work. Go home right this minute. I can handle things."

Sara turned from the griddle. She'd always reminded Mary Jane of Cinderella—blond, blue-eyed and working in the scullery. "What's wrong?" She put down her spatula and moved a stool toward Mary Jane. "Do you need to sit down? Are you having pains?"

"No, it's not me. And the baby's fine." Mary Jane took a deep breath. "Arielle—you know, the mother of the baby..."

"Yes, yes," Shelby said impatiently. "Your nanny. What about her? If she's changed her mind, I will personally—"

Mary Jane's hands started to shake, and she clutched them in front of her as she tried to stop the trembling. "She...was killed in a car accident." As she watched the shock register on the women's faces, the horror of it all came down on her again, and tears welled in her eyes. She gulped back a sob. "But I'm doing—"

"Oh, honey." Shelby wrapped both arms around her and began to rock her back and forth.

"I'm so sorry," Sara murmured brokenly. She came over and began to rub Mary Jane's back. "I'm so very sorry."

Mary Jane fought her tears, but they were winning. "I didn't want...to break down," she said. And then she buried her face against Shelby's uniform and sobbed while Shelby rocked her and Sara rubbed her back.

Finally she was able to bring the tears to a halt and drew away from Shelby with a watery smile. "Sorry."

"Nothing to be sorry about, toots."

"Here." Sara grabbed a paper napkin and handed it to her.

"We need...need to check on the customers," Mary Jane said. "Maybe I'd better go fix myself up a little first."

"Hold on there, sweetheart." Shelby took her arm. "The customers can wait another couple of minutes. When did this happen?"

"Uh—" She tried to think, to figure out the timing. "About four days ago, I guess."

Sara handed her another napkin. "And you just heard?"

"No." Mary Jane tossed the first soggy napkin in the trash and blew her nose with the second one. "Her husband, Morgan, came to my house night before last to tell me. We've been hanging out, trying to come to grips with it."

"Of course you have." Shelby rubbed Mary Jane's arm. "You should have told me when I called. You have no business being in here. Go on back home. In fact, you'll probably need time off to go back there for the funeral.''

Mary Jane sniffed and dabbed at her eyes. "No, I won't. There won't be one. She didn't believe in funerals.''

"Oh." Shelby started to say something, but seemed to think better of it. "Well, regardless. You shouldn't have left her grieving husband to come in to work." She patted Mary Jane's hand. "Go on. Take all the time you need.''

"We can ask Joe to come in and do more of the cooking," Sara said. "Then I can help with the waitressing. Seriously, Mary Jane. We'll be fine here, won't we, Shelby?''

"Absolutely.''

"You guys are the best." Mary Jane took a shaky breath. "But Morgan went back to New York today, and the best thing for me right now is to work. I wanted you to know, though.''

"So you haven't told Lana?" Shelby asked.

"No. You two are the first.''

Shelby gazed at Mary Jane in sympathy. "Do you want me to tell her?''

"That's okay." Mary Jane figured Lana would rather hear it from the source. "I'll go by the shop on my way home.''

"I think you should ask her to spend the night with you," Shelby said. "You shouldn't be alone right now. If she can't do it, I will, but I'm betting she'll drop everything if you ask her.''

"That's an idea." Mary Jane managed a smile. "It's been a long time since Lana and I had a sleep-over. We can stay up all night, eat ice cream from the carton and make anonymous phone calls.''

Shelby returned her smile. "Sounds like fun. I might have to stop by, after all.''

"Me, too," Sara said.

"Shoot, maybe we should see if we can get Beth and Ellie to come and have an old-fashioned slumber party!" Mary Jane gave them both a hug. "Thanks. And now we *really* need to go see about our customers.''

AFTER SEVERAL straight hours of not getting a flight, Morgan was totally sick of the Austin airport, its waiting lounge and its ticketing agents. Everyone had been unfailingly polite, but the planes were just…full. While waiting he'd ingested way too much coffee and not enough food. Some healthy role model he was. Mary Jane could rightly accuse him of being a hypocrite.

How he'd love to listen to her lecture him. How he'd love to hear her voice, period. She could read from the flight departure monitor and he'd be enthralled. Leaving Mary Jane was turning into a production, both mentally and physically.

Without her he couldn't seem to care about anything, least of all his diet. He sat down to wait for yet one more flight with a cup of black coffee and a bear claw.

"I can't get over how busy this airport is," a guy in a business suit remarked as he sat next to Morgan.

"Tell me about it." Morgan bit into his pastry.

"You must be from around here."

He swallowed. "Nope. I'm from New York."

"Really?" The businessman eyed Morgan's shirt, jeans, boots and hat. "You sure look like a Texan, although now I notice your accent's wrong. Thinking of relocating?"

"Nope." Actually, he hadn't been able to think of anything *but* relocating, but he couldn't justify encroaching on Mary Jane's territory. He took a drink of coffee and scalded his tongue.

"I tell you, Austin's booming. The high-tech industry is going gangbusters. I've been down here on business, and I seriously thought of snapping up some real estate. I ran out of time to look, but it would be a damned good investment."

"Is that right?" Morgan forgot about his scalded tongue as he turned to the stranger.

"I sure think so. I may schedule another trip for that very purpose."

"That good, huh?"

"Hey, you see what happened in Silicon Valley. Housing prices there are through the roof. I was thinking a place down here would make a good weekend getaway for the family during the winter when New York's buried under a few feet of snow. Eventually I could sell the property and turn a nice profit. Or who knows? I might decide to retire here. It's a great little city.''

"No doubt about it." Morgan thought about the For Sale sign he'd noticed on the road where Mary Jane had stopped so he could examine the bluebonnets. He remembered the way the hills had turned purple at sunset, and how peaceful he'd felt standing by the roadside, looking at the field of wildflowers in the fading light.

An investment. That wasn't such a bad idea. After all, he was about to become a father, and he'd have to start saving for things like college. The baby would eventually become a young woman, and she'd find a nice guy and want to get married. Morgan had to be ready for that with some spare cash.

Besides, his baby shouldn't spend her entire winter in the snowy Northeast. If they owned a place in Austin, they could fly down for long weekends until the time came to make good on the investment. And it would make it easier for Mary Jane to see the baby.

It would also make it easier for him to see Mary Jane, but he shouldn't think about it that way. That shouldn't be his motivation. He didn't intend to make a pest of himself and interfere with her life. He'd only be doing the prudent thing, the financially responsible thing. He'd only be making an investment.

"They're calling the flight," the businessman said. "Where're you sitting?"

"I'm on standby."

"Oh. Then good luck getting on. Nice talking to you."

"Same here." Morgan watched him walk toward the jetway and made a decision. If they had room for him on this flight, he'd go. But if not, he'd take it as a sign that he needed to stay a little longer and look into the possibility of investing in some real estate.

IT PROMISED to be the slumber party of the century. Limp Bizkit blared from Mary Jane's stereo as another contestant moved to the center of her crowded living room to compete in the First Annual Slutty Dance Contest.

"Don't start without me!" Lana yelled from the kitchen. "Hey, who ate all the Rocky Road?"

"There's another one in the freezer!" Ellie yelled. "Get in here before Shelby chickens out."

"Shelby, Shelby, Shelby," chanted Beth, Ellie's twin.

Mary Jane picked up the chant and started to clap rhythmically. She could hardly believe that a dozen of her friends had dropped whatever they'd planned to do tonight to come over and sleep on her living room floor.

The house was a disaster following the makeover session. Hot rollers, blow driers, curling irons and makeup cases were scattered everywhere. Beth still wore some of a green clay masque across her upper lip like a mustache, and Ellie had allowed Mary Jane to spike her hair so she looked like a punk rocker. Even quiet Sara had joined in the fun and wore an enormous set of false eyelashes.

They'd pigged out on pizza, ice cream and various packages of cookies with no redeeming value other than they tasted terrific. At one point Ellie had made a halfhearted attempt to clean up the food mess, but she'd been hooted into submission. Empty pizza boxes and ice cream cartons sat on every available surface.

Everyone had gathered, in various stages of undress, to stage the dance contest. As Shelby did her version of a bump and grind, Mary Jane laughed so hard her sides began to hurt.

"Your turn!" Shelby cried, gasping with laughter as she pointed at Mary Jane.

Beth started the chant, and everyone joined in. "Mary Jane, Mary Jane, Mary Jane!"

Giggling, she moved to the center of the room. For the occasion she'd worn some baby-doll pajamas she'd had when she was in high school. As the music started, she began a sensuous shimmy that soon had the group applauding wildly. She whirled and wiggled her hips, having more fun than she'd had in ages.

"Doorbell!" someone shouted.

"That's more pizza!" Lana called above the music. "Keep going! I'll get it!" She leaped to her feet and headed for the entry hall.

Mary Jane threw herself into the beat, lifting her hands over her head and trying out every naughty little move she'd ever practiced in front of the mirror as a teenager when she'd fantasized herself as an exotic stripper. Her appreciative audience whistled and stomped, which only egged her on.

"Hey, Mary Jane!"

With a flourish, she whirled toward the entry where Lana stood. Then she nearly fell over. Standing next to her, his eyes bugging out of his head, was Morgan.

She gulped. "What are you doing here?"

He rubbed the back of his neck and gave her a sheepish smile. "Investing in real estate?"

MORGAN'S FIRST THOUGHT, that he'd made a terrible mistake in coming back, was obliterated by the rush of female attention that followed Mary Jane's hurried introduction. Not a single woman ran screaming from the room because he'd caught them in their pajamas. Although a couple casually slipped on bathrobes, most of them didn't seem to care what they were wearing. They were too busy taking care of him.

Over his protests they scurried around to serve him food, pour him something to drink and find him a place to sit. But the commotion kept him from getting a bead on how Mary Jane was taking his return. He was sorry he'd interrupted her dance. Yes, it was a sexual turn-on to watch her shaking and shimmying, but more than that he'd sensed she was dancing her way through her grief.

Good for her. He should have known she'd find a way to slay her dragons, and he didn't want to interfere with that. But God, he was glad to see her. He wished he could tell whether she was glad to see him.

How ironic that he'd planned to meet Mary Jane's friends today and find out whether they would take care of her when he left. Obviously they would.

Introductions took a while, but eventually he figured out the principal players. Lana Lord, Mary Jane's best friend, and Shelby Lord, Mary Jane's boss, had the same red hair because they were two members of a set of triplets. Then came the Maitland twins, Beth and Ellie. Sara worked at the diner with Mary Jane.

The other seven women were buddies from high school who were no longer a big part of Mary Jane's life but were more than ready to swoop in and offer support in a time of crisis. Morgan wasn't surprised by the kind of devotion Mary Jane inspired in her friends. She was an extraordinary young woman.

And so different from the way Arielle had portrayed her. Arielle hadn't been able to say her name without putting the word *little* in front of it. That was understandable, because when Arielle had first taken over the Potter household, Mary Jane *had* been little. She still wasn't very big in terms of stature. But in terms of heart, she was ten feet tall.

Morgan looked around the room at the people who had gathered to help Mary Jane through a difficult time and couldn't imagine anything similar being orchestrated for him or Arielle. Perhaps Mary Jane didn't have a college education or a job with a fancy title, but she was obviously doing something very significant with her life.

In response to questions, he told his story about not being able to get a standby flight and meeting the New York businessman who'd suggested that Austin was a good place to buy real estate. Now that he was explaining his reasoning, it sounded pretty weak.

Strangely enough, nobody pointed that out. They praised his idea as brilliant. Again, he kept trying to sneak a look at Mary Jane to get her reaction, but she avoided his gaze.

"There's the Slattery place, next to Garrett," Lana said. "That would make a wonderful winter home for you."

"Perfect," Shelby agreed. "That area will increase in value, and the house is well-built. Don't you think it would be perfect, Mary Jane?"

Her cheeks grew pink. "Well, I—I guess it would, although that seems like a lot of money to spend."

He was in agony, thinking that she didn't like his idea at all. "Maybe it's a stupid idea."

"No, I didn't say that. It's just so much money for a winter home, that's all." She still refused to look at him. "More pizza?"

"No, thanks. It was great, though." He wondered if she remembered how cozy this house had been the night before when they'd shared a pizza and watched *Toy Story*. Then again, maybe she'd moved beyond that and wanted him gone. "Listen, I didn't mean to break up the party. I'll call a cab and check into a hotel for the night."

"That's silly," Mary Jane said.

His stomach relaxed a little. It was the first thing she'd said that indicated she might want him around.

"Maybe we should all skedaddle," Lana Lord said.

"No!" He could see how much effort had gone into this party. "I'd feel terrible if you all left because I showed up. I'll call a cab."

Finally Mary Jane looked at him. "You can't spend the night in some lonely hotel room," she said.

He looked into her eyes, which had turned to that soft blue he'd come to cherish. "I'll be fine."

"Maybe, but I wouldn't feel right about it. We're all sleeping down here tonight, so you can go upstairs and crash in my bed."

That reminded him of something he'd conveniently forgotten. Mary Jane might need a night of fun and games, but he wondered if that was a good thing for the baby. "If I do that, then you won't have use of the bed."

She gestured toward a sleeping bag in the corner. "I have that."

He had to tread lightly here. She'd created her own method for getting through her bad moments, and that was brave of her. Still, she shouldn't spend a totally sleepless night. "Is that going to be good enough? Considering that you're—"

"Aha!" Shelby said, stepping in. "I get it. He thinks we're

going to keep the little mama-to-be up all night and that's not good for the little one. Am I right?''

"It crossed my mind,'' Morgan admitted.

"Don't worry about a thing,'' Shelby said. "We have a couple more events planned, and then we're tucking Mary Jane in for the night.''

"Wait a minute,'' Mary Jane protested. "I didn't agree to be tucked in.''

"Too bad.'' Shelby wrapped an arm around her shoulders and gave her a hug. "If you think a room full of women are going to let pregnant you stay up all night, then you don't know your friends very well.''

"We'll see about that,'' Mary Jane said.

Shelby glanced at Morgan. "Trust me. It's under control. You can have the bed upstairs and go to sleep without a care.''

Mary Jane seemed ready to drop the argument for the time being. "I'm pretty sure there's a pair of earplugs in my bedside table left over from the week they jackhammered the sidewalk to replace the sewer pipe. Stick those babies in your ears and you'll be out like a light.''

Of course he wanted to stay in this house that was so full of life and fun. The idea of a hotel sounded really depressing. But his conscience bothered him. He hated the fact that he'd crashed her party. "I really don't think I should—''

"Either you do that,'' Lana said, stepping forward, "or we'll all pack up and go home. Take your choice.''

He looked around at the women, and all of them nodded. With a sigh of relief he threw up his hands. "I guess you can't fight city hall.''

"Of course, you don't have to go up and go to bed right away if you don't want to,'' Shelby said.

"Yes, I do.'' He picked up the duffel he'd borrowed from Mary Jane and smiled at her. "Otherwise you're liable to rope me into that dance contest, and I'm a terrible dancer.'' Amid a chorus of protests, he climbed the stairs. He sure loved living in Mary Jane's world.

CHAPTER NINE

MARY JANE watched him walk up the stairs, her mind in a turmoil. He'd come back. To invest in real estate. If that was really his motivation, he was about to turn her life upside down simply for financial gain. With the way she felt about him, having him winter in Austin would be horribly painful.

The minute he'd gone upstairs and closed the bedroom door, her friends clustered around her.

"Oh, Mary Jane, he's adorable," Lana said. "Those sad brown eyes and that cute little grin. His body's not so bad, either, although maybe it's bad taste for me to mention it, with him being a grieving husband and all."

"Poor man," Shelby said. "You can tell he's not quite sure how to cope."

"I wouldn't say that." Mary Jane sent another glance up the stairs to make sure Morgan wouldn't suddenly appear because he'd forgotten something he needed. "Looks to me like he's ready to wheel and deal."

Beth laughed. "Are you saying you *believed* that cockamamy story about coming back so he could invest in real estate?"

"Lame, totally lame," Lana agreed, shaking her head.

Mary Jane glanced around as everyone else echoed the sentiment. "But you all sounded as if you thought it was the greatest idea since sliced bread!"

"Of course we did." Shelby patted her arm. "The man's got nothing back in New York, and he doesn't want to leave Austin and face an empty apartment, so he's grasping at straws. Only a cruel person would point that out at a time like this."

Shelby's comments made sense to Mary Jane, much to her dismay. Morgan was running away from something, not toward something. Away from New York, not toward her. She shouldn't be tempted to think otherwise.

"Besides," Lana said, "you can make sure he doesn't buy something that's overpriced or in a less desirable part of town. Encouraging him to buy the Slattery place won't hurt anything, for example. I'm sure it *will* go up in value, so he's not risking much."

Just my heart. "But all that money for a place he might visit two or three times a year? That's crazy!"

"People do it all the time," Ellie said. "And he'll have life insurance money," she added gently. "A piece of property in Austin might be a solid way for him to put that money to work. When someone is upset, they sometimes make bad financial decisions. This wouldn't be a bad decision. Unorthodox, maybe, but not bad."

"Tomorrow you could take this poor guy to a trustworthy real estate agent," Beth said. "I know a few who would be good."

"Or better yet, why bother with all that?" Lana said. "We know the Slattery place is an excellent buy. Why not steer him straight to that and not have him stumbling into something that isn't as good a deal?"

"That's the best way to go," Shelby agreed. "Call Garrett in the morning and ask him for the agent's name and number on the sign out front. Once Morgan sees that place, he's gonna fall in love with it, guaranteed."

Mary Jane nodded. She was astounded by how quickly the women in the room had become protective of Morgan. But she shouldn't be surprised. After all, she had reacted exactly the same way. Well, not *exactly.* Her friends had no idea what had transpired between her and Morgan that first night, or the sexual tension that had existed between them from that moment on.

Although she loved her friends and usually told them everything that mattered, especially Lana, she didn't think she could reveal this. Even Morgan didn't really understand what had happened between them, and Mary Jane wasn't going to risk telling anyone who hadn't been there, who hadn't felt the wrenching pain or the need to heal it somehow.

If her friends had suspected anything was going on between her and Morgan, they wouldn't have been so casual about him buying a piece of property in Austin and coming here for visits. Mary Jane knew if she intended to protect her secret, she should be casual about it, too.

After all, there were pluses to the idea. She wanted to play a part in the baby's life, and if Morgan had a foothold in Austin, so much the better. She'd see the baby much more often.

She envisioned her relationship with the little girl as falling somewhere between fairy godmother and totally cool aunt. Morgan couldn't be trusted to know about fashions and hair-styles, so Mary Jane would have to stay alert and make sure he didn't turn the kid into a nerd.

Of course he might remarry, and then Mary Jane wouldn't have as much of a say in what went on with the kidlet. She thought about the enthusiastic welcome Morgan had received from her friends. Oh, yeah, Morgan would remarry. He was far more of a hunk than he realized. Arielle hadn't been ex-actly straight with him about his sex appeal. He was loaded with it.

With new insight, she gazed around the room. "Would any of you by chance be encouraging Morgan to buy property here because you'd like to keep track of him...personally?"

A few of the unmarried women in the room, including Lana and Shelby, blushed.

Mary Jane crossed her arms. "Interesting."

"But, hey," Lana said quickly, "you have first dibs, Mary Jane. Though you're probably such good friends that you've never thought of him like that. If somebody's like a big brother to you, you never think of him as sexy."

"Right," Mary Jane said with a straight face.

"But that could change," Lana added. "If so, then you definitely have the field to yourself."

"Don't worry," Mary Jane said. "He's not my type."

Then she moved to the stereo, which had been turned off when Morgan arrived. She punched the power button. "Everybody ready to rock 'n' roll?"

"You bet," Shelby said, "but I'm keeping an eye on the clock."

"Geez," Mary Jane said. "I feel about eight years old." But her complaint lacked any bite. She liked knowing that her friends cared about her that much, even if they were bossy sometimes.

MARY JANE'S BED lost a lot of its appeal without Mary Jane in it. Worse, the pillows were filled with the scent of her hair, and Morgan felt as if he were sharing the bed with a phantom. He much preferred the real thing.

He slept some, but not much. That might have been his fault for not wearing the earplugs, but he'd been comforted by the happy noise downstairs. He'd strained to pick out Mary Jane's voice in the chorus of female chatter.

Once he'd been positive she was the one belting out Ricky Martin's "Shake Your Bon-Bon," and he'd become aroused imagining her down there gyrating around, the way she'd been doing when he arrived. That had been some show, all right. He wouldn't mind a repeat. In private.

Of course that would be a very bad idea.

The next morning he woke to the sound of women calling goodbye as they headed home.

Shortly after that Mary Jane tapped on the bedroom door. "Are you awake?"

"Yep."

"I'm sorry we made so much noise saying goodbye. I was afraid that would wake you up."

He sat up. "No problem."

"Everybody's gone, if you want to come out."

"You can come in, you know. This is your bedroom."

"Oh. Yeah, I guess it is." She eased open the door and gazed at him. "Did you sleep at all?"

"Sure. Did you?" He marveled that she looked so damn good first thing in the morning. Probably had something to do with being twenty-two, or possibly with being gorgeous to begin with. The pink baby-doll pajamas made her look as yummy as cotton candy. When she lifted her arms and combed her hair from her face, he was glad he'd kept the covers over his lap.

"Those party poopers sure enough made me go to bed," she said. "But I guess it was a good thing. I slept like a rock, and from what I heard, most of them stayed up talking for hours after I conked out. This town has its share of secrets. I really hated missing all the gossip about the current status of little Chase Maitland. You remember that whole thing, right?"

"Isn't that the kid who was left on the doorstep of the clinic?"

She nodded. "He supposedly is a Maitland, but there are a ton of unanswered questions. It's been tough on everybody in that family."

"I'll bet. Arielle was a little upset about the clinic getting so much controversial press. She didn't want her baby connected with a place that showed up in the tabloids."

"I remember she said something like that to me, too. I was surprised she'd even care about some stupid scandal. It won't affect the care I'll get at Maitland, and I can't see how it would affect the baby, either."

"That's what I told her." He sighed. "Well, none of that matters anymore, I guess."

She gazed at him. "Listen, I hope you don't think I'm a degenerate for throwing a wild party after you left. Or that I was being disrespectful to Arielle's memory."

"No," he said quietly. "I have a pretty good idea why you'd want to fill the house with friends and turn up the music. It was a good plan. I'm sorry I barged in on it."

Instead of reassuring him that he'd been no trouble, she continued to study him without speaking for several seconds. "Shelby and Lana think you should buy that house next to Garrett's. I don't know if you remember, but that was right past were we stopped to look at the—"

"Bluebonnets. I know. I noticed the sign." He forced himself to ask the next question. "Would you rather I didn't buy a place here in Austin?"

While she continued to regard him thoughtfully, she used one foot to scratch the back of her other calf. He wondered if she had any concept of the voluptuous picture she created standing there, so deliciously mussed from her sleep-over party.

"I guess I wonder why you want to do it," she said.

"I'm not sure I know myself," he answered truthfully. "I feel pulled to this town. To you," he added, deciding maybe they needed to talk about that.

Her eyes darkened, and she gripped the door frame, as if to keep herself in place. "Maybe because of the baby. It might not be me at all."

"Maybe." He committed to memory the image of her standing in the doorway, in case he never saw her that way again. "God knows I'm in no mental shape to make that kind of evaluation right now. But when I couldn't get on a plane yesterday, and the guy next to me in the waiting lounge started talking about real estate investments in Austin, something clicked into place for me."

"But it's a big step, buying property here. Maybe after the baby's born and you've taken her back to New York, a place in Austin won't seem like such a cool idea, after all."

He shrugged. "I could always sell it at that point. But you still haven't answered my question. Would you rather not have me do this? Because this is your territory. If you think this town isn't big enough for both of us, I'm outta here."

"On the noon stage?" she asked with a smile.

"You bet."

Sighing, she turned and leaned against the door frame so she was no longer looking at him. "I don't know what I want," she said.

He gazed at her profile and the perky jut of her breasts under the baby-doll top. Short-term, he sure knew what he wanted, but he wasn't going to have it. He waited for what she had to say.

"Every day I'm more attached to this baby," she said,

"and I'm not sure that's a good thing. Sometimes I think it would be better if you took her back to New York and I never saw her again. That might make it easier to put her out of my mind."

His heart ached. A few months ago the surrogate mother concept had seemed like such a civilized answer to his and Arielle's problem. Now it seemed barbaric that Mary Jane would nurture this little girl inside her body for nine months and then have to give her up to others to raise. Maybe cutting it off clean would be the best way for her to cope with that.

He took a shaky breath. "If that's what you want, that's how we'll play it. As far as I'm concerned, you're calling the shots here."

"Is that right?" She turned her head to look at him. "You mean if I wanted to keep the baby, you'd give her up?"

He blinked. "No! I just meant—"

"See? I'm not calling the shots, after all."

Scrubbing a hand over his face, he blew out a breath. "I can't give up my baby. I'm willing to listen to any other solution you have besides that."

"Tell you what." She closed her eyes and leaned her head against the door frame. "I need a little time to think this over. When I pictured keeping in touch with this baby, I thought I'd have control of how that happened."

"You still would. I—"

"Not if you own a place here. That means you could show up virtually anytime, without having to make arrangements, without contacting me. It would be a whole different ball game from coming for visits once in a while, or me visiting New York."

"You're right. I'll forget the whole thing."

"On the other hand, think of the fun she could have here in Austin, staying at her own place instead of in some hotel room." She opened her eyes and glanced at him. "That's a gorgeous little place next to Garrett's. There's a pond where she could sail boats, although you'd have to watch her close until she knows how to swim. But there's tons of room to run around, and we could build her a playhouse and one of those

wooden gyms that are so popular for kids these days. She
could have a wading pool. And a sandbox.'' Her eyes shone
with excitement. ''Think of it, Morgan. We could make it into
a little paradise for her, a total change from living in a New
York apartment.''

''Yes, we could,'' he said carefully. He didn't think he'd
keep his apartment. He would likely move somewhere in the
suburbs, but he wasn't about to tell her that and spoil her
campaign to rescue the baby from the sterile environment of
his Manhattan high-rise.

He'd also noticed that she'd fallen into using the word *we*
in connection with her dreams for a play yard, so he'd used
the word, too. He couldn't think of anything he'd love more
than having Mary Jane help him with a project like that. But
he wasn't sure it would be fair to her.

''You probably don't want to put that kind of money into
it,'' she said.

''No, that's not it. I think the whole thing sounds great. But
is that what you want?''

She placed her hand over her belly. ''Now that I've pictured her in that setting, I don't think what I want is so important anymore. She should have a place like that, Morgan.
And a wonderful room of her own, with murals on the walls
and games and puzzles and stuffed animals.''

He could create a setting like that in New York, of course,
somewhere in the suburbs. After years of working with kids,
he had lots of ideas, and he could ask any number of his
patients' parents for their input. He should tell Mary Jane that,
so she didn't have the mistaken view that it was Austin or
nothing for this kid.

But he couldn't. He wasn't sure whether it was her obvious
need to follow through with her plan or his need to share the
project with her that motivated him. All he knew was that he
couldn't pour cold water on this. It seemed like the most
hopeful activity either of them had come up with since the
accident.

''Then you'll help me?'' he asked.

She smiled. "Maybe we'd better go look at the house first. You might hate it."

"I doubt it, but you have a point." Fortunately their discussion had cooled his jets and he was presentable enough to climb out of bed. "Do you want first shower?"

"Sure." Her gaze swept over him. "I'm really glad you didn't leave yesterday."

Oh, boy. All his libido needed was a little encouragement. They both had better get more clothes on, and fast. "Me, too," he said quickly, grabbing the duffel he'd left beside the bed. "I think I'll shave downstairs." Then he practically bowled her over as he charged out of the bedroom and pounded down the stairs.

TWO HOURS LATER, as Mary Jane followed the real estate agent up the walk to the front door of the Slattery house, she was glad she'd worn shorts. The blast furnace that would become an Austin summer was heating up already, even in early May.

"You're in for a treat." The real estate agent, Eleanor Burnside, took the key from the lockbox hanging on the brass doorknob. A polished professional in her mid-fifties, Eleanor had no gray in her auburn curls and not a single wrinkle in her pale green suit. "This is a treasure of a house."

"Good," Morgan said from behind Mary Jane. "That will save some time."

"I've heard it's very nice." Mary Jane could hardly wait to get inside the house. She'd been eager to see the place after Lana had raved about it, even though it was obviously beyond a waitress's wages. But even if she couldn't own it, the kidlet might someday, and that was a thrilling prospect.

Eleanor opened the door and ushered them inside.

Although the day was getting warm, the interior of the house was cool and welcoming. Hardwood floors gleamed from a fresh coat of wax. Beyond the entry she glimpsed the living room and the fireplace Lana had told her about.

Made of large river rocks, it looked like something out of a cottage in a fairy tale. Waist-high shelves, perfect for books, flanked the fireplace. Above that, honey wood-framed windows looked out on mature trees. On the basis of that fireplace wall alone, Mary Jane was in love. But it wasn't her place to say anything. She wasn't the person with the checkbook.

Morgan looked around. "Cool," he murmured.

Mary Jane was really psyched that Morgan seemed to have the same reaction to the house she did.

Eleanor smiled in obvious satisfaction. "Would you like me to go through with you, or would y'all rather explore for yourselves?"

"We'll explore for ourselves," Mary Jane and Morgan said together.

Eleanor glanced at them with a smile. "It's nice to see a couple so in sync."

Mary Jane's cheeks heated at Eleanor's assumption they were planning to buy a house together. "Oh, we're not—"

"Always in sync," Morgan finished smoothly, taking Mary Jane's elbow.

"Well, spend all the time you need," Eleanor said. "I have a favorite spot in the back yard under a weeping willow. I'll be sitting in one of the Adirondack chairs, so come get me when you feel you've explored the place enough."

"We'll do that," Morgan said, steering Mary Jane toward the living room.

"Why didn't you tell her we're not a couple?" she whispered once Eleanor was headed toward the back of the house.

"Because I love this place already, and she probably knows that from my first comment. You haven't committed yourself yet. I thought the asking price was a little high, so if Eleanor thinks you have veto power, and you bring up some objections, we might not have to pay top dollar."

Mary Jane grinned. "You mean *you* might not have to pay top dollar. I'm not risking anything on this deal." Not anything financial, at least. Emotional risks were a whole other subject.

Standing in the living room with Morgan while they admired the fireplace, she had no trouble imagining it blazing, and some cushy furniture grouped around it, and a soft rug in front of the hearth, and Morgan and her stretched out on that rug....

She needed to stop this, right now. Easing her arm out of his grip, she stepped away from him.

He glanced at her with that yearning expression that made her brain cells cease to function.

"So you like the house?" she asked, gazing into his warm brown eyes. What an obvious question. But when he looked at her like that, she couldn't do brilliant.

"So far."

"We should go see the rest."

"Guess so. Is that fudge lipstick you're wearing today?"

Her heart began to pound. They were supposed to be looking at a house, not discussing what flavor she had on her mouth. "Caramel."

"I'd better level with you. At this moment, it's not just about the baby."

"I know." Her chest grew tight. "For me, either."

"Maybe it never was."

She felt herself sinking fast. "But you don't trust your feelings, remember? Which is perfectly logical."

"There's nothing logical about the way I'm feeling right now."

"Exactly."

With a groan he pulled her into his arms. And heaven help her, she let him do it. Worse, she dug her fingers into his hair and coaxed his head down. She wasn't going to be able to blame any of this insanity on him.

"I'm wild about caramel, too," he murmured. Then he settled in to prove it.

During their first kiss in her kitchen she'd felt as if someone had pulled the pin on a grenade. This time it was as if someone had detonated a bomb.

In the resulting explosion, they both went crazy trying to get closer, deeper, more completely entwined. Her kissing history included men who'd gone about it sweetly, or wetly, or even loudly. She'd never experienced an encounter like this one, where she and Morgan seemed to collide like asteroids in deep space.

"Mmm," he said, grabbing her by the shoulders as if to set her away from him. "Mmm," he said, diving in for another round.

At last he spun away from her so fast she nearly fell down. Gasping, he leaned both hands against the smooth rocks of the fireplace and lowered his head between them.

Her legs were shaking so much that she decided the better part of valor was to sit on the floor until she recovered a little.

When he finally spoke, he was short of breath. "This... has...never happened...to me."

She could be a smart aleck and ask if he'd never kissed a woman before, but she knew that wasn't what he meant. "Me, either," she admitted.

He lifted his head and glanced at her in surprise. "What are you doing down there?"

"My legs wouldn't hold me up."

Slowly he pushed away from the fireplace and came over to sit cross-legged in front of her. He stared intently into her eyes. "What are we gonna do, Mary Jane?"

"The first thing we'd better do is clean you up. You have caramel-flavored lipstick from ear to ear."

He nodded. "You, too."

She reached for her purse, which had fallen on the floor in the midst of the chaos. Opening it, she took out two tissues and handed him one. "It tastes good, but it's not what you'd call super-hold lipstick. I guess you can't have everything."

He smiled grimly as he wiped his face. "Now, there's a nugget of truth if I ever heard one."

"You missed a spot." She started to reach over to do it for him.

He leaned away. "Better not. Just tell me where it is."

"Left cheek, two o'clock. There. You got it." She scrubbed at her face. Her mouth felt as if she'd blown up about a hundred balloons. And looking at him, she was ready to do it all over again.

He rubbed his hands across his thighs and sighed heavily.

"The thing that worries me is that all this…intensity…might be nothing more than another way of expressing our grief."

"If that's true, it sure gives a whole new meaning to the expression 'good grief.'"

He chuckled. "Ah, Mary Jane. You're an original."

"So are you."

"Me? Nah. I'm just your average, ordinary—"

"Caring, sensitive, loyal—"

"Am I loyal?" His gaze searched hers. "Seems to me a loyal person wouldn't be kissing another woman within days of losing his wife."

"Actually a loyal person might find himself swept up in emotions he didn't understand. He might find himself kissing another woman, but he'd feel guilty about it. Which you do."

"Yep."

"Well, if it makes you feel any better, I feel guilty, too. That first night was one thing. A single incident. But now…now it's becoming a habit with us."

He gazed at her for a long moment. "Should I forget about this house?"

"That's not fair. Don't make me decide. I'm at least as crazy about this house as you are, and I love the thought of the baby playing around in a house like this."

"As much as we've seen of it, that is, which isn't much."

She wadded the tissue and tossed it back and forth between her hands. "Maybe if what we're feeling for each other is only a—what did you say?—an expression of grief…"

"That's what I said."

"If that's what it is, then maybe when the grief wears off a little, we won't feel like tearing each other's clothes off anymore."

He didn't look very convinced. "I guess that's possible."

"If you gave up this great house just because we couldn't control ourselves, and then in a little while that wasn't a problem anymore and you *could* have had the house, you'd kick yourself." She rolled the tissue into a snake.

"Probably. I can't remember ever walking into a house and having it reach out and grab me like this one has."

She looked up from her tissue snake. "Me, either."

"It's a great house."

She grinned. "What we've seen of it, which isn't much."

"Okay. Let's get the house." He pushed himself to his feet and dusted off the seat of his pants. "Start thinking of things to complain about while I go find Eleanor. I'd help you up, but then I'd probably start kissing you again."

"I understand." As he started toward the back of the house, she stood. "But we haven't seen the kitchen, or the bathrooms, or the bedrooms."

He turned. "Under the circumstances I think it would be better if we cut this tour short, don't you? I especially think we should stay out of the bedrooms."

She gazed at him and felt the heat flashing between them. "I see your point. Go find Eleanor."

CHAPTER TEN

NOT LONG AFTERWARD Morgan walked with Mary Jane and a very hopeful Eleanor to Eleanor's Lincoln, which was parked in the driveway.

"So you like it, basically?" Eleanor said.

"I do," Morgan said. "But Mary Jane has some problems with it, as she mentioned." That was her cue, and he hoped she'd come up with something.

"I'm worried about how dust will collect in the crevices of the rocks on that fireplace," she said.

Morgan almost laughed. The fireplace had been the thing they'd both been crazy about, and he knew dust was the last thing she'd care about with such a gorgeous natural look.

"I could ask the Slatterys how they cleaned it," Eleanor said. "Anything else?"

"The grounds will take a lot of maintenance," Mary Jane said.

"True," Eleanor agreed. "I assume you'll have to hire someone to help with it." She glanced at Mary Jane. "You live here currently, correct?"

"Correct."

"And will you be living part of the time in New York, as well?" she asked.

Eleanor seemed to be struggling not to offend, Morgan realized. Perhaps she thought he was buying a house for his mistress. He didn't care for that interpretation.

"Mary Jane is a good friend," he said to Eleanor. "She'll be helping me set up this house as my winter getaway, and I trust her judgment. I would never buy anything if she had any reservations about it." And that speech didn't do anything to clear Mary Jane's reputation, either, damn it.

"I see," Eleanor said.

"What I mean is—"

"It doesn't matter," Mary Jane said quietly, putting a hand on his arm.

"But—"

"Seriously." She gave him a sunny smile.

She didn't care about her reputation, he thought with amazement. And of course she wouldn't. She'd been willing to walk around pregnant with no wedding band on her left finger. Her friends knew the truth, but strangers didn't.

Mary Jane didn't show much yet, so Eleanor probably hadn't guessed her condition. But soon it would be obvious to anyone. Mary Jane met the public nearly every day in her job, and as the pregnancy progressed she'd probably get rude questions, or even worse, no questions and rude stares. She didn't care.

It was a revelation to him. "Okay," he said, regarding her with admiration. As he reached to open the car door for her, a man on horseback rode up the drive. Well, he sure enough was in Texas, Morgan thought, if social calls were being made on horseback.

"Garrett!" Mary Jane hurried over to the guy.

"How're you doing, Mary Jane?" He dismounted and gave her a hug.

Morgan remembered then that Garrett was the man who lived next door, Shelby and Lana's older brother. The guy wore shades and a straw cowboy hat, so Morgan couldn't see his coloring, but his facial features were an older, more masculine version of Shelby and Lana's. With Lana being Mary Jane's best friend, Morgan wondered how friendly Mary Jane and Garrett were. That hug had set his teeth on edge.

"Garrett Lord, I'd like you to meet Morgan Tate," Mary Jane said, turning to him.

"Tate." Garrett stuck out his hand, and his grip was brief and impersonal. "Lana told me you might be interested in the Slattery place."

"He's buying it." Mary Jane's enthusiasm contrasted strongly with Garrett's reserve. "Well, if the Slatterys accept the offer, of course. This is the real estate agent, Eleanor Burnside. Eleanor, this is—"

"Mr. Lord and I have met," Eleanor said with a formal smile. "I held an open house a couple of weeks ago, and the parking got a little out of hand. I'm afraid we encroached on Mr. Lord's property. But with the sale of the house, you won't have to worry about that again."

Morgan thought about the evening he'd walked into a field of bluebonnets that technically belonged to the reserved Mr. Lord and figured that Mary Jane had been his ticket on that trip. Judging from Lord's stern expression, if Morgan had tried such a thing on his own, he might have been met with a loaded shotgun.

He decided it was time to institute a good-neighbor policy. "You sure won't have to worry about a parking problem if I end up owning the place," he said. "I'll only be coming down from New York once in a while, and I can't imagine I'll be throwing any parties."

Garrett's mouth curved in a faint smile. "Then you'd better stay away from this gal." He put an arm around Mary Jane. "I understand you had a wild one going last night."

Morgan nearly groaned as he thought how that would sound to Eleanor. But Mary Jane didn't care what other people thought, he reminded himself. That was his hang-up, not hers. He also wanted to shove Garrett's arm off Mary Jane's shoulders. Her bubbly personality didn't fit with Garrett at all.

"Morgan knows all about that party," Mary Jane said with a grin. "He hid upstairs while it was going on. I'm sure he didn't get much sleep."

"So you're staying at Mary Jane's?" Garrett asked.

"Yes," Mary Jane said.

Morgan would have loved to echo that statement and make it sound as if he and Mary Jane were very cozy, even though that would support Eleanor's suspicions. But he didn't.

First, he had no business staking any claims on Mary Jane. He was in no position to interfere in her life any more than he already had. And second, after the kiss by the fireplace, he realized that he couldn't spend another night under the same roof with Mary Jane without making love to her.

"I have been staying there, and making use of her couch," he said. Well, that had been true for about two hours one night. Maybe Mary Jane was strong enough not to care about her reputation, but he couldn't help wanting to protect her. "But now that it looks as if I'll be sticking around until I close on the house, I'll probably move to a hotel." He glanced at her. "I've inconvenienced you enough."

"I can recommend a good one," Eleanor said. "Many of my clients from out of town have stayed there."

Questions upon questions lurked in Mary Jane's blue eyes. "It's really no trouble for you to stay with me," she said.

"It's better if I book a hotel room." He looked into her eyes and hoped she'd get the message. Another night together would only have one outcome.

She held his gaze. "Well, if you're sure."

"You could stay with me," Garrett said.

Morgan and Mary Jane turned in surprise.

Garrett looked almost as surprised that he'd made the offer. Then he shrugged, as if he couldn't do anything about it now. "I have room in my main house," he said. "And you could get to know the area while you're waiting for the closing. I could loan you a horse."

Morgan nearly choked. "I don't—"

"A gentle horse." Garrett's faint smile appeared again. "If you're going to buy a piece of property out here in horse country, it'd be a real good idea if you learned to ride."

"He's right," Mary Jane said. "When the baby comes, you'll want to teach her, too. Kids love horses."

"Baby?" Eleanor said. "I didn't realize you had a child, Mr. Tate."

Mary Jane turned to her. "Well, you see, I—"

"She's still very young," Morgan said.

"Oh." Eleanor looked at him as if she longed to ask more questions but knew she was liable to overstep if she did. "A child would be very lucky to have this house and grounds to roam in."

"Yes, she would," Mary Jane said wistfully.

Her tone tore at Morgan's heart. She so wanted to mother this little girl.

"I guess it's settled then, Tate," Garrett said. He sounded friendlier than he had before. "Come on out and I'll get you acclimated."

Morgan could see that if he didn't accept Garrett's offer he'd lose face in front of his new neighbor. He'd also look like a coward in front of Mary Jane, which was worse. He was going to have to stay at Garrett's and learn to ride one of his horses. He'd been on a horse maybe once in his life. Or maybe it hadn't even been a horse. Might have been a pony. A pony tied up to one of those pole things that went around in a circle.

"Okay," he said. "I appreciate the offer. I'll take a cab out here this afternoon."

"You'll do no such thing," Mary Jane said. "Taking a cab out here would cost a fortune. I'll drive you."

Not having a vehicle in Austin was becoming a real problem, Morgan realized. In New York he hardly ever drove a car, but out here cabs weren't the best way to get around.

He glanced at Mary Jane. "Thanks, but I think I also need to buy a car. Maybe we could do that this afternoon."

"A *car?*" She looked flabbergasted.

"It's a good idea," Eleanor said. "You could find a used sedan for a reasonable price, leave it parked in the garage when you're not here, and then whenever you come down from New York, you're all set."

Instantly he realized a used sedan wasn't what he needed at all. If he planned to own a place in horse country, he needed to think about his image. "Scratch that. I need to buy a truck." From the corner of his eye he could see that Garrett Lord, macho rancher, approved of that statement. "A big truck," he added for good measure, and watched Garrett's head incline the slightest bit in agreement.

"A big truck?" Mary Jane stared at him. "But you won't be here that much, and—"

"And when I am here, I need to be able to drive around. And I might want to haul things." Yeah, that sounded good. He'd never hauled anything in his life, but now that he said it, he knew it was something he'd have fun doing.

"Absolutely," Garrett agreed, looking even friendlier. "You have to buy furniture for that house, and there's no reason to pay the delivery fee if you can haul it yourself."

"Hold it." Mary Jane stood with her hands on her hips and looked at him as if he'd lost his mind. "You are going to spend thousands of dollars on a big truck so you don't have to spend a few dollars on delivery fees? What kind of logic is that?"

Morgan glanced at Garrett, knowing he had an ally. "Makes sense to you, right?"

"Sure does."

"Then it's settled. We'd better head on back now, so Eleanor can get started on the paperwork." He glanced at Garrett. "I'll see you this afternoon."

"You might want to check at Buck's," Garrett said. "He usually has some decent trucks on the lot. Tell him I sent you."

"I'll do that. Thanks." Morgan opened the door for Mary Jane.

"Men," she mumbled as she got in the front seat next to Eleanor.

After closing the door and climbing in the back, Morgan glanced out the window and gave a friendly wave to Garrett. The guy had mounted his big brown horse, and Morgan had to admit he looked pretty good sitting up there. Women seemed to like that cowboy hero type. A New York pediatrician was a long way from fitting that image.

He hoped to hell Mary Jane and Garrett didn't have something going on between them. Much as he loved the house, what he'd seen of it, he didn't relish the thought of living next door to Mary Jane's boyfriend.

ELEANOR WHISKED THEM back to her office, and Mary Jane spent the ride listing as many objections to the house as she could make up, considering she'd seen the entry and the living room and had a quick peek into the sunny kitchen. The bedrooms were still a mystery.

Once they'd arrived at the real estate office, Morgan named the figure he was willing to pay for the house, considering all the points that Mary Jane had brought up. The amount seemed staggering to Mary Jane, and though she was all in favor of Morgan getting a bargain, she hated the thought that he'd decide against the house if the Slatterys wouldn't come down on the price.

"I don't know if the Slatterys will accept a lower offer, but we'll try," Eleanor said as she settled them in chairs in front of her large desk and picked up a sheaf of papers. "As I understand it, this is a firm price. There's a lot of architectural detail in that house. For example, the window seat in the master bedroom is a wonderful touch."

"Window seat?" Mary Jane asked eagerly. She adored the idea of a window seat—a place to sit and read, crochet something for the baby...dream.

"Why, yes." Eleanor glanced at her with a puzzled expression. "Did you miss that?"

"I guess we did," Morgan said. He looked at Mary Jane. "You like window seats?"

"Oh, yes. Think of being curled up there on a rainy afternoon with a good book, or just to watch the raindrops running down the windowpane. You can be so cozy, and yet the outside is right there, and—"

Too late she remembered she was supposed to be the one who wasn't excited about the house. She cleared her throat and did her best to sound nonchalant. "They're okay. This one must not have been very cool if we didn't even see it." Glancing at Eleanor, who had a cat-who-ate-the-cream smile on her face, Mary Jane decided she'd definitely blown her cover by raving on about the wonders of window seats.

She was also afraid Morgan would be annoyed, but instead he continued to gaze at her with tenderness.

Then he did the most amazing thing. He turned to Eleanor and told her not to submit a lower offer, after all. He'd pay the asking price for the house so they could get the purchase taken care of without haggling or delays.

Mary Jane grabbed his arm. "But, Morgan—"

"It's worth it," he said, smiling at her.

"So you're really buying it, lock, stock and barrel?"

His smile widened into a grin. "Yeah."

"Oh, Morgan!" She leaped from her chair and leaned over to give him a big hug. The minute she breathed in his familiar fragrance and felt his arms tighten around her, she realized that hadn't been a good idea. Obviously the chemistry lesson she'd been given beside the fireplace hadn't taught her anything.

While she still had a few brain cells working, she backed quickly out of his arms and away from his chair. "I don't think you'll be sorry," she said, sounding very breathless.

He looked at her, his eyes filled with a soft light. "No chance."

Very aware of Eleanor watching them, Mary Jane returned to her chair and sat down demurely, but her cheeks felt hot. "I've never been with someone when they bought a house," she said by way of explanation. "It's very exciting, isn't it?"

"Under the right conditions," Eleanor said with a smile. "This is a special house. It was built with great love. But as much as they cared for their house, the Slatterys care for their children more. The kids' jobs took them to California, and there was no chance they'd ever move back to Texas. Once both parents retired, they decided to move to California, too. I know they hoped someone would buy the house who loves it as much as they do."

"I think there's a good chance of that," Morgan said.

"I think so, too." Eleanor turned to her computer. "Now, let's get things rolling."

"Did their kids grow up in that house?" Mary Jane asked. Eleanor kept typing. "I believe they did."

"Well, personally, I think they were nuts to leave Austin,

which means their folks have ended up selling the family home. But their loss is our gain. I mean *your* gain, Morgan.''

"Our gain," he said, sending her another one of those tender looks. "And the baby's gain. I guess the first thing we'd better think about is outfitting the nursery."

As she thought about that, her heart expanded another notch. She'd been dying to outfit a nursery and she hadn't even realized it. Now she would get to. Then she remembered that Morgan couldn't hang around indefinitely fooling with this house.

"We might not have time before you go back," she said. "I'd hate to slap stuff in there without thinking it over, wouldn't you?" As she said that she realized she'd been thinking over a nursery plan for at least a month, but she'd never let herself admit it. Rainbows. She envisioned a room filled with rainbow colors, rainbows painted on the wall, on the crib, the changing table and the big wooden rocker.

"I'll call Chuck from your place," Morgan said. "Maybe I can buy a little more time."

"And I'm going to have to get back to work, too," Mary Jane reminded him. "I know what Shelby said, but I'd feel bad sticking Georgette for too long."

His expression dimmed. "You know, I sort of assumed...but I was probably wrong. Never mind. You don't have to worry about the nur—"

"But I want to," she said quickly. "I really do. It's just that I have to do it after work or on my days off."

"I don't want you overworking yourself. That would defeat the whole purpose."

She gazed into his eyes and wondered what color eyes the baby would have. Arielle's had been gray. Once Mary Jane had known the baby was a girl she'd automatically given the kidlet gray eyes and blond hair, like Arielle. But brown eyes would be nice on the little girl. Soft, compassionate eyes like Morgan's.

"I really want to help with the nursery," she said. "But if it means you have to stay longer than you should to accommodate me, then maybe I won't be able to. Unless you want me to work on it after you're gone." That didn't sound like much fun, although it was better than nothing.

"I'm not sure I trust you not to overdo it," he said with a grin. "I picture you getting started after work, getting involved in painting or something, and not knowing when to quit."

Not long ago she would have thought he was being overprotective and anal. Now she knew this was the way he showed he cared, not only for the baby, but for her. "Just put Shelby on it and I'll be monitored every hour."

"Let me talk to Chuck," he said. "Then we'll decide what to do."

Eleanor's printer surged to life as she turned to them and pushed a pen across the desk toward Morgan. "Ready to buy a house?"

He picked the pen up without hesitation. "You bet I am."

MORGAN COULDN'T believe how he was flinging money around. He'd always been on the conservative side when it came to finances, and he'd just bought a valuable piece of property without making a counteroffer, and a shiny red pickup for the sticker price. And he hadn't had a moment of regret.

He followed Mary Jane home from Buck's and parked in front of her town house. Then he got out and circled the truck, admiring it from all angles. He'd always wondered why men bought trucks that cost as much or more than a luxury car. Now he knew. Driving a truck made a guy feel cool.

Leaving her Beetle in the drive, Mary Jane walked to the street and watched him, arms folded. "That's a pretty expensive rig you plan to park in a garage for most of the year."

He glanced at her. "I couldn't resist it. I've never had a truck."

"I could tell." She walked closer and lowered her voice. "Listen, I didn't want to say this in front of the salesman, but I'm worried about you."

"You are?" He looked at her in surprise. "I can drive a truck. It's easier than I expected, in fact."

"No, I mean...you're still recovering from a terrible shock. Now, the house was one thing. I can see how that could work out great for the baby. But this truck isn't for the baby."

"Nope."

"Maybe you shouldn't be buying stuff like this until... well, until you're sure you're not doing it to...I don't know...compensate or something."

He gazed at her earnest expression and wanted to kiss her again. He backed up a step to avoid the temptation.

"Now I've offended you," she said.

"No, you sure haven't. I appreciate your concern. But let me tell you how I see this."

"Please do. Because I'm worried. That truck is so *red*."

"Do you like it?"

"Why, sure I do, but that's not the point. I didn't put out a gazillion dollars for it. You did."

He loved the way her hair turned all gold and shiny in the sun. "When I first got here you took me out shopping for clothes, and you talked me into getting these." He gestured to his shirt, jeans and boots.

"See, I knew it! I created a monster. Now you think you have to have a house and truck to match!"

Maybe he shouldn't laugh, but he couldn't help it. She was adorable. "Maybe you did create a monster, and maybe I've totally gone off the deep end, but I don't see it that way. I feel as if you've given me the courage to break out of a mold that was getting too tight and confining. All my life I've been conditioned to be conservative, to only like what was elegant, tasteful and...*boring*. God, so boring."

"You mean you were conditioned by your parents," she said.

He looked into her eyes and decided to risk some heresy. "And by Arielle."

He could tell she had some trouble with that. The struggle showed in that expressive face of hers, and he could well imagine she didn't want to admit anything negative about her idol.

Glancing away, she stared at the red truck for a long time. Finally she spoke. "She would have hated that truck."

"Yes."

She turned to him, her gaze anxious. "That isn't why you bought it, is it?"

"No. I like to think I'm more mature than that. I bought it because *I* like it. Remember when you asked me if I'd ever run around the back yard shooting at the bad guys when I was five years old?"

She nodded.

"Of course I did, but when I wasn't doing that, I pretended my bike was a truck. A bright red truck." He waved a hand toward the curb. "Just like that one. I realized when I decided to buy it that I didn't have to please anybody but myself. I kind of thought you'd like it, too, but if you hadn't, that would have been okay. This truck is for me."

Her smile came like sunshine from behind a cloud. "That's good. That's very good."

He couldn't help but smile back. "I think so, too. And who knows? I might get down here more than you think I will. I might drive this truck a lot."

"That would be nice," she said, continuing to smile at him.

Yes, it would, he thought. Very nice.

CHAPTER ELEVEN

THE SECOND they walked into the town house so Morgan could pack up his stuff and call his office partner, Mary Jane understood why they couldn't spend another night there together. The air instantly became thick with unspoken needs. At this rate they wouldn't be able to spend five minutes alone, never mind an entire evening. Good thing he was leaving.

She watched him walk to the phone and pick up the receiver to call New York. She wanted to be that receiver, cupped in his skillful grip and held close to his sweet, sweet mouth. In her imagination she grabbed the phone, slammed it into its cradle and kissed him hard. The maneuver had every chance of accomplishing her goal of seducing him senseless. She'd seen the way he looked at her.

But she didn't know what would happen after the seduction was completed. Right now things were good between them, although sexually a little tense. If they were careful and didn't put themselves in the wrong situations, they should be able to join forces to create the perfect nursery for the baby. Then Morgan would go back to New York. He had to. He had a profitable medical practice there, one he'd been building for several years.

Mary Jane's friendship with Beth and Ellie had given her inside information about the workings of Maitland Maternity and the medical community in general. When she'd started her job at Austin Eats she'd waited on enough doctors and overheard enough conversations to know how precious a good practice was. You didn't throw it away without a mega-spectacular reason. She didn't think sex with her fit that category.

Morgan might be enjoying his Texas experience, and he'd want to come back when he could, but his life would still be centered in New York. She had no faith in the staying power of this attraction, which could have so much to do with timing and not enough with the two people involved. She had a sneaky suspicion that once New York got its hooks into Morgan again, once he'd overcome the shock of losing his wife and settled into a new routine with work and maybe even a social life, he'd forget all about this lust he felt for a young waitress in Austin.

So she wouldn't seduce him now, and she wouldn't seduce him in the future. But damn, he was a tempting sight, standing in her living room in his snug jeans and cool Western shirt. His butt got cuter the more she looked at it.

She'd better stop looking at it. As he connected with his office, she went out the back door to check on the bird feeder.

After she'd filled the little glass and wooden house with seed, she sat on one of the two plastic Adirondack chairs she'd bought for her patio. The Slattery back yard had real wooden ones. Apparently they'd left them for the new owners, which was very accommodating of them.

Now that she thought about her glimpse into the new house's kitchen, she remembered a screened porch in the back. That would be a great place to sit about now, as the day was coming to an end. If she had her choice, she'd furnish it with wicker and fat cushions. Damn, but she could have a field day picking out stuff for that house. And spending more of Morgan's money.

Despite what he'd said about having plenty, he was getting dangerously free with his money, and she'd have to steer him to less expensive furniture stores or he'd run through his savings and the life insurance before he was done. That wouldn't be good for the baby.

As if the kidlet knew she was being thought about, she gave a solid little kick.

Mary Jane placed her hand on her tummy. "Your daddy bought you a play house today," she said. "You're gonna love it, too. At least I think you will. The living room was pretty terrific, but I didn't completely check out the rest. Lana says it's wonderful, though, and Lana wouldn't lie.''

The baby nudged her, more a gentle bid for attention than exuberant.

"You like this time of day, don't you, sweetie?" Mary Jane said. "Me, too. Everything winds down, people come home to their families...." She paused as an old fantasy played through her mind. When her mother was alive, she'd lived in that kind of world, where the little family of three gathered at the end of the day to share a meal. After her mother's death, her father hadn't come home much, and Arielle had fallen into the habit of taking them both out for fast food.

"I think Morgan will come home to you, kidlet," Mary Jane said as she rubbed a hand across her pregnant belly. "I don't think he's the type to forget about you. You'll be fine." She wanted to believe it, even though the thought of this baby stuck in that stark Manhattan apartment curdled her blood. But this house Morgan was buying would help.

MORGAN HUNG UP the phone and headed in the direction he'd seen Mary Jane go. She'd left the sliding glass door open, closing only the screen. He started to slide the screen back to go out to tell her what Chuck had said, when he heard her voice and paused.

Stepping into the room so she couldn't see him, he eavesdropped shamelessly on her conversation with his baby. His throat closed at the wistfulness in her words. And he knew for sure that if he took this baby to New York with him, he might as well rip out Mary Jane's heart.

But he couldn't give up the baby or his own heart would break. There had to be a solution. If he trusted this feeling between them the solution would be obvious. Unfortunately, he didn't trust his feelings. Or hers. And they both had to be very careful, because they weren't only affecting themselves with the decisions they made now. An innocent, unborn child's life hung in the balance, too.

Do no harm. He'd always taken that oath seriously. But sometimes it seemed that no matter which road he took, someone would be harmed. He needed more time, and Chuck had been able to give him that. He opened the screen door and went out to the patio.

She glanced up with a smile of welcome.

Somehow, in two short days, that smile had become essential to him. He couldn't imagine how he'd make it through his routine in New York without it. At least he wouldn't have to face that prospect immediately.

"What did Chuck say?" she asked. "Must not have been too bad. You look pretty cheerful."

He sat in the chair next to her and leaned back. This was what it would be like to come home to Mary Jane every night and share the news of the day. He felt a surge of excitement at the prospect. But maybe he'd be excited about coming home to anyone, anyone at all. Nobody liked being alone. "I've been replaced," he told her.

"What?"

"Not permanently."

"Oh." She fanned herself with her hand. "Don't scare me like that. I pictured us taking the truck back and canceling the deal on the house."

"I don't plan on that. One thing I seem to have a lot of these days is money. And despite the fact you think I'm spending it like a drunken sailor, I'm still in very good financial shape."

She glanced at him with some surprise. "You mean you could, like, buy a whole other house?"

"Yeah. Ridiculous, isn't it? But all Arielle and I did, really, was work. Except for our honeymoon, we didn't even travel that much. She was eager for me to build my practice and she made sure the right people heard about me. I take care of some very wealthy little kids. I don't make as much as a heart surgeon, mind you, but I do more than okay."

She shrugged. "Then I'll stop worrying. So who's replacing you?"

"Chuck heard about a young woman who wants a temporary clinical position until her husband finishes graduate school in June. Then they'll be moving to Chicago. Chuck's talked to her and thinks she's excellent, so he said if it was okay with me, he'd let her fill in until I came back."

"Wow, that was lucky. Like fate or something."

He turned to look at her. "Do you believe in that kind of thing?"

She met his gaze. "Is that a loaded question?"

"I don't think so." He had to chuckle at her serious expression. "I think I'm just curious. What could be loaded about it?"

"If I told you I believe that everything happens for a reason, that would mean I must think that Arielle's accident happened for a reason. And I refuse to accept that. It was a stupid accident, that's all. I'm not going to pretty it up and say it was part of some grand plan. That would be insulting to her."

"I agree." He loved the way she talked to him, opening up her mind and letting him in without any thought of hiding.

"But sometimes when things happen, like this woman being right there, needing a job for the very time you'd like to take a leave from the office, it seems kind of spooky, don't you think?"

"I do. Like the guy showing up at the airport at the end of a frustrating day of not being able to fly out. It was like I was supposed to stay until he could get there and tell me about the real estate opportunities in Austin."

She regarded him steadily. "But you didn't come back to make a fast buck, did you?"

"No. If I had, I'd have tried to drive a harder bargain today."

Her eyes glowed with the kind of admiration that could make a guy feel ten feet tall. "I wanted you to get a bargain, Morgan. But I have to admit that when I heard about the Slatterys, I decided they probably put a fair price on the house. They don't sound like greedy people, and I think they deserve what they're asking, considering they have to give up that beautiful place."

"I think so, too. I can hardly wait to have the closing and get the keys. But we can start looking for furniture before that. Do you think you can stand having me around a little longer?''

Her blue eyes softened. ''You know I didn't want you to leave in the first place, and I'll have a ball helping you buy stuff for that house. But you have to go back to New York sometime.''

''I know.'' It would be so easy to lean over and kiss her. He forced himself to stay where he was. He watched a little brown bird fly to the feeder. ''It won't be easy, walking into that apartment. It wasn't very cozy under the best of circumstances. I can't imagine myself living there anymore. Maybe I can get out of the lease.''

''You probably do need to get a different apartment.''

''Yeah.'' And an apartment was still the most sensible place for him to live, even with the baby. After seeing the house today, though, he couldn't get very excited about a new apartment, even if it turned out to be cozier than the last one. Maybe he'd outgrown apartment living.

But moving to the suburbs would be a big hassle considering that his practice was in Manhattan. If Mary Jane had agreed to come and be the baby's nanny, then he'd be willing to endure the commute. But that had been a dumb idea from the beginning. She would end up as a nanny-mistress until such time as they both discovered the sexual excitement was gone. Then she'd be SOL.

He wondered if the time Chuck had given him was enough to ride out this attraction and put him and Mary Jane on a friends-only basis. ''You'd better give me directions again so I can find my way back to Garrett's.''

''Right.'' She got out of her seat. ''Stay there and relax. I'll get a piece of paper and draw you a map.''

Staying put was the best plan, he decided as he watched her go into the kitchen. Following her would have predictable results. Out here on the patio he was able to control himself a little better. There were walls between each of the small yards, but they were only five feet high, and besides that, the second-story windows would make for excellent spying. A neighbor wouldn't have to work very hard to see what was going on in Mary Jane's yard.

She came back with a hand-drawn map and handed it to him. "This should get you there. I also showed you the route to Austin Eats, in case you want to come in for a meal."

"I could do that, couldn't I?" The prospect cheered him up.

"I'd be honored if you would." She returned to her seat.

He studied the map, folded it and tucked it in his shirt pocket. "You know, I was thinking that if we didn't live under the same roof, this tension between us might ease up a little."

"God, I *hope* so."

Her fervent statement made him laugh as he glanced at her. "That bad, huh?"

"I've never wanted sex so desperately—and not had it—in my entire life."

"Me, either."

She grinned at him. "And you're not even pregnant, so you can't blame your hormones."

"No, but maybe I'm developing that empathy fathers are supposed to have. Maybe my ankles will start to swell."

"If they do, you're doing that on your own. I don't intend to let my ankles swell."

He couldn't help looking at her trim ankles and sandal-clad feet. And there were those sexy red-painted toes with the silver stars winking at him. All that expanse of bare leg began to work on his imagination and made him feel a little grumpy. "Good luck keeping your ankles from swelling, given your job. Are you sure you won't consider quitting?"

Her smile faded. "No, Morgan, I'm not quitting. If staying here longer means you're going to start nagging me about that, then maybe you should head on back to New York, after all."

He gazed at her. His frustration had so many faces. He wasn't allowed to make love to her, and now he wasn't allowed to make life easier for her, either. She had no idea how much money he had, especially considering the huge life insurance check that would be waiting for him when he arrived home. All that money, and the mother of his—no, the woman carrying his child—insisted on working in a diner, where she spent a good part of her day on her feet.

Her expression softened. "You really should come in for a meal tomorrow," she said. "I think if you saw the place, you might understand why I want to work there. It's not just another greasy spoon."

"I never said—"

"I know, but you're acting as if that's what you think. It's a primo place to work, and lots of people know it. Shelby has a drawer full of completed job applications, and she could replace me in a minute."

"But surely she could hold a spot for you."

Mary Jane shook her head. "Nope. The diner does a booming business and she likes to keep the level of service up. If someone quit when I was ready to come back, then I might get on again, but the help doesn't tend to quit. Not only do I want to be a waitress, but I specifically want to be a waitress at Austin Eats. I don't want to lose my place there."

"I see." He wondered if her story would be the same if she didn't have to support herself. If someone offered her a year to be home with this baby, would she take a chance on getting back on the staff at Austin Eats after that time was up? He believed she would. After years of watching mothers, he knew a natural when he saw one.

Arielle had not been a natural. He'd never admitted that to himself, and it came as a shock. She'd portrayed herself as a mothering type of person when she'd recounted her tales of being a nanny for Mary Jane. He'd accepted her self-evaluation without question. In fact, her professed mothering talents had been one of the things that had attracted him.

Yet as he looked through new eyes it seemed as if Arielle had been more a puppet master than a true mother to Mary Jane. Oh, they'd been intimately connected, all right, but Arielle had always been the one who'd pulled the strings.

Mary Jane sighed. "You hate my career choice as much as

Arielle did, don't you? I can see disapproval written all over your face."

Instantly he tried to erase the frown that must have given her the wrong idea about what he was thinking.

"I don't disapprove of your career," he said. "I have no right to approve or disapprove, anyway. I just feel…helpless. Like there's nothing I can do to help you through this pregnancy. I can't even offer to be your birth coach, because I won't be here long enough to take the classes with you, and you might go into labor before I can get here." He really hated that thought. But first births were so unpredictable, and after this long absence he'd feel guilty saddling Chuck with another one in four months.

Mary Jane clapped her hands in apparent delight. "Too perfect! My magazine was right on!"

"What magazine?"

"I'm subscribing to a pregnancy magazine, and one of the articles was about fathers who feel as if they're not included in the process. They warned against the dangers of this, because then the daddy isn't ready to bond with the kid when she comes out, because he's been out of the loop for nine months." She brought one knee up and hooked her arms around it, balancing her sandal on the seat of the chair as she rested her chin on her knee and gazed at him.

In another month she'd have trouble doing that, he thought. He hoped she was prepared. Some women got cranky when they lost their figures so completely. "I can see how that would happen," he said. "I encourage the dads to bring the kids in for well-baby checks at least as often as the moms."

"Good for you. I was worried about that bonding thing with both you and Arielle, to be honest. That's why I sent all those ultrasound pictures and Polaroids."

He recognized the true mother's instinctive urge to help her child get a good start in life, even if it wasn't technically *her* child. "Did it ever occur to you that if it happened, it was our problem, and you didn't have to worry about it?"

"No."

"I didn't think it would. You've had a stake in this baby from the beginning, haven't you?"

She nodded. "I didn't expect to. At first I tried not to." She looked away and then shot him a furtive glance. "I wondered if I should take you up on the offer to buy me some appointments with a head doctor."

"The offer's still open, but if you want my opinion, your head's in fine shape."

She laughed. "You're in no condition to judge. You're probably more screwed up than I am."

"Probably," he said with a grin.

She continued to gaze at him, and gradually a soft glow appeared in her eyes. "Well, screwed up or not, you're looking damned good to me right now."

He could almost hear the flick of a match and imagine it being touched to a waiting bonfire. "Ditto."

"You'd better get on your horse and ride out of here, cowboy. Git while the gittin's good, as they say."

"You're right." Summoning willpower he'd learned at his mother's and father's knees, he stood. "I'll get my stuff and vamoose."

"Don't bother to say goodbye."

He gazed at her. She looked so relaxed and available. "All right. Will you be okay alone tonight?" God, he didn't want to go.

"Who says I'll be alone? Lana is usually ready and willing to take in a show, and I think there's a Ben Affleck movie in town."

So he could be replaced by Ben Affleck. He tried to remind himself that Mary Jane's resiliency was the saving grace in this whole crazy mess. "Then I guess I'll take off."

"Will you come to the diner tomorrow?"

"Sure." He would eat all his meals there if he could get away with it. But that might come across as too obvious. Just maybe. "If you're not too tired, we could go out tomorrow night and look at baby furniture."

"That would be cool."

"Okay, then." Still he lingered.

"Take off, Morgan."

"Right." Turning on his heel, he went inside the town house. Moments later he walked out the front door, locking it behind him. As he drove away, he felt as if a huge rubber band stretched from him all the way to Mary Jane.

CHAPTER TWELVE

ALTHOUGH MARY JANE went to the movies that night with Lana, she turned down Lana's suggestion of another sleepover. Mary Jane felt it was a point of honor to get through a night by herself, alone in her own bed, to prove that she could.

It took her entire collection of stuffed animals sharing the bed with her, but she managed to stave off the nightmares. She rolled several of her animals up in a towel and pretended the lumpy bundle was Morgan sleeping next to her. It wasn't much of a substitute, but at least it didn't turn her on, either. Because she was very tired, she finally fell asleep.

She greeted the next morning with a feeling of triumph. Maybe she hadn't slept well, but at least she'd slept. And today Morgan was coming to the diner.

Unfortunately they hadn't settled on any particular time. That had been an oversight on her part, she realized as her pulse leaped with anticipation every time the diner door opened. By midmorning she was a nervous wreck. In the process of making a fresh pot of coffee she nearly scalded herself.

Shelby dumped the plates she was carrying into a plastic bin and took Mary Jane by the shoulders. "Are you sure you should be here?" She studied Mary Jane's face. "You still have dark circles under your eyes. Maybe you need more time before you jump back into the routine."

Mary Jane took a deep breath. "I'm fine. I slept all alone in my own bed last night. I just need to slow down, is all."

A gleam of curiosity lit Shelby's green eyes. "If you say so."

As Mary Jane tried to interpret the look, she went over what she'd just said to Shelby that might have aroused her boss's interest. And there it was, the incriminating remark. I slept alone in my own bed last night. She'd been so proud of herself that the words had slipped right out. But a person didn't usually say that unless she'd been doing otherwise recently. Uh-oh.

"Lana said that Morgan is buying the Slattery place," Shelby said.

"Yep. Sure is." Mary Jane thought Shelby was skating too close to some things she wasn't ready to admit, even to herself. "Guess I'd better go finish busing number four."

"Okay." The wheels seemed to be spinning furiously in Shelby's mind, but she didn't make any more comments.

Mary Jane grabbed a damp cloth and hurried to booth four. Maybe if she blew right past Shelby's curiosity, Shelby might drop the whole matter. Probably not, but it was worth a try.

From the corner of her eye she saw a tall, broad-shouldered cowboy come through the door of the diner. Her heart beat faster until she turned to look more fully at him and realized he wasn't Morgan.

The man approached the booth she was cleaning. Funny how people did that when other booths were available. For some reason, booth four was popular, maybe because it had the best view through the pass-through into the kitchen, and diners liked to watch their food being cooked.

Mary Jane smiled automatically. "Welcome to Austin Eats. I'll have this booth ready in two shakes of a lamb's tail."

"Take your time, ma'am."

Texas born, Mary Jane decided. She liked trying to guess where people were from by their accent. Morgan's clipped New York accent gave her a real charge because it was so different from what she heard every day. As if she needed one more thing to turn her on where Morgan was concerned.

She pocketed her tip and gestured toward the booth. "If you'd like to have a seat, I'll be right back with your silverware. Would you like some coffee?"

"Yes, ma'am. That'd be great."

"Cream?"

"No, thank you. Just black." He sat in the booth with a sigh and pulled the menu out of its holder.

That deep sigh tugged at Mary Jane's heart. She'd also learned to read moods, and this fellow had some big problems, judging from that sigh. Even though it wasn't yet eleven in the morning, maybe she'd recommend a hot fudge sundae with the works. The guy could probably use it.

By the time she'd returned with his coffee and silverware he had the menu closed in front of him. Giving him another encouraging smile, she took her order pad out of the front pocket of her apron. "What can I get for you this morning?"

He nudged the brim of his hat and glanced at her. He was nice-looking, probably in his mid-forties. "To tell the truth, ma'am, I'm not all that hungry. Maybe I'll stick with the coffee."

She tapped her name tag. "You can call me Mary Jane."

"And you can call me Harrison." He smiled, but his eyes still looked sad. "I'll stick with the coffee, Mary Jane."

"May I make a teeny tiny suggestion, Harrison?"

"Okay."

"How about the Austin Eats Super-Deluxe Hot Fudge Sundae?"

He looked startled. "Now?"

"Anytime's a good time for chocolate."

Sure enough, the years slipped away as his expression turned to one of anticipation. The little boy in him still loved ice cream, apparently, although the grown man thought it was a silly idea.

"I make them myself, and they're unbelievable," she said. "You only live once." She'd been saying that for years to her customers at the diner without really thinking about it. Now, after what had happened, the words made her chest hurt a little. But she needed to remember those words and keep on saying them. She hadn't realized how important they were.

"You're right." Harrison looked much happier already. "I'll have the sundae."

"Good. I'll be right back." This was one of her favorite parts of the job. She'd always loved the stainless steel refrigerated compartments where the ice cream was kept, the scoop, the thick fudge, the pressurized can full of whipping cream.

Ever since Sara had taken the job as cook, Mary Jane enjoyed making ice cream treats even more, because while she worked on one, she could talk to Sara through the rectangular opening into the kitchen. "Hey, Sara," she called. "You did a primo job on that four-top that wanted all those substitutions. Thanks."

"I sort of liked the challenge. So I made the meals to suit them?"

"Apparently."

Because the lunch rush hadn't started, Sara had time on her hands. She came over to the pass-through to watch Mary Jane and chuckled when she saw what she was up to. "I see you talked somebody into a hot fudge sundae again."

"Yep. He needs it, too. Looks like he lost his best friend."

"Where is he?"

"Booth four. Don't look like you're staring, though. I'd hate to embarrass the poor guy."

"Okay. Thoughtful of him to take booth four so I can get a good look at him." Sara glanced into the diner with a show of nonchalance. "You mean that big cowboy?"

"He's the one. His name's Harrison."

"Funny, he doesn't look like a Harrison. But he's very attractive."

"I guess so, for an older man."

"I must go for that type, because I think he's gorgeous. Oops, he looked over here. He might have caught me. How embarrassing. I'll pretend I'm doing something right by the window." Sara turned away but continued to talk to Mary Jane. "Is he still looking?"

Mary Jane turned so she could peek over her shoulder. "Yep."

"Shoot. I know he saw me."

"So you glanced at him. So what?"

"I'm afraid it might have been more than a glance. Something about him really appeals to me. Maybe I do go for that older-man type. Maybe that's a clue about who I am."

"Maybe." Mary Jane gazed at her in sympathy. When Sara had taken the job at Austin Eats many months ago, she'd had amnesia, and no one knew her real name. But she was a heck of a cook, and a very nice person. Mary Jane liked her a lot. "Still no glimmers?"

"No. And you can't imagine what that's like, Mary Jane, to have no idea who you are, to have no history."

"You're right. I can't imagine it. But I have to believe you'll remember. You just need more time." She positioned a cherry, stem pointing up, in the exact center of a swirl of whipped cream.

Sara straightened her shoulders, as if determined not to let her situation get her down. "I'm sure you're right."

"I'm right. Well, gotta take the prescription over to the sad cowboy." Mary Jane winked at Sara. "Try not to drool on the French fries, okay?"

"Maybe he lost his true love," Sara said. "Check for a ring."

Mary Jane laughed. "I'll do that." She put the sundae on a plate covered with a paper doily, picked up a long-handled spoon and headed toward booth four. Instead of the smile of delight she expected from the cowboy, he was still staring intently toward the kitchen and barely seemed to notice that she'd put the sundae in front of him.

She hoped he wasn't offended because he'd caught Sara looking at him. "Ta-da!" she said, waving her hand toward the sundae.

He glanced at the treat. "Oh. Thanks, Mary Jane. That looks nice."

It wasn't the response she'd hoped for. Some people actually clapped when they were presented with one of her sundaes. He must be offended about Sara's obvious interest.

Maybe she should acknowledge the fact and get it out in the open. "I'm sorry if you caught our cook staring at you." She looked to make sure he didn't have a wedding ring on. No ring. Maybe his ego could use a boost. "She'd kill me for telling you, because she's on the shy side, but the truth is she thinks you're attractive."

"Is that right?" Instead of sounding pleased about it, he seemed royally ticked.

"Don't be angry with her," Mary Jane said softly. "She has amnesia, and she's trying so hard to get her memory back. Searching for every clue. Maybe she thought—"

"Amnesia?" The cowboy looked at Mary Jane in astonishment, all trace of irritation gone.

"Yes." Mary Jane was glad she'd changed the cowboy's attitude. Sara would die if she thought she'd made him mad, and Mary Jane felt very protective of Sara's feelings. "She showed up about nine months ago. Didn't know who she was or where she'd come from. We call her Sara because we don't know her real name."

"That's terrible."

"I know. But she's a great cook and a hard worker. She's become a good friend, so I'm hoping she'll figure out who she is soon. It's driving her nuts."

"I'll bet." The cowboy was so intent on watching Sara in the kitchen that his sundae was in danger of melting and dribbling over the side of the dish.

"Well, I'll leave you with your ice cream," Mary Jane said, hoping the statement would remind him of the special treat he was ignoring.

"Okay. Thanks again." He made no move to pick up his spoon.

With a shrug Mary Jane left. You could lead a man to a hot fudge sundae, but you couldn't make him eat. Besides, any minute the lunch crunch would begin and she needed to be caught up and ready for that. She wished she'd warned Morgan not to arrive right in the middle of it. If he did, she wouldn't have a second to spare.

A little past noon every booth was filled and only a couple of stools at the counter were available. At moments like this Mary Jane shifted into high gear, taking orders with lightning speed and delivering food in a smooth rhythm she'd developed over the years. Shelby called it her perpetual motion mode, and Mary Jane took great pride in being unflappable.

But when Morgan limped through the door with a bandage

across his forehead, she nearly dropped the tray of shakes and burgers she was carrying to booth two. With her arms full of food, there was nothing she could do but deliver the order while Morgan made his way to one of the available stools and sat down.

Damn that Garrett! He'd put Morgan on the wrong horse, most likely. She would like to wring his neck. He should have seen right away that Morgan was a greenhorn and given him that fifteen-year-old gelding that couldn't get out of a trot. Garrett would have some explaining to do. He—

"I had the onion rings and she had the fries," the woman at the table said, switching the plates Mary Jane had placed on the table. "And mine was the chocolate shake."

Mary Jane looked at the table in dismay and realized she'd completely mixed up the orders. "Oh, I'm so sorry! Of course you did." Blushing, she rearranged everything.

"No problem," said the woman. "You're busy. It happens."

"Not to me," Mary Jane said, irritated with herself. She never did this. She was famous for her ability to match up orders and customers correctly. "That's my personal motto—you get what you order. Now, is there anything else I can do for you folks?"

"Uh, give us the straws in your apron pocket?" the woman asked.

"Of course." Her cheeks heated as she took out the straws she'd put there specifically to go with the shakes. All her automatic moves were deserting her simply because Morgan was sitting on a stool somewhere behind her and he was hurt. "I'm sorry I'm so spacey."

"Don't worry about it," one of the women said. "My sister and I just came from a visit with my new granddaughter over at Maitland. Nothing could upset us after getting a look at little Ashley."

She flashed the women a big smile. "Congratulations. That's wonderful news. Give that baby Ashley a kiss for me when you see her again, okay? I'll be back to check on you in a bit!" Then she whirled, ignored a signal from booth six and made straight for Morgan's stool.

She tapped him on the shoulder.

He put down his water and swiveled to face her. "Hi."

Now she could see a bruise forming on his cheek, as well. "What the heck happened to you?"

"I—"

"Don't tell me. I can guess. That Garrett should be shot." She raised her voice to summon Shelby, who was racing back and forth behind the counter, serving customers. "Did you see what your brother did?"

"I think it was a horse, not my brother," Shelby called.

"It wasn't Garrett's fault," Morgan said. "I was—"

"Mary Jane!" called one of the regular customers, a pediatric nurse. "We're outa coffee over here!"

"Gotta go," she said to Morgan. "Don't leave."

"I thought I'd eat," he said, looking amused.

"Good. Get the mushroom burger. You won't be sorry." Then she hurried behind the counter, grabbed a coffee carafe and headed for booth one.

She didn't have time to check on Morgan again for nearly fifteen minutes. Having him in the diner was ruining her concentration, and she'd goofed up another order already, but she didn't want him to leave. She had to find out exactly how he'd ended up on the injured list.

"How're you doing?" she asked as she paused for a minute behind his stool. She noticed with satisfaction that he'd ordered the mushroom burger.

He glanced over his shoulder at her. "This is good. Very good."

"Told ya. Save room for a sundae."

"Oh, I—"

"On the house. Be back soon." She was falling behind on her orders. Once you got behind during the lunch crunch, you were dead meat. Finding the time to make him a sundae wouldn't be easy, but she was determined to do it. It was one of her skills, and she wanted to show it off. Besides, a hot fudge sundae was just the thing to take his mind off his injuries.

Garrett was so going to hear from her about this. He was in deep trouble for mussing up her Morgan.

MORGAN WATCHED Mary Jane run her legs off taking and delivering orders, and he congratulated himself on having the foresight to come in when the place was hopping. This way he could correctly evaluate the strain she was under, and she wouldn't be able to give him a snow job about her work being a piece of cake.

It wasn't. He'd waited tables during his undergrad days, and he remembered how exhausting the job could be even if you were young. And Mary Jane was pregnant. With his kid. That had to give him some leverage to convince her to cut back, even if she didn't quit entirely.

She zipped past him like the Roadrunner being chased by Wily Coyote. "Ready for that sundae?" she called over her shoulder.

"Not yet!" he called back. He could see how frazzled she was. Stopping to make him a sundae was ridiculous.

But damn, she looked cute tearing around this place in her snug white uniform, her ponytail bouncing in time to the tunes pouring out of the jukebox. He'd bet she was a cheerleader in high school. Cheerleaders hadn't attracted him back when he was in school. All that energy and emotion had made him nervous. Now, though, he wanted to soak it up, maybe even wallow in it. No doubt about it, the accident that had taken Arielle's life seemed to have wiped out the man he used to be.

This new man drove a cherry red pickup, wore a Stetson and rode a horse. Sort of. Thinking of his baptism as a rider made him smile. It took a real greenhorn to fall off Garrett's gentlest horse, but Morgan had claimed that honor.

Poor Garrett had been horrified and begged Morgan to give it up, but he'd been determined to get back on. Unfortunately, in the process he'd confused the horse, and the bewildered animal had accidentally stepped on his foot. Morgan was pretty sure he had a broken toe, but not much could be done besides taping it, so he was determined to forget about the pain.

Besides, he and Garrett had become friends, and that was more important than a broken toe. After discovering that Garrett wasn't romantically interested in Mary Jane, Morgan had been more than willing to be friendly.

He'd eventually ridden the horse, although Garrett had refused to let him leave the corral. Morgan could hardly wait to try again. He could hardly wait to get a little mud and grime on his truck, too, so it looked like it belonged. The five-year-old who had ridden an imaginary horse through the back yard still existed deep within his soul, and he was having a great time getting to know that kid again.

Mary Jane appeared at his elbow. "You've finished your burger. You must be ready for the sundae by now."

He wondered if she realized how out-of-breath she was. The hair at her temples was damp from sweat and curled in little ringlets around her forehead. Her lipstick was completely gone, and her cheeks were pink from exertion. She wore a combination of scents, from the sweetness of chocolate syrup to the tang of fried onions. Delicious.

If only he could haul her out of here, take her home and put her to bed. And climb in with her.

"Why don't you wait until it slows down?" he suggested. "Then maybe you'll have time to talk to me."

"I do want to talk to you. That Garrett has some explaining to do."

Morgan smiled. "Don't jump to conclusions."

"Mary Jane! We need our check over here!" called a guy from the far corner.

"Be right there!" She gazed at Morgan, her attention going to his bandage and the bruise on his cheek as indecision flickered in her blue eyes. "Are you sure you'll be okay sitting here a little longer? You really look like you could use a sundae right now."

"Do I?" He figured she was misinterpreting his lust for her as lust for an ice cream treat. That was okay.

"Yes, you look positively ready for hot fudge. Why don't I—"

"Yo, Mary Jane!" shouted another customer.

"Why don't you take care of everybody else first? I'm fine here."

"Okay. If you're sure."

"I'm sure." He wanted to talk to her, too. She couldn't keep up this pace for the next four months.

The diner cleared out faster than he'd thought it would. Within a half hour only one booth was filled, and two customers besides him were sitting at the counter.

Mary Jane cruised behind the counter, dodging Shelby in the process. "*Now* I can make you that sundae! I assume you want everything on it?"

The old Morgan would have skipped the nuts and asked her to go easy on the whipped cream. But the new Morgan was in charge today. "Sure. Everything. By the way, have you had any lunch yet?"

"Not yet."

Shelby turned to her. "Why don't you let me make his sundae and you go sit down at the counter. Sara can get your plate ready."

"That's okay." Mary Jane plopped a second scoop of vanilla ice cream in the tall sundae dish. "I'll finish this."

"If you insist." Shelby looked amused. "Sara, can you fix Mary Jane a BLT and hold the B? And stick a banana on the plate, too."

Mary Jane glanced at Shelby. "A BLT with no B? What the heck's that?"

"Good for you."

"Ugh. I thought I'd have a mushroom burger."

Shelby shook her head. "You eat way too many of those. You need your fruits and veggies."

Looking over her shoulder at Morgan, Mary Jane made a face. "See? I told you there was nothing to worry about. They boss me something terrible around here."

"Good," Morgan said. But whether Shelby looked out for

Mary Jane's diet or not, there was still the matter of being on her feet for hours at a time.

Yet he could see that she was very good at what she did. More than good. An artist. He sensed the creative energy going into her work as she made his sundae. And watching her was an erotic experience for him. As she ladled on the thick fudge sauce it slid between the plump mounds of vanilla, melting the ice cream as it went. It occurred to him that warm, sticky chocolate would make a good body paint.

He couldn't believe he was having thoughts like that. Kinky had never been a part of his repertoire, but spending time with Mary Jane was bringing out all sorts of hidden facets in his personality. He had a feeling she would be willing to get messy in order to have some fun.

Then she picked up the can of whipping cream. As she squirted it in an artful pyramid, he had no trouble picturing her putting that can to great use on a certain part of his anatomy. And then she'd have to lick it off....

Depraved. That's exactly what he was becoming, and he needed to get control of himself. Mary Jane needed someone to watch out for her welfare, not someone to dream up exotic love scenes with her in them.

"There you go." She set the sundae on the counter in front of him and gave him a long-handled spoon.

He admired the symmetry of the whipped cream, the blend of brown fudge and vanilla ice cream showing through the clear sides of the glass, the even sprinkling of nuts on top of the clouds of cream and the bright cherry sitting perfectly balanced on top. "It's so beautiful I hate to eat it," he said, glancing at her.

She looked incredibly proud of herself. "You have to eat it. It tastes even better than it looks."

"I'll bet." But he was thinking about her, not the ice cream treat. Her expression was so adorable he wished he could snap a picture to keep with him.

"Here's your lunch, Mary Jane," Sara called, putting a plate on the pass-through. "Heavy on the lettuce."

"Thanks, I think." Mary Jane took the plate and put it on

the counter next to where Morgan was sitting. Then she came around the counter and slid onto the stool beside him. "You haven't taken a single bite!"

"I was waiting for you."

"Well, I'm here. Dig in!"

He was aware of her gaze on him as he pushed the spoon into the sundae, getting it far enough in to reach some of the fudge. Bringing up a dripping spoonful, he put it in his mouth. Then he closed his eyes with pleasure. It tasted like Mary Jane's kiss.

"Good, huh?" she asked eagerly.

He opened his eyes. She sat there anticipating his certain praise, and her face looked as if it were lit from within. He'd never had anyone look so happy about creating something special just for him, and his throat closed at the sweetness of it.

As he looked into her sparkling eyes, the truth came over him. He wasn't going to get over Mary Jane. Not in a few weeks, not in a few months, not ever. She'd taken up residence in his heart.

"I'll bet it's so wonderful you're having trouble finding the words to describe it," she said. "Sometimes my customers are speechless with delight over my hot fudge sundaes."

He cleared the hoarseness from his throat and smiled at her. "That's exactly my problem," he said. "I'm speechless."

"I knew it. Eat up. It'll fix whatever ails you."

Somehow Morgan didn't think so.

CHAPTER THIRTEEN

MARY JANE bit into her sandwich. She was hungrier than she'd wanted to let on. And a minor but annoying ache had developed in the small of her back. Worst of all, her feet hurt, which meant that, doggone it, they were probably starting to swell. Served her right for boasting to Morgan about keeping her ankles slim and trim throughout this pregnancy.

But she had more important things to think about. After chewing and swallowing her first bite, she turned to him. "I get the impression you're trying to protect Garrett, which is noble of you, but I'll hear the story sooner or later, so you might as well tell me now. He put you up on Tigger, didn't he?"

He licked a glob of fudge from the back of his spoon. "Nope. He put me up on Pooh."

"*Pooh?* Pooh bucked you off?"

"I wish I could say that. I fell off all on my own. Too macho to hold on to the saddle horn, and I didn't have my feet firmly in the stirrups. When Pooh went right, I went left. Hit the fence on the way down."

"Ouch," Shelby said as she put the coffee carafe back and came over to where they sat. "Do you think you should see a doctor?"

"Yeah," Mary Jane said. "Did you have X rays? You could have a concussion. You really should see a doctor."

He smiled. "I am a doctor," he reminded them, "and I know the signs of concussion. I don't have one."

Mary Jane shook her head. "Not good enough. You should go next door and get an X ray. Wouldn't they give you one free out of professional courtesy or something like that?"

"I don't need an X ray," he said.

"Yes, you do. My friend Ellie's the hospital administrator over there. Ask for her and tell her I sent you. Even though it's a maternity clinic, Ellie will slip you in."

"Mary Jane, I really don't want to get an—"

"And what about your foot?" she added. "You were limping when you came in."

"Pooh accidentally stepped on it."

"Double ouch," Shelby said. "Pooh's not a small horse."

"So I suppose you have a broken toe or two, besides a concussion," Mary Jane said. The thought of Morgan being hurt made her tummy ache. The only way she knew how to handle it was to lecture him. "You need to get that checked out, too."

"I agree," Shelby said. "And if they won't do it for free out of professional courtesy, like Mary Jane said, then I'm sure Garrett's insurance will pay for it. He must have been fit to be tied, having you get hurt like that. I'm surprised he didn't drive you to the emergency room himself."

"He did want to do that," Morgan admitted. "I talked him out of it. For one thing, I wanted to ride that darned horse at least once around the corral."

Mary Jane groaned. "So after you fell off, conked your head and broke some toes, you got back on?" If this was the way he planned to behave, she'd have to keep a closer eye on him. She hadn't thought of him as reckless, but maybe she'd been wrong.

"I did." He gave her a triumphant look. "And I rode that horse. Even at a trot."

"With a concussion."

"I don't have a concussion."

"We don't know that, do we?"

He rolled his eyes. "Okay, if you're going to keep after me, I'll go next door and get an X ray."

"I'm going to keep after you, so you might as well."

"Me, too," Shelby said. "We'd all feel better if we knew you were okay. Garrett would, too, I'm sure. He'd hate to think he'd caused serious injury to his new neighbor."

"I'll go. I've been curious about the place, anyway. It has a fantastic reputation in its field."

"I thought you were going to say you're curious about the baby left on the back steps," Shelby said. "I'm sure that made the news, even in New York."

"Yes, but I'd forgotten about it until Mary Jane mentioned it yesterday." Morgan shrugged. "I figure that's a private matter for the Maitlands to work out. I'm interested in the clinic."

"I'm sure Ellie would love to show you around," Mary Jane said. "*After* you get some X rays."

"I'm really not going to get out of this, am I?" he asked with a good-natured grin.

Mary Jane shook her head. "I know Ellie. She'll take one look at you and escort you straight to the lab to get those X rays."

Morgan glanced thoughtfully from Shelby to Mary Jane. "You know, I've seen the statistics, and Austin's technically a large city, but ever since I arrived I've felt as if I'm in a small town, the way everyone is so concerned about each other."

"That's Texas for you," Mary Jane said.

"Well, whatever it is, I like it."

She told herself not to put too much store by his statement. Right now he'd probably like anything that wasn't connected to New York, which was linked in his mind with tragedy. Still, having him praise her hometown felt good. Arielle had made her think she was a hick for preferring Austin to New York, but Morgan seemed to think Austin had a lot to recommend it.

Morgan finished his sundae, and she was gratified to see him scraping the last of the hot fudge and melted ice cream from the bottom of the dish. But with his sundae finished, he had no more reason to hang around, and with his injury he might not feel like looking at baby furniture after work.

She might as well prepare herself not to see him again today after he left the diner. Gradually they'd wean themselves from each other. Then when he left for New York, she wouldn't miss him much. Right. That was as likely as snow on the Fourth of July.

Still, she needed to pretend that she wasn't sitting here basking in the joy of having Morgan around. ''Guess I'll get back to work or I'm liable to get canned.''

''Yeah, that'll happen,'' Shelby said. ''You sit a little longer, Mary Jane. I'll finish up with booth two.''

''I should probably—''

''Hey.'' Morgan put a detaining hand on her arm. ''It's not a good idea to question the boss, right, Shelby?''

''You should *never* question the boss,'' Shelby said. ''Give me the ticket for booth two and stay and keep Morgan company a little longer.''

Mary Jane was having so much trouble trying to ignore the warmth of Morgan's touch that she didn't have any energy left to protest. She took the ticket out of her apron pocket and handed it to Shelby. ''Thanks, Shel.''

''Don't mention it.'' Shelby winked before she walked around the counter and toward booth two.

If Mary Jane thought Shelby hadn't noticed her interest in Morgan, that hope was dashed with Shelby's wink. Chances were Lana and Shelby had talked about it already and were making bets on what would happen next.

Morgan took his hand away, but he didn't rush the process. ''You work very hard,'' he said.

She glanced into his eyes. ''In this business that's what you want. When it's slow, then the job gets boring fast. Plus, the more customers I serve, the more tips I make. The time goes zipping by, and before you know it the day's over and you have a pocketful of money.''

''And you don't get tired?''

She had the darnedest trouble with honesty. No matter what, she couldn't seem to tell fibs, especially to Morgan. ''Sure, I do. But I'll bet you get tired, too. I've heard about your fourteen-hour days.''

''But I'm not pregnant.''

Her jaw tightened. ''We've had this discussion, and I don't intend to quit.''

"Okay. I accept that. I can see you love your work, and another waitressing job wouldn't take its place. But couldn't you cut back on your hours, at least for the next few months? From what I've seen of Shelby, she'd go along with that."

The prospect didn't sound too bad to Mary Jane, except that she couldn't afford the pay cut. "There's the little matter of my car payment and my rent," she said. "In fact, the landlord has warned me it'll be going up when the lease expires." The minute she brought up the subject of money she knew it was a mistake. Now he was going to try to give her some.

He would never understand that if she took money from him, she'd feel as if she'd sold the baby. Even she knew it wasn't a logical position, but logic wasn't her strong point these days.

She decided to head him off at the pass. "Look, Morgan, I can't accept money from you beyond my medical expenses. I realize that sounds ridiculous to you, but that's the way it is. And this job will work out fine. I don't always work as hard as I did this lunch hour. As you see, the place is quiet now."

"I wasn't planning to offer you money," he said. "I know you won't take it."

"Good."

"When does your lease expire?"

It wasn't at all what she'd expected him to say. "Next month. Why?"

"Are you totally committed to that town house?"

"I haven't found anything I like as well, if that's what you mean. It's convenient to everything, like this place and shopping and my friends. Besides, anything cheaper would be more cramped." She smiled. "And wouldn't have a place for a bird feeder."

He nodded. "It's a nice place. You probably wouldn't want to consider what I was thinking about, anyway. The town house really is perfect for you. I'm just being paranoid about this job of yours."

"Probably." Now he'd aroused her curiosity. "What were you thinking about?"

"Nothing. It's probably not for you. Maybe I can work something out with somebody else. Maybe even Lana would be interested."

The jealous flash that whizzed through her was uncomfortable and unwelcome. "Interested in what?"

"House-sitting." He glanced at her. "Bad idea, huh?"

She stared at him. "You don't need someone to house-sit." And if he did, it sure as hell wasn't going to be Lana.

"I think I do. Somebody needs to monitor the automatic watering system to make sure the plants are okay. And I'm thinking of buying a horse."

"A *horse?*"

"Yeah. I'm sure Garrett could help me find a good one, and I loved the riding this morning, Mary Jane. Just like you said, I've always wanted to be a cowboy, but I'd shoved the idea to the back of my mind. Now that I have the clothes and the truck and the house in the country, I want a horse."

She shook her head in disbelief. "A horse."

"You said it would be good for the baby to learn how to ride. She needs her own horse for that. In fact, I might eventually have two horses."

"I truly have created a monster," she said. "Morgan, a horse is a very expensive proposition. I don't care how much money you make, it's foolish to buy a horse that you'll only lay eyes on a few times a year. The horse will get barn sour, and you'll have made a huge investment and get a bad-tempered horse in the bargain."

"That's why I need a house-sitter. Someone who would exercise the horse. I don't mean you at this point. You should stay off horses for now, but after the baby's born, you could—"

"You really are serious about all this, aren't you?"

"Yes." He regarded her solemnly. "I know you think I'm bonkers, and that it's all because of Arielle's death...."

"That's exactly what I think. Maybe instead of looking for

baby furniture while you're here, we should research the mental health professionals in the area.''

"I can understand why you'd think I'm crazy." He looked deep into her eyes. "But I'm not crazy, Mary Jane. I feel as if I'm getting a grasp on who I am, who I might have become, with different influences. A whole new world is opening up for me, and I'm having a hell of a time."

When he looked at her like that, her tummy started doing flip-flops. That look was what made her start thinking of kissing and...other things. She found this transformation of his fascinating and very, very sexy. "That's great, Morgan, but I think you should wait on this horse business," she said.

He smiled. "I wasn't planning to buy one this afternoon, if that's what you're worried about. I might even wait until after you have the baby. But I still like the idea of a house-sitter. The inside needs live plants and...and someone sitting in the window seat more than three or four times a year. The house shouldn't be empty so much."

"Then maybe you shouldn't have bought it," she said gently.

"Logically you're right, but the minute I walked into that house I felt as if I'd come home. I had to have it."

"I know what you mean. I—" She paused as a group of teenagers came in and took over their favorite booth. She knew and liked these kids, and they'd expect her to wait on them. "I'd better go," she said.

"I'm glad I kept you sitting down as long as I did," he said. "Will you feel up to looking at baby furniture after you get off?"

"Sure." Her tiredness seemed to have disappeared with the fairy-tale prospect of living in that house.

"I'll come back a little after three. We can talk more about this house-sitting thing then."

"Okay."

He moved his plate, looking for a ticket. "Shelby didn't ever give me a bill."

"Shelby didn't intend to give you a bill."

"But—"

"Let her comp you," Mary Jane said. "She's glad you're here helping me through this, and this is one way she can show you."

"All right." He took some money out of his wallet and tucked it under the plate. "But the least I can do is leave a tip." He gazed at her. "Take care of yourself until I get back."

"I'm not the one who bonked myself on the head trying to act macho."

He grinned at her. "Aw, shucks, ma'am. It's only a flesh wound."

"I want a note from the doctor to that effect."

"I'll see what I can do. See you soon."

Mary Jane watched him leave the diner and waited until she was sure he was headed over to Maitland before she took the order pad out of her apron and started toward the group of teenagers. She would give her eyeteeth to live in that house. She had a sneaky suspicion he knew that.

A HORSE. Morgan realized how inventive he could be when it suited his purpose. Ever since he'd decided to buy the Slattery place he'd been trying to figure out how to get Mary Jane to live there. She belonged in that house. He'd seen that from the first moment they'd stood together in front of that fantastic fireplace.

A house in the Hudson Valley was all wrong for her, but this place was perfect. Her light-filled, passionate personality fit the personality of the house. He'd come up with the house-sitting idea right away, but it had seemed like a flimsy pretense until the horse angle had popped into his head.

Everything was falling into place. Mary Jane could live rent free in the house, which should allow her to cut back on her hours at the diner. He could help her move in before he left. Then maybe he'd be able to make it down a couple more times before the baby was born.

As he climbed the steps up to Maitland Maternity Clinic's front entrance, a sudden thought brought him to a stop. If he and Mary Jane hadn't moved past their sexual attraction to each other by the time he came back for a visit, that could be a little awkward. Well, they'd have to move past it.

Then another thought hit him. Assuming he and Mary Jane managed to put their relationship on a friends-only basis, she would want to start dating once the baby was born. If she was house-sitting for him, she would be within her rights to bring her dates to the house. He wasn't wild about that idea. He wasn't wild about her dating, period. But maybe he'd get used to it as time went by. He really had no choice.

Moments later, as he stood in the waiting room at Maitland Maternity, he thought he already understood why the place had such a good reputation. The hospital was obviously busy, and the voices he heard were cheerful, but the underlying atmosphere was of calm competence. Maybe the pastel color scheme contributed to the feeling, as well as the soft music in the background.

From where he stood he could see the entrance to a small coffee shop, another door leading into a gift shop and a third for the day-care center. But his principal interest lay down the hall where the labor, delivery and recovery rooms were located. Now that he was here, he was eager to see everything. He approached the receptionist, gave his name and asked to see Ellie, as he'd promised Mary Jane he would.

"Is this about a position at Maitland, Dr. Tate?" the receptionist asked.

A position at Maitland. The concept sent a quiver of anticipation through him. But that would be ridiculous. He'd worked his tail off to build up that practice, and it was worth a mint. A sane person didn't throw something like that away for a salaried position at a clinic, even one as celebrated as Maitland.

"No, no, it's not," he said. "I just wanted a quick tour." He decided not to mention the X ray until he saw Ellie. Maybe she'd agree that he didn't need one.

The receptionist buzzed Ellie's office. A moment later she smiled at Morgan. "She'll be right down, Dr. Tate."

"Thank you." *A position at Maitland.* It was unlikely there were any openings. And he couldn't leave Chuck in the lurch like that. Except Chuck might not look at it that way. He could take over the entire practice, hire someone young and hungry to help carry the workload and be in a wonderful financial position. Come to think of it, Chuck might love the idea, so long as he had time to get everything set up.

But it would be truly dumb for Morgan to consider it. He'd done the hard part, building the practice. Word of mouth had taken over, and before long he'd have to start cutting back on new patients. With the income he generated, he was looking at a cushy life-style for some time to come. Early retirement was a given. Nobody walked away from something like that.

When Ellie stepped off the elevator and came toward him, Morgan almost didn't recognize her. He'd met her dressed in pajamas at the slumber party, but she looked crisp and professional in her tailored suit.

She smiled at him. "Morgan! What on earth did you do to your head?"

"Fell off a horse," he said with a sheepish grin.

"Have you had anyone look at it?"

"Me."

Ellie clucked her tongue. "If you're like most doctors I know, you think that's good enough. Before we start the tour, I want you to come with me and we'll get a quick X ray."

Morgan almost laughed. "Mary Jane figured you'd say that."

"Mary Jane and I go way back," Ellie said. "We know each other pretty well. Come on, let's get you taken care of."

"I'm sure it's nothing." Morgan walked beside her down the hall.

"Nevertheless, it'll be good to know for sure. I hear you're buying the Slattery place."

He glanced at her in surprise. "Word travels fast around here."

She smiled. "In certain circles. I was glad to hear that you'd be a property owner, because it might give me more leverage in convincing you to come and work for us."

Morgan blinked. "Oh, I don't—"

"I know," Ellie said. "You have a lucrative private practice in Manhattan, and we can't match the kind of money you're making. But after meeting you the other night I did some checking, and you have impressive credentials. If you hadn't come in of your own accord, I was planning to have Mary Jane drag you over here. I wouldn't be doing my job if I didn't at least try to recruit you while you're in town."

Morgan was beginning to wonder if he had a concussion, after all. In spite of all the reasons he shouldn't consider what Ellie was suggesting, he was beginning to seriously think about it. Maybe he did need to have his head examined.

CHAPTER FOURTEEN

BY THE TIME Mary Jane finished her shift at Austin Eats and Morgan hadn't arrived, she began to worry that he really did have a concussion and Ellie had recommended he go for more tests. She decided to wait a few more minutes, and then she'd call Ellie.

It was the changing of the guard at the diner. Sara had gone home and Joe had taken over the cooking duties. Shelby had temporarily left Georgette in charge of the counter while she ran some errands.

Business was slow, and Lisa, the teenager who waited tables four afternoons a week, had launched into the story of her big date the night before. Mary Jane was so busy keeping an eye on the front door that she barely heard a word the girl said.

"And he *so* wanted to go out again," Lisa said. "And I was all, why do you want to go out again? We, like, fought the whole time."

"That doesn't sound like much fun." Mary Jane watched the clock. A couple more minutes and she'd call Ellie's office to find out what the situation was with Morgan.

"It was a hideous evening," Lisa said. "The only thing is, he's way cute. Oh, darn, there's that weird couple. I hate waiting on them. They creep me out."

Mary Jane recognized Janelle Davis and Connor O'Hara. Janelle claimed to be the mother of the baby left on the steps of Maitland nine months ago, and Connor O'Hara was apparently the father of the little boy *and* Megan Maitland's nephew. He hadn't known about Janelle's pregnancy, and now he wanted to make it all up to her and get married. Mary

Jane had her doubts about the whole thing, especially considering that Connor was allowing his aunt to finance the wedding. It didn't seem like a very manly thing to do.

"If the stories they're telling are true, they'll become a fixture around here, so we may as well get used to them," she told Lisa. "And they're customers, so you'd better go take their order."

"I don't trust them. And that guy is, like, middle-aged, but he keeps checking me out and acting all studly. Gross."

Mary Jane had the same reaction to the couple Lisa did. On the surface they were nice looking and dressed well, but something about them was a little off. Mary Jane wasn't usually suspicious of people, but in this case she couldn't help it.

Janelle seemed to be well on her way to proving she was indeed the mother of little Chase. But Chase was a valuable kid to be connected to, and as far as Mary Jane was concerned, Janelle and Connor seemed far too eager to assume their place in the Maitland family.

Before she'd become pregnant, Mary Jane might not have been so sensitive to another woman's mothering style. But now she was, and Janelle didn't strike her as the motherly type at all. Besides, from what Beth and Ellie had said, Janelle was having an amazingly tough time coming up with birth records. Mary Jane knew red tape was a reality, but she wondered if Janelle could be stalling.

Megan Maitland, the matriarch of the family, was treating Janelle and Connor like royalty, that was for sure. She'd planned a big June wedding with all the trimmings, and Mary Jane figured the huge rock on Janelle's left hand had been bought with Maitland money, too. Everyone in the Maitland clan was buzzing about what could turn out to be the social event of the year.

Through her friendship with Ellie and Beth, Mary Jane had known Megan Maitland for a lot of years, and the woman wasn't stupid. She wanted to be welcoming to her long-lost nephew and the mother of his baby, but she was obviously keeping a firm hold on that baby until Janelle came up with some official documents. Mary Jane would be surprised if anyone pulled the wool over Mrs. Maitland's eyes for very long.

JANELLE LOOKED nervously toward the kitchen as she sat in a red vinyl seat opposite Petey. "I don't like coming in here, Petey," she said quietly.

"Watch yourself. You'd better keep calling me Connor while we're out in public like this."

"Okay, *Connor*. You're sure she's not on duty right now?"

"Look through there into the kitchen." Petey ran a hand through his thick hair. "There's an old guy back there. She's not on evenings this week. I've checked. I know her schedule better than she does. Anyway, they have the best lemon meringue pie in the city here."

"You and your pie are gonna get us in trouble yet. The more she sees us, the more she's liable to remember who she is. And once that happens, we're toast." Janelle glanced up quickly as a teenager way too perky for her own good came to take their order. "I'll have black coffee and a piece of cherry pie," she said quickly.

"Black coffee and lemon meringue," Petey said.

"Coming right up," the teenager said.

Janelle thought the kid's smile looked fake. Well, the brat probably hated her job. Janelle had sure hated service jobs, too. But those days were over.

Petey leaned toward her and lowered his voice. "Look, maybe you're right, Janelle. This while thing is getting risky. We've already raked in a lot, enough that we won't have to worry about money for a long, long time. Let's cancel out of this gig. Any minute now those idiot Maitlands are going to figure out that you don't have any damn birth records for precious little Chase."

Janelle's features hardened and she leaned back against the booth. "I may be getting a little antsy, but that doesn't mean I'm ready to give up on our chance at the mother lode. We've been over this a million times. If we can make it as far as the wedding, the gifts are just going to pour in."

"You're so sure we'll get cash, but I got my doubts, babe. I ain't risking my neck just to get a goddamned silver gravy boat that once belonged to Great Aunt Beulah."

Janelle chuckled. "It's not the gravy boat I'm going for, sweetheart. It's the gravy. The Maitlands owe me big time— and I'm not leaving till I get my fair share."

MARY JANE finally decided to go into Shelby's office and call Ellie when Morgan walked through the door all smiles, like a kid who'd just come in from the playground. From his cheerful expression she would have thought he hadn't been to Maitland at all except that he had a new bandage on his forehead.

She hurried toward him. "Are you okay? I was worried sick."

"Worried?" He looked confused. "About what?"

"Your head! And your broken toe. Honestly, Morgan."

"Oh, that! My head's fine. I knew it would be. And they retaped my toe, although they said my job was fine. Ford told me to hang on to the saddle horn next time."

"Ford Carrington?" Then she realized that Ellie must have introduced Morgan to Ford, who was Maitland's top pediatric surgeon.

"Heck of a nice guy," Morgan said. "Turns out he went to med school with Chuck. They pulled a few pranks together, too. Now I have some things to blackmail old Chuck with. What a small world."

"Sure is." Except the world seemed huge when she thought of him living in New York and her living in Austin. She didn't like to think about Morgan in his old office joking around with his partner. Forgetting about her. But fortunately Morgan was so excited about his visit to Maitland that he didn't pick up on her sadness.

"They have a fantastic setup over there, Mary Jane," he said. "Top-of-the-line equipment, great staff. I met Abby, your gynecologist."

"Beth and Ellie wanted me to have the best, so they set me up with their big sister."

He nodded. "I'm glad. The whole family thing they have going on over there is something to behold. I had no idea that the clinic was truly *Maitland* Maternity. I guess that's one of the secrets to its success. Anyway, Abby told me you're coming along great. I know you're going to love having the baby there."

She wondered if he'd be by her side. Despite his good intentions, he might not make it. "Aside from a few pesky labor pains, I'm sure I will."

"With the atmosphere they have in that clinic, I'll bet even labor pains are easier. I can see why women come from all over the country to have their babies there. Oh, and Beth showed me through the day-care center. What a terrific setup. I got some ideas for the nursery." He paused long enough to glance at her. "But first I need to ask if you're still up for shopping. We don't have to if you're too tired." He looked so hopeful that she'd want to go.

And she did want to shop for the nursery. That would take her mind off the idea of him leaving. Besides, his excitement energized her. Obviously he was as happy with his work as she was with hers, and she loved seeing that side of him. "Sure. But it's getting really hot and muggy out. I'd like to zip home and change clothes first."

"I'll follow you. Then we'll take the truck. Garrett said if we found things we wanted we could store them at his place until we get keys to the house."

"Okay. I'm parked in back. I'll meet you at the town house."

"Right." He started to leave and then turned to her as if remembering something. "Oh, and I saw that baby, the one all the fuss is about. Chase, I think his name is. Cute kid."

Mary Jane moved closer to him and lowered her voice. "Connor O'Hara, Mrs. Maitland's nephew, is over in booth four with Janelle Davis, the woman who says she's the baby's mother."

Morgan studied the couple. "Ellie said there was a problem with birth records, but it's hard to believe it would take this long," he murmured at last.

"Anything's possible, but something about the whole setup seems fishy to me."

"They have a lot to gain. It took me about five seconds to realize that Maitland Maternity is a gold mine for the family, although it's obvious that's not why they're all so dedicated to it. That's the best part—everybody's working for love, not financial reward. But I can understand why being part of that family would be a very attractive prospect for someone who cared about money."

Mary Jane glanced at Janelle and Connor eating their pie. "I would guess they do. I only know one thing about them for sure, and it's enough to put me on guard."

"What's that?"

"They're lousy tippers."

MORGAN FOOLED with the bird feeder, tightening the wire hook holding it, while Mary Jane changed clothes. It didn't take his mind off her being up there removing clothes, but at least while he was outside in the patio he couldn't hear her doing it. He had to admit the weather was getting quite warm and humid on this May afternoon. Waiting inside her air-conditioned town house would be more comfortable. But not safer.

He'd be fine once she'd changed clothes and they could get on their way, he told himself.

Wrong.

When she came out to the patio to find him, he nearly swallowed his tongue. Her cotton tank top was sliced off just beneath her breasts, and her low-slung pants hugged her hips. In between was a nicely rounded, incredibly sexy, bare pregnant belly.

She took one look at his face and started back into the house. "Okay. It's too revealing. I'll change."

"No, wait!"

"I saw your face. You were shocked that I'd show my tummy like that. I was wondering if I dared wear these pants, but nothing else feels comfortable and it's so warm today. I should probably get some maternity clothes, but I've been resisting doing that.''

"Mary Jane, you look fantastic. What you saw on my face wasn't disapproval.''

"It wasn't?''

"No.''

"Then—''

"Never mind.'' He wasn't about to explain what his expression had meant and he didn't dare stay out on the patio with her any longer or the neighbors would get a real show watching him worship her tummy the way it should be worshiped. He headed into the house. "We'd better get going before the stores close.''

"The one I was thinking of stays open late,'' she said as she followed him through the door and reached to flick the lock closed. "It's a great discount place.''

He figured she was thinking of his pocketbook again. But this was a fantasy shopping trip, one he'd been dreaming about for years, long before he'd had a baby on the way, and he didn't want to spoil it by considering price.

"We can go to the discount place last,'' he said. As they headed out the front door, he heaved a sigh of relief that he'd escaped her town house without seducing her. But seduction wasn't far from his mind. When she turned and leaned toward the door to lock the dead bolt, he admired the sexy curve at the small of her back. He wondered if she had on the fudge-flavored lipstick this afternoon or if she'd chosen caramel. Or if there was a third flavor he hadn't experienced.

But he couldn't kiss her to find out, so he settled for treating her like a princess. "Let's go to your favorite baby furniture store first, so we can see how much we're saving at the discount place.'' He had no intention of buying anything but what she loved.

"That's an idea.'' She shoved her keys into a trendy little shoulder purse and started down the walk toward his truck. His truck. Watching Mary Jane, pregnant with his baby, walk toward that big red truck was one of those perfect moments he hadn't experienced very often in his life. He paused to appreciate it before he followed her.

"How do you know I have a favorite baby furniture store?" she asked over her shoulder.

"Just a guess." He suspected she was dying to go all out on this baby business, but she'd probably held back because she didn't think it was her place. He was prepared to give her full rein.

"Well, I do have a favorite," she confessed as he opened the passenger door for her. "I've been there about ten times already."

"And it's not the discount place." He gave her a hand into the truck, and for one glorious moment he touched the warm skin at her waist. He almost groaned with delight.

"No, it's not the discount place. If you insist we can go to my favorite store first."

"I insist."

"Okay. I'll direct you."

"Great." He closed the door and walked around the front of the truck. He'd love to have her direct him, but not to the furniture store. That first night she'd taken charge and directed him to the most heavenly spot in the universe. He wanted her to direct him there again, and he was beginning to wonder if he'd ever get over it.

Ellie had offered him a job, and he hadn't turned her down flat. He'd told her he'd think about it, and he couldn't decide whether to tell Mary Jane about the offer. Sooner or later she'd find out, considering the way news traveled around here.

He didn't know how Mary Jane would react. For one thing, if he took the job it would blow the whole house-sitting caper out of the water. He wanted Mary Jane in that house. Nothing else seemed right to him.

There was an obvious solution to this convoluted mess, but a solution like that shouldn't be proposed in haste. Although his heart soared at the idea, he wasn't sure if it was the most selfish one he'd ever come up with. Mary Jane was only twenty-two. She deserved more experiences before she made forever-after commitments.

Swinging into the cab, he breathed in the scent of new upholstery and the wildflower scent of Mary Jane. He'd had a ball driving this truck the past two days, but now he knew what had been missing from the experience.

"This is a very nice truck," she said. "I can see why you fell in love with it."

"I've already thought of a drawback, though. With no back seat it's no good for a little baby."

"My car would take a baby seat," she said. Then she blushed. "Of course that has no bearing on anything."

"When I'm down here it would be very handy. I appreciate the thought." He wished they didn't have to dance around this whole subject, but for her sake, they needed to. With her hormones going crazy, she didn't know what she wanted. He started the engine and the radio came on.

"You're listening to *country?*"

"Sure, why not?"

"You're from New York, that's why not!"

"What's the matter, don't you like country?"

"I *love* country, and in Austin it's practically against the law to listen to anything else. It's only that I'm surprised you've got it on by choice. I hope you don't think you have to, or anything."

"I found out I like it, but mostly I think it goes with the truck. Probably goes with the truck better than I do."

She gazed at him. "I'd have to say you look mighty fine driving this truck, Morgan. As if you'd been driving one forever."

He put the truck in gear and glanced at her. "Thanks. Then maybe I can get away with it. Now where's this baby furniture place?"

SEVERAL HOURS LATER, boxes containing a crib, a changing table and a rocking chair decorated with rainbows were safely stored in Garrett's garage. Mary Jane settled back in the truck's passenger seat as Morgan pulled out of Garrett's drive.

She'd been completely dazzled by the shopping trip. Morgan had refused to consider anything that didn't fit her dream for the nursery. Then he'd treated her to dinner at a restaurant far too fancy for her outfit, but one she'd secretly been dying to try. She hadn't felt self-conscious about how she was dressed after he'd promised her that she was the most fascinating woman in the room.

He turned down the volume on the radio. "This has been a long day for you. I hope I didn't wear you out by dragging you out to buy furniture."

She laughed and leaned her head against the seat. "Are you kidding? I loved every minute." She had taken Morgan to her friend Lana's shop, Oh Baby! Lana had been thrilled to show them her very best, and for a few hours Mary Jane had felt as if she, Morgan and the baby were a real unit. It was a very special feeling, indeed.

"I really like the rainbows," he said.

"I'm glad. Do you realize we bought all that stuff without ever looking at the bedrooms? What if the one that's perfect for the nursery has wallpaper full of pastel hydrangeas?"

"I take it that would be bad."

"It would be *terrible*. You'd raise a daughter who would think pastels and primary colors look good together. She'd grow up with no color sense, have no idea how to dress herself, become a hopeless outcast in high school and require hours and hours of counseling to reprogram her."

He chuckled. "Then we'd better check out the situation. I might have to hire somebody to replace the wallpaper, because we're not returning those rainbows." Pulling to the side of the road, he checked for traffic and made a quick U-turn. "Let's go look at the bedrooms."

His dedication to her vision of rainbows thrilled her to her toes. "Did you get keys and not tell me? If you have keys and you didn't say so, I might have to strangle you."

"No keys. But today I bought a flashlight for the glove compartment. We'll peek through the windows."

"What a cool idea. I suppose technically we'll be trespassing."

He pulled into the drive and headed for the darkened house. "You can stay in the truck if you're chicken. I can report back on the wallpaper situation.'' He stopped the truck and opened his door.

"And the snake situation."

He slammed the door shut. "The *what?*"

She couldn't help laughing. "You're out west now, pardner. When it warms up, the snakes come out."

"What kind of snakes?"

"Boa constrictors," she said with a grin.

"Okay, now I get it. You're playing with the greenhorn's mind, right? Well, I happen to have seen a few documentaries on the Discovery Channel. Boa constrictors live in the jungle." He glanced at her. "Don't they?"

She took pity on him. "Yeah, they do. But seriously, we do have rattlesnakes. We'll use the flashlight to make sure we don't step on one by accident."

"Or maybe we should forget about the whole thing."

"Now who's chicken?"

"I'm thinking about you walking around out there in your sandals," he said.

"I'm an Austin girl. I can take care of myself."

Opening the glove compartment, she took out the flashlight. "And I've been dying to see what the rest of the house looks like. Let's go." She opened the door, whipped the light over the ground and hopped down.

"Mary Jane!" He leaped from the truck and ran after her as she started toward the house, sweeping the ground with the flashlight beam as she walked. "Let's forget this. It's probably a bad idea. Let's go get you a big piece of chocolate cake for dessert instead."

She turned to him. "Chocolate cake is good, but some things are even better than chocolate cake. Looking into the windows of this house and visualizing how the nursery furniture will look is one of them. Come on. I'll protect you."

Muttering under his breath about taking foolish chances, Morgan walked beside her toward the house.

From a lifetime of living in Texas, she'd become used to the creatures that shared the place with her. She wasn't about to go walking through high grass in the dark, but the area around the house had been beautifully maintained. The grass was clipped short and the bushes had been trimmed several inches off the ground. If any snakes were around, she'd be able to see them instantly.

But she thought Morgan's concern was kind of cute. "I'm guessing this is a bedroom." She pointed the flashlight beam at a window.

"Probably is." Morgan seemed to have relaxed a little.

She had to angle the flashlight beam before they could see anything. "Looks like white walls to me, and hardwood floors, like in the living room."

"Yep." Morgan stood close to her and cupped his hands around his eyes as he peered into the room. "Looks like a bath through that door."

She became very aware of his body, which brushed against hers as he shifted his weight to get a better view. She felt the need to make small talk. "This room faces south, so it'll get shade in the summer and sun in the winter. That would be perfect for a nursery."

"Winter sun's good." His voice sounded deeper than normal. "Ready to go back?"

It was probably a good idea, she thought. Tramping around in the dark with Morgan could be dangerous, and not just because of snakes. "I'd love to see the window seat," she said.

"We could come back tomorrow."

"Just a quick peek." She backed away from the window and started around the end of the house, making sure no reptiles lay in their path.

"Okay." Morgan sounded resigned to his fate as he followed her.

"I promise we can leave after that." She really needed to see that window seat. It was one of the main features that drew her when she tried to decide if she should house-sit for him. Maybe it would be a dinky window seat, and then she could be more objective about the house-sitting proposition.

Turning the corner of the house, she saw a generous bay window. Damn, if that was the window seat, she was hooked.

It was the window seat. A shaft of moonlight came through the trees, giving her a view of wide cushions on a beautifully crafted base tucked inside the curve of the window. She sighed softly.

"Is that what you had in mind?" Morgan asked, coming to stand beside her.

"Oh, yes." She looked around at the backyard trees that would give plenty of privacy to anyone sitting there. Or two people sitting there. An image of making love on that window seat took hold of her and wouldn't let go.

"You belong there," Morgan said. His voice had taken on that husky quality again.

Her heart pounded with anticipation as she turned to him. Yes, it was dangerous standing here with him in the dark. And so exciting she couldn't bear to leave. "I do want the house-sitting job," she said.

He gazed at her. Although the darkness hid his expression, his quickened breathing gave a clue as to what he was thinking about. "I'm beginning to wonder if it's such a good idea."

"Are you?" She lifted her face to his. "Why?" She knew why. She was tempting him, and she knew it. She couldn't seem to stop.

"Mary Jane." He spoke her name like a plea for help.

She wasn't in a charitable mood. Her pulse raced out of control as she moistened her lips and moved closer to him. "Yes?"

CHAPTER FIFTEEN

MORGAN HAD BEEN so sure he could maintain his control, right up to the moment when he lost it.

And he really lost it. He nearly lifted Mary Jane off her feet as he crushed her against his chest. The flashlight dropped to the ground with a soft thud as she wrapped her arms around him.

That was all the encouragement he needed. Taking a breath, he delved deep into her mouth. Cherry. The flavor tonight was cherry. He was wild about cherry. He was wild about the warmth of her bare back against his palm. Sliding his hand under the short top, he found the catch of her bra. With hardly a moment's hesitation, he released it.

He heard her breath catch, and then she eased slightly away, silently inviting him to touch her. If only she hadn't been so eager, he might have had a chance of regaining some part of his control. But when he reached under her top and closed his hand over her breast, she moaned with happiness. That moan made him forget everything but the tension that had been building for days.

That tension soon had him leaning down and nuzzling her top and bra aside. Her nipple was tight and hard by the time he found it with his tongue. He shouldn't be doing this, shouldn't...couldn't help himself. Surrendering to a drive stronger than conscience, he filled his mouth with the fullness of her breast.

Whimpering, she dug her fingers into his scalp and urged him on. As if he needed urging. She tasted of sweet innocence and wild abandon. So much warm, perfumed skin to explore.

He moved from the glory of her breasts down the valley between her ribs.

Dropping to his knees, he kissed the soft swell of her belly. His baby cradled inside Mary Jane. It was a potent combination, and desire settled heavily between his thighs. Yet he knew he would deny himself the pleasure of making love to this woman. He might be weak, but he wasn't that weak.

He indulged himself as much as he dared. Grasping her hips, he brushed his mouth against her skin here, and here, and over here. Turning his head, he rubbed his cheek against her tummy, loving Mary Jane, loving the baby she carried.

Her whispered words drifted in the night air. "I want you, Morgan."

"I want you, too." He swirled his tongue inside the depression made by her navel.

"Come home with me."

He leaned his forehead against her belly, breathing hard as he fought with his demons. Finally he placed one last kiss on that inviting expanse of skin and rose slowly to his feet.

"I would give ten years of my life to be able to make love to you tonight," he murmured.

"I'm not that expensive."

"You're even more expensive than that. I'd have to give away all my self-respect, too." Gently he searched out the loose ends of her bra.

"It's too soon, isn't it."

"Yes." Easing the garment into place, he kissed her tenderly while he fastened it. Then he stepped back and straightened her top.

"It doesn't feel too soon."

"I know."

She took a shaky breath. "Maybe we're in a situation where time is compressed."

"Maybe. Or maybe we're in a situation where we're not thinking clearly." He reached out and cupped her face in both hands. "But you do tempt me, Mary Jane Potter."

"I can tell." She covered his hands with hers. Then she traced the plain gold band that circled the fourth finger of his left hand. "You know what people say at times like this—that she would want you to be happy. I think she would, but maybe—"

"Maybe not this happy," he finished. "And certainly not this fast. When I can think, I know that, but sometimes I forget to think."

"Do you...do you still feel married?"

His chest tightened. It was a fair question, and he didn't have an answer. His reaction to Mary Jane wasn't the response of a man who felt committed to his late wife. And yet, he hadn't been able to take off that ring. Mary Jane was very smart to have zeroed in on the fact that he still wore it.

"I have an idea," she said softly.

"I'm listening."

"We've been together pretty constantly ever since you got here."

Not constantly enough for him. He would have liked to stick to her like a burr. He was afraid he was obsessed. "That's true."

"Maybe we've become too fixated on each other, like baby ducks who bond to the first thing they see after they're born."

He had a bad feeling about what she would suggest. "How do you unfixate a baby duck?"

"Keep them away from whatever they've bonded to." She let out a long breath, as if she didn't like what was coming, either. "I think we should see what happens if we take a break from each other."

He'd figured he wouldn't like it. And he didn't. Didn't like it at all. But he thought she was probably right to suggest doing this. "For how long?"

"A few days. Maybe until you close on the house. Do you think you'd be able to find enough things to do for a few days?"

"Sure." He had no idea what, but if that's what she wanted, he'd come up with activities. Maybe he'd volunteer a few hours at Maitland. Maybe he'd work on his riding skills. Maybe he'd decide whether to take off his wedding ring.

"Then it's decided," she said. "When you close on the house, you can call me, and we'll…we'll see where we are."

"Okay." He fought the panic he felt at the thought that after he took her home tonight, he wouldn't see her tomorrow or the next day or the next. But that panic was exactly what she was trying to cure. Panic wasn't a good emotion to build anything on. He took a deep breath and stepped away from her. "Time to get you home. You and that baby need your rest."

DURING the next few days Mary Jane thought of that silly cure for a headache, where you were supposed to hit yourself on the foot so the pain made you forget your headache. Apparently that's what she'd done to herself. She missed Morgan so much that she forgot to miss Arielle.

"You don't look like a happy person," Sara remarked one morning when Mary Jane went in the kitchen to hunt up some herbal tea to drink during her break.

Mary Jane opened the foil packet and took the tea bag out. "You know, I've gone with a few guys, even thought I was in love a couple of times." She put the tea bag in a mug. Morgan would be so proud of her for drinking this tea. She thought it had antioxidants in it. "But I've never felt like this before," she said, glancing at Sara.

Sara looked up from the chopping block where she was mincing onions. "And how is that?"

Mary Jane tried to explain it. "Maybe like this tea bag. It has so much potential to be a great thing. Well, maybe not that great. Medium great. Semi medium great. It's only a tea bag, after all. But you get nothing out of it until you add hot water."

Sara chuckled. "And Morgan's the hot water." She took a steaming saucepan and poured the water carefully into Mary Jane's mug.

"Oh, he is *so* the hot water." Mary Jane laughed as she dunked her tea bag. "I'm liking this comparison more and more. He's hot water and he's getting me in hot water."

"But if you're a tea bag, that's your destiny," Sara said,

grinning. "And by the way, I think you're a great tea bag, not a semi great one."

"Thanks, I think. But what if it's not Morgan's destiny to make tea? I mean, hot water can be used for so many things. He's such a great guy, Sara. Right now he's interested in me, but I can see what that's all about."

"So can I." Sara scraped the minced onion into a bowl. "You're beautiful, talented, funny—"

"Oh, Sara, he could have beautiful, talented and funny any day of the week. Especially now that I've talked him into showing off his cute butt. That was probably a mistake on my part." Maybe now she understood why Arielle hadn't wanted Morgan to think he was sexy. That way she'd had a better chance of keeping him to herself. But that wasn't playing fair.

"Anyway," she continued, "Morgan could have anybody. He thinks he wants me because I'm carrying this baby, and because he needs someone right now to comfort him."

"I think you're selling yourself short." Sara turned to get a spatula. "And I think... Oh, my God. There's that guy again. That Harrison Smith."

Mary Jane looked through the pass-through and noticed the man she'd served a hot fudge sundae to a few days ago. "You found out his last name?"

"Shelby did. He came in one evening when I wasn't here and he asked about me, so Shelby thought it was only fair to ask him a few questions, too. I guess he found out about my amnesia somehow." She gazed pointedly at Mary Jane.

Warmth rose to Mary Jane's cheeks. "Okay, so I did sort of tell him about that. He was looking all mad at you, so I told him, and it changed his whole attitude. I'm sorry if you didn't want me to, but I thought it was a good way to explain why you might have been staring at him."

"Great. Now he thinks I'm a few slices shy of a loaf."

"No, he doesn't! I told him you were constantly looking for clues to your past."

"Which is true." Sara's gaze softened. "I'm not really sorry you told him. Shelby says he's been around for a while.

He's here checking out Maitland as a possible place for his grandchild to be born, and she definitely thinks he's single.''

Mary Jane patted her apron pocket. "Want to go take his order?"

"Oh, no, I couldn't do that!"

"Why not? He sounds interested, and you're definitely interested. He's not allowed in the kitchen, so if you don't go out and say something to him, then never the twain shall meet, as they say.''

"I couldn't go out there and take his order. He'd know I was doing it on purpose."

"So?''

"So what if he's a serial killer or something?"

Mary Jane laughed. "I haven't known too many of those, but this guy isn't giving off serial killer vibes. If you won't go take his order, I'd better. The poor guy probably came in for food as well as to stare at you. Want me to slip him your phone number?"

Sara looked horrified. "Absolutely not!"

Mary Jane set down her tea. "Okay, but this is starting to remind me of junior high. Maybe you could arrange his French fries in the shape of a heart." With a wink at Sara, she went to take the mysterious Harrison Smith's order.

Not long afterward one of her favorite customers came in and took a seat at booth five. She approached him with a smile. "Hello, Mr. Blake."

"I've told you a million times to call me Hugh," the silver-haired man said. "Am I going to have to get a court order?"

Mary Jane laughed. He was the Maitland family's lawyer, and she'd known him since she'd been in elementary school. "When I first met you I was supposed to call you Mr. Blake, so it's hard to change. But I'll try. Can I get you a hot fudge sundae?"

"You sure can. With everything that's been going on at Maitland Maternity this past while, it's enough to make me come in for a sundae every day of the week."

"Be my guest," Mary Jane said. "I sure hope everything gets sorted out for poor little Chase and his parents."

"Oh, it will." Hugh Blake's blue eyes twinkled. "In any case, all the activity keeps me on my toes. And it is my job to watch out for the family's welfare."

"I'm sure Mrs. Maitland is grateful to have you on her side."

The older man's expression softened. "I like to think so," he said.

"I'm sure she is. Now, if you'll excuse me, *Hugh,* I'll whip you up the best hot fudge sundae in the state of Texas."

ONCE MORGAN contacted Ellie about volunteering a few hours at the clinic, he had no trouble filling his time. He hadn't considered the proximity of Maitland to the diner, though. Thinking of Mary Jane working right next door made their self-imposed separation that much worse.

He wished he'd thought to tell her about working at the clinic so he wouldn't be the only one suffering. A better man wouldn't want Mary Jane to suffer, but he wasn't that saintly.

A couple of times he considered going over for a cup of coffee. Other people at Maitland did it all the time, and he'd been invited to go along. But then he'd ruin the experiment, and he was determined to tough it out because he could see the value in being away from Mary Jane. He was gaining perspective he wouldn't have otherwise.

His need for Mary Jane didn't diminish. If anything, it intensified the longer they were apart. But without Mary Jane around, he could think about his marriage to Arielle. After some struggle, he was able to set aside the tragedy of her death long enough to look at the emptiness of his life with her.

He might not have seen it if the change hadn't been so abrupt, if he hadn't been rocketed immediately from life with Arielle to life with Mary Jane, from artsy black-and-white prints to the colorful fun of Sunday comics. No surprise that he'd been drawn to the artsy black-and-white world Arielle represented—his parents lived in that world, too. Now that he understood that he had a choice, his choice was the Sunday comics.

Finally he could admit that he hadn't much liked the man he'd been turning into. Arielle's horrible and undeserved fate made it damned near impossible to think negative thoughts about her. But...she'd been a snob. And he'd fallen right in with her behavior.

Only certain restaurants would do, only certain people should be cultivated as friends. She'd advised him to build his practice around children of the wealthy and influential, and he'd gone along with her. Art buyers had been prime candidates, and those with both children and "exquisite taste," as Arielle had termed it, were quietly steered in Morgan's direction.

At Maitland he met all kinds of people. Some were rich and famous, while others were barely scraping by. The second category had been the reason Megan Maitland had established the clinic, and she made sure nobody on the staff forgot the clinic's roots. Morgan discovered he loved working with plain folks.

He also discovered that in his off hours he loved working with horses. Arielle would never have understood his immense satisfaction in mucking out a stall and spreading it with clean straw. She would have said he was wasting time and potential on a mundane job like shoveling manure, that he hadn't invested all those years in med school to sweat like a common laborer.

But Morgan enjoyed every minute of the time spent caring for the horses, and the more familiar he became with them, the more comfortable he was when he climbed in the saddle for a riding lesson. As the days went by, he felt less like a fake when he put on his boots, jeans and Stetson.

Gradually he created mental distance between his former life in New York and his new life in Austin and began to see the shape of an altered future shimmering in the distance. Maybe it was a mirage, but he didn't think so. He saw himself working happily at Maitland and coming home to a rural life that included dogs and horses and satisfying physical labor.

And Mary Jane. But that was the part he agonized over. With every passing day he was more convinced that she was right for him, but he might not be right for her, even if she thought so now. He had to remember that her hormones were out of control and her thinking was probably fuzzy. And she was, after all, only twenty-two. The phrase "robbing the cradle" was old-fashioned, but it kept running through his mind.

He and Arielle had been selfish to ask Mary Jane to have their child. He couldn't compound that selfishness by tying her to a commitment she might regret in four months when her body chemistry stabilized. No, he needed to distance himself from Mary Jane, at least for the next few months. He wouldn't give up his dream of eventually moving to Austin, but he wouldn't implement it anytime soon.

Mary Jane didn't have to know he was considering the move. He would tell her he was returning to New York and he'd be back when the baby was born. He would break the news after Eleanor called to set up the closing on the house.

And finally, Eleanor did call. The closing was set for Friday, two days away.

He thought carefully all day Thursday about what he wanted to say. Telling Mary Jane about his decision over the phone might seem impersonal, but it would be kinder to both of them in the long run. That evening he drove to a pay phone beside a convenience store rather than call from Garrett's house, where he might be overheard.

Heart pounding and throat dry, he dialed Mary Jane's number. All he got was her answering machine. He'd forgotten about the cute, silly message she had on it.

Hi. This is not the real Mary Jane. The real Mary Jane is out doing the social butterfly thing and will call you back. You can make that so much easier by telling her who you are and what your phone number is. She's developing her psychic powers but they're not fully operational yet.

That perky message further convinced him that he was doing the right thing by backing away from their relationship. Social butterflies needed to be free, and all that stuff. But he didn't want to talk to a machine. Telling her about his decision on the phone was one thing. Putting the news on her answering machine was just plain cold.

Frustrated, he drove around for an hour, went to the same phone booth and tried again. Still the answering machine. He glanced at his watch. It was getting late. Social butterfly thing, hell. She should be home resting, especially if she'd spent the day at the diner. Damn it, where was she?

Dialing again, he decided to put a message on the machine. It was too late for her to call him at Garrett's anyway, so she'd have to get back to him the next day. This wasn't working out the way he'd hoped. He had his speech ready and he wanted to deliver it and get it over with.

He listened to her message again and took a deep breath. "Hi, Mary Jane." Her name sort of stuck in his throat and didn't come out as casual-sounding as he would have liked. He cleared his throat. "I'd like to talk to you when you—"

"Hello? Morgan?" Her voice sounded funny, sort of clogged up like she was sick.

Instantly he was worried. "Mary Jane? Do you have a cold or something?"

"No, no. I was…watching movies. That's why I put the machine on."

Instead of being out doing her social butterfly thing, she'd been home crying over a movie. Tenderness washed over him. He remembered her cache of weepy videos. Laughing with her about those tearjerkers had been a high point of his visit.

But there had also been that moment when they'd stopped to look at the bluebonnets. That ranked pretty high, too, and making a chocolate cake had been fun, and playing gin, and sleeping tucked in with her and a million stuffed animals. And kissing her. Oh, God. Kissing her had been the best.

"Morgan? Was there something you wanted to talk to me about?"

"Yes, I, uh… What were you watching?"

"*Titanic.* I got to the part where they're floating in the water together, and he's making her promise… Oh, Morgan, it's so…sad. And I know what's going to happen." She sniffed.

He couldn't tell her what he'd planned to say. Not when she'd been sitting there watching doomed lovers floating in the Atlantic and crying her eyes out. He wondered why she was putting herself through such misery.

She spoke again. "I probably shouldn't be telling you about it. I didn't mean to depress you."

"No problem." If she insisted on watching that kind of movie, he didn't think she should be doing it alone. "Is Lana with you?"

"No."

"Why not?"

"Because. The thing is, I sort of... Oh, never mind. Are you ready to close the sale on the house? Is that why you called?"

"Yes."

"Have you been thinking about us?"

"Yes."

She met his answer with silence. "See, that's why I've been watching sad movies. To get ready."

His chest constricted with pain. He couldn't do this over the phone. He'd been an idiot to think that was the best way to handle it. "I'm coming over," he said.

"Okay." Her voice sounded very small.

"I'll be right there."

"Okay. Bye."

Damn. Damn, damn, damn. Right when he needed Mary Jane to be tough and resilient, she was going soft on him. He jumped in the truck and drove straight to her town house, running yellow lights all the way. Somehow, he had to make her see that this was best for both of them.

CHAPTER SIXTEEN

WHEN MORGAN CALLED, Mary Jane was wearing her total comfort and elegance outfit for warm summer nights—teal silk pajamas with drawstring pants that accommodated her growing tummy and a boat-necked tee that settled gently over her sensitive breasts. She'd found the set on sale a year ago at the Maitland Maternity gift shop.

Although the outfit was obviously designed for someone who'd recently had a baby, Mary Jane hadn't seen any reason any woman wouldn't adore it. She certainly did. But even on sale, the washable silk had been out of her price range. Hope Logan, a friend who ran the shop, had called her two days later and told her she'd cut the price of all the sale merchandise another twenty percent.

Mary Jane had suspected Hope had lowered the price so she could afford the pajamas, and although they still hadn't been cheap, Mary Jane had splurged. Lately she'd wondered if buying the outfit had announced to the universe that she was interested in having a kid. Not two months later Arielle had called to suggest the surrogate mother project.

At the time Mary Jane had laughed and said she already had the postpartum PJs taken care of. Recently she'd discovered they worked great for this stage of the pregnancy, too, and they seemed to go perfectly with a night of watching *Titanic* and bawling her eyes out.

Titanic was the grand finale in the Tragedies on the Tube Film Festival she'd been conducting since she and Morgan had decided not to see each other for a while. Her theory was that if Morgan took Option A and decided she was not for him, she'd be totally cried out and therefore wouldn't embarrass herself when he broke the news. If, on the other hand, he went for Option B and thought they might have a future together, then she'd be more than ready for some joyous news after several nights of angst.

Judging from his tone when he'd called, he was choosing Option A. When a telltale lump formed in her throat, she wondered if she was totally cried out, after all.

Turning off the movie, she glanced at her outfit and wondered if she should change into something else. No, by God, she wouldn't change. She wasn't in the mood to make this easy for him by greeting him in sexless fleece or flannel. Besides, it was too warm a night for that. Let Morgan deal with her in nearly transparent silk.

Then she took inventory of the living room. Crumpled tissues lay on the coffee table next to an empty pint of caramel fudge ice cream and a nearly empty bag of chocolate chip cookies. Pig-out city revealed.

Grabbing everything, she headed toward the kitchen to toss it. She threw the tissues in the garbage and started to drop the ice cream carton in after them when she noticed there was a good tablespoon, at least, of melted ice cream in the bottom. If she dropped a cookie in there and mashed it up with a spoon, she'd have something luscious to put in her mouth to ward off the depressing emotions she felt coming on.

She'd barely accomplished that when the doorbell rang. Still chewing her treat, she walked toward the front door. She couldn't help but remember the first night he'd arrived on her doorstep. A doorbell ringing late at night would probably freak her out for quite a while. At least this time she had a pretty good idea of what he intended to say and was as prepared as possible. Answering the door with a mouthful of chocolate and caramel helped some.

She looked through her peephole to make sure Morgan was the person standing on her front porch, and then she opened the door.

He wore his cowboy clothes with a lot more confidence than he had the day he'd bought them, she noticed. He also wore his hat, even though it was nighttime and he didn't need

it to shade his eyes. Wearing the hat after dark meant he'd
truly crossed the line to cowboy land, she decided. She wondered if he planned to dress that way in New York. If he
walked around Manhattan looking like this he'd have women
following him down Fifth Avenue.

She had herself to blame for that. He'd arrived in Austin
clueless about his babe-magnet factor, a guy who didn't even
realize he had a sexy butt. She hadn't been able to leave well
enough alone, and now he probably knew how yummy he
looked in those jeans. Damn it.

His eyes got kind of wide when he looked at her outfit,
though. Well, good. Let him take that mental picture up north.
Then immediately she felt guilty for her lousy attitude. He
would be going to that sterile apartment with the black, white
and gray color scheme that Arielle had thought was so sophisticated. It probably was sophisticated, but it wouldn't lift
Morgan's mood any. No doubt he was convinced he was doing the right thing. The poor guy had enough to handle without adding sexual frustration.

She finished chewing her treat and swallowed. "Come in,"
she said, stepping back. "I was just on my way upstairs to
get a robe. Do you want something to eat or drink? Why don't
you go on back to the kitchen and help yourself? There are
some carrot sticks in the fridge." They were carrot sticks
she'd ignored during her film festival, but maybe he'd think
that was what she'd been chewing on when she answered the
door. She started toward the stairs.

"Wait."

She glanced over her shoulder and discovered he hadn't
come inside yet. Maybe he didn't intend to. If he delivered
his kiss-off speech on her front porch he could make a quick
getaway.

The thought of him reciting his goodbye speech and then
leaving immediately made her chest hurt, but he might have
the right idea. Goodbye speeches could get messy, especially
when it came to making that exit. Sometimes just navigating
through a doorway was damn near impossible. This way he
could turn and leave, and she could close the door quietly, or

slam it, whichever she felt like after hearing his reasons, and then it would be over.

Taking a deep breath, she squared her shoulders and went to the door. Cool air-conditioned air was sifting out the door while warm night air sifted in, but thinking about the electric bill wasn't very noble at a time like this. Another spoonful of crushed cookies and melted ice cream would sure go good right now.

"I've, uh, come up with a plan," he said. His gaze grew hungrier by the minute as it kept straying to her breasts.

She started to feel sorry for him again. Then she remembered she *had* offered to go cover up. "Okay."

He cleared his throat. "Are you still interested in house-sitting?"

She weighed the options in her mind. Living in his house and knowing he'd put himself out of her reach would be frustrating. It would also hurt her pride. But if she let those things bother her, she'd never know what it was like to read a book in that window seat or lounge in the backyard under the willow tree.

"You're not interested." He sounded very disappointed.

She thought about it some more. The house would be a connection to him. You never knew what was around the bend. People could change their minds. "Yes, yes, I am interested. At least for now."

"Good." He nodded. "That's very good." He was obviously trying hard to ignore her sexy outfit and keep his attention focused on her face. He was failing. With each guilty glance at her silk-covered body, his eyes grew darker, his breathing more ragged.

She tried hard not to pity him, but he looked so miserable she couldn't help it. Actually, she pitied them both. He was trying to be grown-up and sensible about all this, and it wasn't his fault that he was breaking her heart in the process. "You can leave a key with Garrett," she said softly. "He'll help me move my things over."

"What?" He glanced up, his gaze hot. He'd been caught

staring directly at her chest, and he seemed to have lost track of the conversation.

She could probably seduce him, but she decided that would be beneath her. "You're flying to New York right after the closing, aren't you? You're not staying until the end of the month, like you planned."

The heat faded from his eyes and he looked totally unhappy. "Yeah, I'm leaving. I think it's the best thing for me to do. Better for both of us."

Although she'd expected this, it was a blow. She managed a little smile. "Then I guess you discovered during our separation that I'm resistible."

His gaze swept over her, and a muscle tightened in his jaw. "Don't I wish."

"I must be. If I do say so myself, this outfit is outrageous. And you're resisting."

"For your own good!"

"Oh, *please!* People say stuff like that to hide the real reason for things. At least be honest with me."

Anger flared in his dark eyes. "You don't need me in your life right now, Mary Jane," he said tightly. "Give me credit for seeing that, at least."

"And who are you to decide what I need? Who made you my keeper?"

"You need someone to be! You're pregnant and you're hormonal. You can't trust your emotions to guide you, so someone else has to—"

"That is the most patronizing piece of bull I've ever heard in my life." She stepped across the threshold and pointed her finger at him. "Now let me tell you how *I* see it. Maybe you think you're watching out for my welfare, but that's not the main issue. In the past few days you suddenly realized that a waitress who is determined to stay in Austin doesn't fit in with your life plan. But you can't say that, because it would hurt my feelings, so you're making this all about me."

His jaw muscles worked as he stared at her in frustration. "That is so wrong."

"I don't think so." She lifted her chin. "Treat me like an

adult for once. Have the courtesy to tell me that your practice makes too much money to consider moving here, so we could never have a future together. Be honest and admit that you think I'm basically too young for you, that chemistry isn't enough to build a relationship on and you're not willing to have an affair.'' She took a breath and lowered her voice. ''I do appreciate that you're not willing to have an affair. I think.''

Fury raged in his eyes. ''You want me to treat you like an adult?'' He took one threatening step forward.

She refused to be intimidated. Whatever he dished out, she could take. ''Give it to me straight, Morgan.''

Jaw clenched, he stared at her. ''All right.'' His voice was low and tense. ''Then get inside. What I have to say isn't something I care to broadcast to the neighbors.''

Startled, she backed up a few steps before realizing she'd just obeyed an order.

Before she could consider the wisdom of that, he stepped into the entry and closed the door. Then he clicked the lock into place. The metallic click echoed in the sudden silence.

''Morgan?''

When he turned to her, his gaze was intent, all confusion gone. ''You're right,'' he said. ''I haven't treated you like an adult. I've been protecting you from what I've been feeling. At first that was because I didn't trust those feelings. But I've had a lot of time to think recently, and I believe that what I want and need from you is real, and not just a result of losing Arielle.''

Her heart began to pound. She forced herself to try to stay rational, in spite of a look in his eyes that heated her blood. ''Or maybe it has to do with me carrying your baby.''

''Icing on the cake. But even not pregnant with my kid, I'd want you, be crazy to hold you, make love to you.''

She could barely breathe. ''Oh,'' she said softly.

He held up his left hand. ''I took the ring off, Mary Jane.''

''Oh,'' she whispered again, her heart racing.

''But I was going to leave town, give you space. Let you

have time to get unpregnant and then…then I was going to see how you felt about me.''

"And…" She swallowed. "And what are you going to do…now?''

"Now?" He tossed his hat to the couch. Then he closed the distance between them and scooped her up in his arms. "Now I'm going to take you upstairs and make love to you until you can't see straight.''

She thought she might faint from happiness. "Cool." No one had ever picked her up like this, literally sweeping her off her feet. She could understand why it made women go bonkers. Strong arms, solid chest, sweet scent of man all around her.

But as he started toward the stairs she realized it was a long climb. "There's always the couch.''

"Nope, we're going to do this right." He was breathing heavily, but he was still climbing. "Finally.''

Cradled in his arms, she could feel the rapid thump of his heart. "But are you sure you should be carrying me? What if your back goes out or something?" Now that the prize was within reach, she didn't want any heroics on his part to ruin it.

"Look, I may be past thirty," he said, puffing away, "and I know that seems ancient to you, but I think I can manage to get your saucy little butt into bed without dropping you, so— Oh, God. I didn't think about the baby." He lowered her to her feet one step above him. "Oh, geez. If I'd dropped you, then something could have—''

"It didn't." She cupped his face in both hands. "And I felt like I was smack-dab in the middle of *Gone With the Wind*.'' Then she treated herself to a kiss, meeting warm lips and an even warmer tongue. Her knees began to buckle. The guy definitely knew what to do with his mouth.

Before she could sag too far down on the steps, he wrapped his arms around her and pulled her close. Being carried was nice, but this was better, with all their significant body parts in direct contact. Feeling more liquid by the second, she snuggled in and kept kissing.

A groan rumbled in his chest as he slid both hands up her
back under the loose top, then down over her silk-covered
bottom to tuck her in even closer. She felt the imprint of his
belt buckle against her tummy. But she was more interested
in the imprint of what was below the belt buckle.

He lifted his mouth a fraction and struggled for breath.
"You taste like...chocolate and...caramel. Again."

"Essential snacks," she murmured.

He peppered her face with tiny kisses. "You have...
to...watch that."

She arched against him, her breathing ragged as she reveled
in the shower of kisses. "I'd rather kiss than eat. Hint, hint."

"Sounds like a plan." With a moan he delved deep into
her mouth.

Judging from the bulge in his jeans and the moisture gathering between her thighs, they'd never make it to the bedroom. She began popping open the snaps on his shirt so she
could run her hands over his chest.

There was nothing boyish about Morgan's body, and that
thrilled her. His broad chest sprinkled with hair was every
inch a man's, and all the more exciting as a result. Even the
scent of him seemed more mature, more erotic than the in-
experienced young guys she'd dated. He was a seasoned
lover, and she'd discovered a taste for good seasoning.

He lifted his head. "We should go into your—"

"Stairs are nice." She finished with his shirt and started
on his belt buckle.

"But you need—"

"You." She unzipped his jeans.

"A bed."

"Later." In an inspired move she slipped her hands inside
the waistband of his briefs and slid to a sitting position, pulling his jeans and briefs down as she went. The maneuver gave
her perfect placement.

Mary Jane.

She wrapped both hands around his solid penis. No wonder
he'd felt so wonderful deep inside her that first night. She

caressed him lovingly, and then she leaned over to kiss the straining tip.

He made a strangled sound low in his throat.

Glancing at him, she took him slowly into her mouth. He closed his eyes and shuddered. Sliding his trembling hands through her hair, he pressed the tips of his fingers against her scalp as he gasped in reaction.

She loved surprising him, shocking him, torturing him. He tasted salty and male and potent, so very potent. With every movement of her tongue he moaned softly, until the moment he tightened his grip and pulled away. Shaking like a leaf, he knelt on the stair in front of her and captured her mouth with his.

With a sigh she leaned back, bringing him with her. His erection lay thick and hard against her inner thigh, but he held his weight away from her as he fumbled with the tie at the waist of her silk pants. In his haste he pulled it into a tight knot. Muttering a soft curse against her mouth, he tried to undo it while balancing himself with one hand propped on the step.

She chuckled softly, breathlessly. "Let me," she murmured, shoving his hand away.

His breath was hot against her neck as he pushed the front of her silk shirt up, exposing her breasts. "Hurry."

"I'm trying." Her fingers weren't working much better than his. "We put this off way too long."

"You're telling me." He leaned down and kissed the tip of each breast. "I want you so much I'm dizzy. Look at you. Look at those beautiful, rosy nipples of yours." He began sucking gently.

"Oh, Morgan..." She had to give up her work on the knot as the tug of his mouth at her breast made her weak with desire.

He continued the sweet suction until she was so stoked with sexual energy she figured she would glow in the dark. At last he released her nipple but continued to flick his tongue over the tip, sending little shock waves through her system. He lifted his gaze to her face. "Good?" he whispered.

She struggled to speak. "The...best. I've never...I've never been affected...like this. I don't know...why."

His gaze warmed even more. "That's easy. You're going to have a baby." He cupped her breast, squeezing gently. "So perfect. So ready to give."

A deep sorrow cascaded through her. "But I'm not going to—"

"Shh." Easing upward, he brushed his lips against hers. "I think you are."

"But—"

He cut off her protest by settling his mouth over hers. And as his tongue thrust intimately inside, he loosened the knot at her waist as if he'd suddenly become Houdini. The silk gave way easily, slipping down and over her hips with just the slightest help from her. One little wiggle, and the garment was gone.

And Morgan was back, bracing his arms on either side of her, easing the tip of his penis into her heat. He slowly ended the kiss and looked into her eyes. "I told myself this might never happen again."

Her gaze holding his, she gripped his buttocks and guided him forward. "So did I."

"You feel so right." His breath caught as he settled deep within her. "So very right."

"We fit." Her body hummed with pleasure as he began to move.

He stroked her with a lazy rhythm, but there was nothing casual about the look in his eyes. "We do," he said, sounding awed. "This is..."

"Perfect," she said breathlessly.

"Yes." He increased the tempo.

"Like..." She moaned as the delicious friction urged her higher. "Like the first time."

"Yes." His gaze darkened. "Like the first time."

"We were good together."

"So good I tried to forget." His voice grew hoarse as he pushed them both closer to the edge. "I couldn't. Because I belong here." He shoved deep. "Right here."

She gasped as the first tremor rocked her. "I want you...there. Oh, yes, there. Again. There."

His words punctuated his sure thrusts. "I know...you do...for now."

"For al—"

"For now." He buried himself within her. "That's all I need."

The rush of a powerful orgasm left her without words. As her cries of pleasure mingled with his heavy groan of release, she reveled in the feeling of completion as his hot seed poured into her. But magical as that feeling was, she knew it was not enough.

CHAPTER SEVENTEEN

MAKING LOVE on the stairs. If anyone had told Morgan six months ago that he'd be making love to a woman in such a wild and crazy place he would have laughed in disbelief.

But, damn, what an outstanding idea. Keeping his torso lifted away from her so she wouldn't have to bear his weight on the uneven surface, he gazed at Mary Jane lying nearly naked beneath him. Her silk top was pushed up to her neck, so she might as well have been wearing nothing.

The light in the stairway wasn't great, but good enough that he could enjoy the view. His glance skimmed over her high, plump breasts, the delicate valley between her ribs and the graceful curve of her pregnant belly. Below that, surrounded by soft curls, his penis was still imbedded deep within her. He should probably move away and get her into bed, but he hated to break that precious connection.

Slowly his attention returned to her face. Her cheeks were flushed and she'd have a case of razor burn tomorrow. If the look in her eyes was any indication, she wouldn't care. She was gazing at him as if he'd just finished creating the heavens and the earth. He couldn't remember seeing that much satisfaction on any woman's face before. And of course he wanted to see if he could duplicate his efforts. But not here.

"This is a first for me, doing it on the stairs," he admitted. "I sure hope your back's okay."

She smiled. "My everything's okay. More than okay. We loved that."

"We?"

"The baby and me." She placed her hand over her tummy. "She's dancing."

"You're kidding."

"Nope. Feel." Curving her hands around his back, she urged him down so his stomach rested lightly against hers.

Sure enough, he could feel that baby. It was sort of like lying on a shiatsu massage unit. Except instead of rolling nodules, the pressure came from a foot, or an elbow, or a knee, all belonging to his baby. His little girl.

He gazed into Mary Jane's eyes as he continued to rest lightly against her belly and absorb the soft nudges of the child she carried. "While I'm still inside you and lying on top like this, I almost feel as if I'm right there with her," he said softly.

"You almost are," she said.

"You're sure I didn't do any damage?"

She shook her head. "I'm no masochist. I would have stopped you if you were hurting me or if I thought there was a problem with the baby."

He rubbed his stomach gently across hers, and the baby seemed to kick in response.

"She's talking to you," Mary Jane said.

"Yeah?" He could stay like this for hours, but he had to get Mary Jane off these stairs. Carpeted or not, they weren't the same as an innerspring. "What's she saying?"

"She's saying, 'Hello, Daddy.'"

His heart swelled with emotion. Gratitude to Mary Jane for nurturing this baby was part of it, but he knew that wasn't the most significant thing he was feeling. He dared not speak of what his heart was telling him. Not yet. He'd already revealed more than he intended tonight. Now Mary Jane knew the depth of his passion. The rest, words that had the power to change their lives forever, would have to wait.

With great reluctance he eased away from her. "I feel like Adam being kicked out of paradise," he murmured. "But you shouldn't keep lying on these stairs."

"There's more paradise where that came from," she said. "Unless you're planning to call it a night."

He hadn't really figured out what would happen next. "You

need your rest," he said, thinking he should leave. He was already a far luckier man than he deserved to be.

She gazed at him. "That doesn't mean you have to go home. I'm greedy, Morgan. Now that you've shown me that the first time wasn't a fluke, I want to make love again." Her glance drifted downward. "If you're up to it," she said with a wicked smile. "And I do believe you are."

His heart began to pound with renewed desire. "I—"

"And after we make love again, I want you to sleep with me tonight and make love to me in the morning before we have to get up."

Oh, he could do that. He could so do that. And then leaving would become more and more difficult. "I'm not sure that we should—"

"Why not? Is there any medical reason?"

He knew there wasn't. Not with a young mother-to-be as healthy as Mary Jane. She could probably make love until the week she delivered, so long as her partner was careful and used positions to accommodate her. His penis twitched at the prospect of making love to Mary Jane as she grew more rounded and ever more desirable. But it wasn't part of his game plan.

"No medical reason," he said.

Her gaze challenged his. "Did you or did you not have a good time just now?"

"I had a wonderful time, and you know it."

"Me, too. Absolutely wonderful. And I didn't think about this before, but making love is very convenient when a woman is pregnant."

"Convenient? I'm not sure what you mean."

"Well, it's not as if you have to worry about knocking me up."

He chuckled. "True." But she was right that their love-making was simple and straightforward. Because she was pregnant, there was no agenda except giving each other pleasure. He wasn't trying to make a baby, nor was he trying not to.

"And so everything's more fun, don't you think?"

''No doubt.''

She smiled. ''Then come to bed with me and we'll do it again.''

He was helpless in the face of temptation. He would spend the night with her and make love to her the next morning, too. But then—then he would have to be strong.

MARY JANE dreamed that Morgan was kissing her all over. His warm, wet mouth traveled from her earlobe to her throat, to her collarbone, then to her breasts and down her inner arm to the tender place inside her elbow. He moved on, and she squirmed at the tickling sensation of his tongue dipping into her navel. Lovingly he stroked her belly before easing down to her feet.

No man had ever licked her toes, but in her dream Morgan did that, and she discovered that she loved it. His tongue slid into the crevices between each one, and the sensation reminded her of the friction of his penis gliding deep inside her. Then he sucked gently on each toe. She grew warm and damp with anticipation.

Guiding her legs apart, he thoroughly kissed the backs of her knees. By the time he ran his tongue up her inner thighs, she knew what to expect next. Some dream she was having. Or maybe not a dream. She trembled on the brink of waking, not wanting to give up this excellent dream unless...unless it was real.

When she felt his warm breath stir the curls covering her most intimate secrets, when he kissed that sensitive place with deliberate care, her lashes fluttered open. The room was filled with the soft light of dawn. This was no dream. Morgan was giving her a treat.

Suspended halfway between sleep and wakefulness, drifting in a sensual haze, she closed her eyes. Lying on the bed limp and relaxed as a rag doll, she allowed Morgan to do as he would with her. He seemed to know *exactly* what to do with her, and he apparently required no participation from her to achieve his ends. He might even think she was still asleep and her body was automatically responding to his touch.

What a wild sensation, to be coaxed and kissed awake in every sense of the word. He cupped her belly with both hands, caressing her lightly as he continued his assault right where it counted the most. She was in heaven.

He used his tongue with the finesse of a master, and she grew slippery and hot in no time. Tension wound through her, tightening the muscles that had been loosened by sleep. Lying still was no longer an option as his tongue continued to work its magic.

Being quiet lost its appeal, too. She began to pant and squirm, although she was careful not to dislodge him. If he stopped she would be reduced to begging.

He didn't stop. He drove her right over the edge, wringing moans of ecstasy from her lips as waves of sensation rolled relentlessly through her, leaving her once more limp as a rag doll.

Moving beside her, he kissed her full on the mouth, giving her a taste of her own passion, and just like that, she was ready for him again. She arched against him in invitation.

He rolled over her, positioned himself between her thighs and in one sure thrust claimed her.

She opened her eyes and discovered she was looking directly into his.

"Good morning," he murmured, angling his body so he pressed gently against her tummy with each easy stroke.

"Yes, it is," she murmured, cupping his bottom and wiggling closer. "At least so far. I'll take you over an alarm clock any day."

His voice grew husky as he continued his lazy rhythm. "I woke up and saw you lying there, and I...couldn't help myself."

"Don't control those urges on my account."

"I don't seem to be able to."

"Good." She wound her legs around his, locking them closer together.

"Ah, Mary Jane." He picked up the rhythm. "That feels so good. Like you really want me inside you."

"Read my lips. I really want you."

"I'd rather kiss your lips." Leaning down, he captured her mouth with firm intent. Then he lifted his head and smiled at her, his eyes alight. "There's something better than fudge and caramel lipstick."

"There is?"

Her breathing quickened as his steady thrusts brought predictable results. Satisfaction was so easy to come by with this man.

"Yeah. Pure Mary Jane." He leaned down to pleasure her mouth again while he continued pleasuring the rest of her.

The combination brought her to the brink of orgasm in no time. Clutching his head, she urged him to break the kiss, wonderful though it was. "I need...room," she said, panting.

"Room?"

"Room to yell. I'm about to yell, Morgan."

"That's what I'm after." Looking into her eyes, he shifted his angle slightly.

And that was all it took. Wham, she was going wild, arching upward, yelling out all sorts of craziness. Maybe even something about love, but she was too far gone to be sure.

Then it was his turn, and his groans echoed through the bedroom. She might not have been totally aware of what she had said in the ultimate moment of release, but she certainly heard what he said. And although he cried out her name, he didn't use the L word. And oh, how she wished that he had.

MORGAN TOLD HIMSELF to put no importance on Mary Jane's declaration of love. Nobody should be held accountable for what they said in the grip of a powerful orgasm. Nothing had changed, really. He still had to leave Austin and give her space. Room. She'd wanted room to yell just now. She needed more room, period. Boxing her in would be unforgivably selfish on his part.

Yet that's exactly what he wanted to do. Her words of love ran through his mind in a continuous loop as he cuddled with her. She didn't bring up the matter, though, which probably meant she hadn't realized what she'd said.

He kept the tone of their interaction light as they finally

climbed out of bed. Following their previous pattern, she went in to shower and get ready for work while he dressed and headed downstairs to make breakfast. All the while he rehearsed his speech.

But he waited until she'd eaten her scrambled eggs and toast before he delivered it. Knowing what he had to say had taken away his appetite, so he made up some story about planning to eat later and instead sipped some instant coffee he'd made for himself. He wasn't setting a good example for her, but he was afraid he'd choke on anything solid.

After she finished, she took her plate to the sink, and he picked up his mug and stood, knowing this was the moment he'd been dreading.

"So you have the closing on the house today," she said, rinsing the plate and putting it in the dishwasher.

"Yes. At eleven."

She turned to him. "So I guess we could go over there tonight, then." There was a cautious look in her eyes, as if she'd guessed that wouldn't be happening.

He kept forgetting how easily she picked up on a mood. He set his mug on the counter and walked to her. Taking her by the shoulders, he gazed into her eyes. Such a clear, honest blue.

She swallowed nervously. "You're still leaving, aren't you?"

"Yes, I'm still leaving."

Backing out of his grip, she lifted her chin. "None of this made any difference to you?"

His chest felt as if it were filled with lead. "It made a huge difference. Now I know exactly what I'll be missing."

"But your practice calls." She sounded bitter.

"No, not the practice. I'm seriously thinking of giving it up. Ellie offered me a job with Maitland, and I'm considering it."

Her eyes widened. "You *are?*" Light began to suffuse her face. "You might *move* here permanently?"

"I might, but I'm worried about the impact on you."

She looked as if he'd just slapped her. "Oh, I get it. You

want to move here, but you don't want to be involved with me, and you're afraid that would be awkward. Well, don't worry. I won't—''

"No, damn it!" He grabbed her again and stopped just short of shaking her. "Don't you see? I desperately want to be with you! But I don't think it's fair for me to swoop in and take over your life!"

She gazed at him and finally shook her head, as if trying to clear it. "Morgan, you're doing it again. Making my decisions for me. Did it ever occur to you that I might love for you to take over my life?"

"Now, maybe." He massaged her arms gently. "That would be natural, when you're carrying this baby. But once you've had her you could easily wake up and wonder what you'd saddled yourself with. I couldn't bear that."

For several long seconds she studied him. "So what are you planning to do?"

"Ellie said the offer stands. She'd be glad to have me join the staff whenever I can arrange it, whether that's in one month or one year. I think the decision should be made after you've had the baby. In the meantime I'll go back to New York and take care of things there. The two of us will have more time to think this through."

Her voice quivered slightly. "Do you need more time?"

No. He glanced away, unable to look into her eyes and tell her a lie. "I need to take care of some things back in New York. For one thing, I'm definitely moving out of the apartment. I need to get started on that."

"Then I'll go with you."

His gaze swung quickly to her. "You can't do that. Your job—"

"I don't mean permanently. I mean for the weekend." Her eyes were soft with compassion. "You're not the only one who can be protective, Morgan. I'm not letting you walk into that apartment by yourself."

A lump stuck in his throat. He wanted her there by his side more than she could imagine, and he felt cowardly as a result. "I'll be fine."

"Maybe you will, and maybe you won't. I'm coming with you. I also think there's something else we need to do. Arielle didn't want a funeral, but you and I need to have...what's that word?"

"Closure."

"That's it. Closure. Maybe we could come up with something for the two of us that wouldn't go against Arielle's wishes."

He knew in his gut that she was absolutely right about closure. He needed to find a way to say goodbye to Arielle, but he hadn't considered that Mary Jane had the same need. "Since we're talking about something symbolic anyway, maybe we could handle that here," he said, "so you wouldn't have to make the trip."

"I don't think so. I think you need to take me back to New York with you, Morgan, for lots of reasons."

As he looked into her eyes, he knew she'd reached within herself and come up with some age-old wisdom he couldn't deny. "Only if you'll let me cover all your expenses. You've been incredibly stubborn about that so far, but I won't consider this unless you'll let me foot the bill."

She hesitated, and at last she nodded. "Okay. And thanks. I'm afraid it would put a real crimp in my budget."

"Do you want to leave this afternoon?"

"As long as I can clear it with Shelby, yes, I would. I think we need to get this done."

"You're probably right."

"I am right. We can leave today and I'll come home Sunday. Then if you're determined to play martyr and stay there until the baby's born while I enjoy your beautiful house here in Austin, I'll try to live with that."

He almost smiled. When she put it like that, his decision to spend the next four months in New York sounded righteous and downright stupid, which was what she had intended, of course. But in four months her outlook might undergo a drastic change. He didn't want to tie her down and then have her long to be free.

MARY JANE had made the plane trip to New York twice, once for Arielle and Morgan's wedding, and once for the procedure that resulted in her pregnancy. Both had been filled with excitement and an air of celebration. Remembering those trips as the plane touched down at JFK that night, she felt the first wave of sadness hit.

As if sensing her mood, Morgan took her hand. "You really don't have to do this. I can book you on a return flight and you won't even have to leave the airport."

She laced her fingers through his and looked at him as the plane taxied in. Although she wanted to be there for him, she was feeling a little queasy at the idea of going to the apartment tonight and facing all those reminders of Arielle. It had been a long day, and her energy wasn't very high. She kept forgetting that she didn't have the stamina she used to have before she became pregnant.

Besides that, she wondered if Morgan had thought about how he'd feel staying with her in the apartment for the next two nights. Would he be offended if she slept in the guest room? She didn't know about him, but climbing into the bed he'd shared with Arielle would totally creep her out. And having him spend the night in the guest bed with her sounded pretty tacky, too. In the rush of making arrangements to leave, she hadn't considered whether they would make love on this trip, but the answer seemed to be no.

"Seriously," Morgan said. "I was crazy to agree to bring you. I think you should go back. This isn't good for you or the baby." Morgan didn't look so chipper himself. The closer they'd come to their destination, the more weariness and anxiety had settled into his expression.

She couldn't desert him at a time like this. "I'm not leaving," she said.

"You're right," he said immediately. "I don't know what I was thinking. You shouldn't make the flight again so soon. I'll book you into a hotel for tonight and you can go back first thing in the morning."

"That's silly. I can certainly—" Then she paused as a crazy idea came to her. "Morgan, let's both stay in a hotel.

I know it's ridiculous and more expensive, but who says we have to sleep in the apartment? We can go there in the light of day to take care of things, can't we?''

His expression brightened immediately. ''Would you be suggesting we stay in the *same* hotel?'' he said with a tiny smile.

''I was hoping we'd be staying in the same hotel *room*,'' she said.

His smile widened. ''Mary Jane Potter, you are a brilliant woman.''

CHAPTER EIGHTEEN

MORGAN CALLED from the airport and was lucky enough to locate a room at a decent hotel in midtown Manhattan not too far from the apartment. Booking a hotel room in his hometown felt extremely weird, but the more he thought about it, the more he realized how fitting it was. From the moment Arielle had died in the crash, New York had ceased to be his hometown.

Knowing he wouldn't have to spend another night in the apartment brought him tremendous relief, and Mary Jane was a real genius for thinking of the hotel idea. He'd stay there even after Mary Jane left, until he could find another apartment. Now that he was leaving the place for good, he could admit that he'd never liked it.

Lifting Mary Jane's small suitcase, he took her arm and guided her to the taxi stand. His next hurdle would be riding past the spot where Arielle had been killed. He'd done it once when he'd taken a taxi to the airport the night he'd flown to Austin, but he'd been numb at that point. He was no longer numb.

He took comfort in the knowledge that at the end of this taxi ride would be an anonymous hotel room, not the apartment he'd fled in a panic. And he'd have Mary Jane to hold on to. He trembled to think what this return trip would have been like without her, and he tried not to think about how drab his life would be when she left on Sunday.

Giving the taxi driver the hotel's name, he helped Mary Jane into the cab and climbed in after her. She snuggled against him, and he wrapped an arm around her with a sense of gratitude. Mary Jane would help keep the goblins away.

"We have to go past the place where she died, don't we?" she murmured as the cab left the airport.

"Yes."

"I want you to show me."

His arm tightened and he glanced into her shadowed face. "Are you sure?"

She nodded.

"There's nothing there, nothing much to see," he said. "Just the road and a field next to it."

"But you'll never forget the way it looks, will you?"

He wished he could, but it still haunted his dreams. "No, I'll never forget it."

She touched his cheek. "That's why I want to see. I want to share that with you."

He covered her hand with his and turned his head to place a kiss in her palm. Thank God for the dark interior of the cab, which hid the tears gathering in his eyes. In his life he'd never had trouble finding people who wanted to share his successes, but he'd never found someone who was willing to share his pain.

As the cab approached the curve in the road where Arielle had skidded out of control, Morgan asked the driver to slow down.

Beside him, Mary Jane tensed.

"There." Stomach churning, he pointed across the road to the spot where the car had gone off the pavement. The guardrail hadn't been replaced yet, and it remained a twisted reminder of the accident. He'd never forget the sight of Arielle's convertible lying upside down in a ditch, the canvas top flattened. "She was going too fast, apparently, and skidded on a slick spot. The car flipped."

Mary Jane stared into the darkness and shivered. "So nobody else was in the accident? I never thought to ask."

His throat felt very tight. "Nobody else."

As the cab continued down the highway, Mary Jane turned to look out the back window. Her voice was unsteady. "She must have been going really fast."

Morgan swallowed. "The cops said she was definitely speeding. And talking on her car phone."

"She did love that thing." Mary Jane shook her head. "And she was always in a hurry, too."

"Yeah, she was." When he'd first met Arielle he'd been attracted to all that energy, but over the years he'd found the pace she set exhausting. There had been no time to talk, let alone to sit quietly without talking. He'd begun to suspect that just being with him hadn't been enough for Arielle, because she'd avoided it so carefully.

Mary Jane turned to him. The light from oncoming headlights sparkled in her tear-glazed eyes. "I hate that it happened."

"I know." He cupped her cheek with his hand. "Me, too."

"But..." She sighed and closed her eyes. "No, I can't say that. It's too horrible."

"You can say anything to me." And he had a good idea what she was thinking, because he was thinking it, too.

She opened her eyes and looked at him for a long time. "If Arielle hadn't died, I wouldn't have had this time with you. There, I've said it. And I'm probably a terrible person for even thinking such a selfish thing."

He stroked her cheek with his thumb. "Then that makes two of us."

MARY JANE hadn't spent much time in hotel rooms. The senior class trip to Disneyworld had been pretty much the extent of it. Checking into this elegant little hotel in Manhattan was a far cry from sharing a double-double at the Disney Hotel with three high school girlfriends.

The desk clerk didn't know quite how to take Morgan, which made Mary Jane grin. In his Austin-bought duds he looked like a cowboy, but he had the sophisticated moves of a New Yorker. He'd handed her suitcase right over to somebody the minute they'd been helped out of the cab.

She never expected to see it again, but sure enough, soon after they let themselves into the room, someone knocked on the door and, presto, there was her little suitcase. The person who brought it even offered to hang up her stuff.

"No!" she said quickly. "I mean, no, thank you." She couldn't imagine having a stranger rummaging through her belongings.

Morgan slipped the man a couple of bills as he was heading out the door.

"That was a complete waste of money," Mary Jane said as the door closed after the guy. "I could have carried that suitcase, considering we came up here in an elevator." She took off her light jacket and hung it in the closet. "Next time let me carry it, okay?"

"Nope." Morgan smiled at her. "Bellmen have to make a living, too. Are you hungry? We could order up something."

"You mean room service?" She couldn't imagine something so decadent, and he was acting totally casual about it. "At this time of night?"

"Sure." He set his hat brim-side-up on the dresser. Someone, probably Garrett, had taught him how to handle a Stetson. Then he picked up a leather-bound folder and began leafing through it. "We didn't have much on the plane. What are you hungry for?"

"Chocolate cake."

He glanced at her with amusement. "Fresh fruit would be better."

"If we're going to make someone go to all the trouble of bringing us food, it is definitely not going to be fresh fruit."

Morgan laughed and picked up the phone. "Maybe you're right." He punched in a number and ordered one piece of chocolate mousse torte and an assortment of herbal teas.

Mary Jane stood next to him and peered over his shoulder at the room service menu. "Yikes! Is that what it costs?"

He hung up the phone and closed the menu before turning to her. "You're worth it."

"Morgan, at Austin Eats you could order an entire dinner *plus* chocolate cake for what one piece of chocolate mousse torte costs at this place."

He took her gently by the shoulders. "You're in New York

now. Everything's more expensive. It's a shock to you, but I'm used to it. To be honest, that torte doesn't cost as much as I've paid at a couple of restaurants I could name."

She thought about that. If prices were that much higher, then wages must be higher, too. Arielle hadn't made a lot of money at the art gallery. That meant Morgan had been pulling down a hefty income for them to be able to afford to live here.

She gazed at him. "Are you sure you should consider giving up your practice? I'll bet Ellie can't pay you anything close to what you're making here."

"No, she can't." He grinned. "But as you just pointed out, I wouldn't pay as much for chocolate cake." His grin faded. "Or are you trying to tell me you'd rather I didn't move to Austin after the baby's born?"

"Are you crazy?" She moved closer and cradled his face in both hands. "I want you to move to Austin next week. But I don't want you to commit financial suicide, either."

He took her into his arms and pulled her close. "I'm only going to say this once, because it's not very pleasant. Arielle cared a lot about how much money I made. Getting ahead financially consumed her, and I fell into that pattern, too. Now that she's gone, I'll never let money have that much control over me again."

She started to protest what he'd said about her best friend. "She didn't really—"

"I didn't think you'd like hearing that," he said. "I'm not even asking you to believe it. But it's true."

Mary Jane thought back over recent conversations she'd had with Arielle, and she had to admit a lot of them had centered around money. Arielle had said many times that Morgan was doing very well financially. She'd talked about when they'd be able to buy an apartment on Park Avenue West and a country home in Connecticut.

"Maybe it was because she had to struggle so much as a kid," Mary Jane said.

"That's what I thought, too. I figured once we reached a certain level, that fear of poverty would go away." Morgan rubbed the small of her back. "But her need for money and prestige seemed to grow the more I made and the higher we climbed socially. I don't know if I ever would have made enough or been important enough to satisfy her."

Mary Jane's heart was wrenched. She'd always thought of Arielle as having it all. Instead she'd had so little self-confidence that she'd needed all sorts of props to feel good about herself. "Poor Arielle," she whispered, looking into Morgan's warm brown eyes. "She wasn't happy."

"No. And I didn't know how to make her happy."

Mary Jane felt her loyalty shifting. Morgan had been trying so hard to please Arielle and he'd been getting nothing but more demands. "I can't imagine why she didn't appreciate you more."

Morgan's gaze warmed another notch. "You're going to get yourself in trouble, talking like that."

"I'm already in trouble."

His head lowered. "Yeah, me, too."

Pleasure zipped from her head to her toes at the thought of another one of Morgan's kisses.

But a knock at the door came at the exact wrong time. With a light brush of his lips over hers, he released her. "There's our chocolate cake."

Room service might not be such a wonderful idea, after all, she thought in frustration, if the servers had no better sense of timing than that. But when she caught a glimpse of the linen-draped cart being wheeled in with a rose in a bud vase, a silver teapot and delicate china, she was enchanted.

Morgan signed for the food while she walked around the little cart in wonder. She could learn something from the presentation, she thought. She wondered how they made the chocolate curls decorating the frosting, and if she should add that to her hot fudge sundae preparation. The way they'd swirled chocolate and cherry sauce together on the plate was a work of art. Of course, any food looked better on china so fragile you could almost see through it.

"Are you planning to eat that or look at it?"

She glanced up and met Morgan's grin with one of her

own. "I'm not used to this, so bear with me," she said. "I'm trying to figure out how they made this design in the sauce. Professional curiosity." She studied the torte again.

"When you're finished ogling the food, may I make a suggestion?"

"Suggest away." The trick was to swirl the white chocolate sauce on the plate first, she decided, and then drop some cherry sauce on top, and maybe use a toothpick or a thin knife to—

"Let's eat the cake in bed."

That got her attention. She looked up and discovered he'd taken his shirt off and was reaching for the buckle of his belt. Her heart began to pound, and she lost all interest in sauce design. "That's an idea," she said, totally absorbed in the subtle movement of his pecs as he unzipped his jeans.

"Naked."

She kicked off her shoes and started on the buttons of her blouse. "That's an even better idea."

MORGAN VOWED to forget about everything but Mary Jane for the rest of the night. He discovered that naked was his favorite way to eat chocolate cake and that Mary Jane had some very interesting ideas for ways to enjoy the chocolate mousse filling. They played and made love far into the night, and slept late the next morning.

Between room service and the charms of Mary Jane, he would have been content to stay in bed for the rest of the day, but Mary Jane finally made him see that the sooner they went to the apartment, the sooner they could come back to their temporary love nest. Still, it was nearly noon before they hailed a taxi to take them to the apartment building.

They held hands, and at first Morgan tried to make conversation. At least the weather was good, he thought, the sky blue and the air warm. He wasn't sure he could have endured a rainy day. Still, the memories worked on him the closer they came to the apartment, and he ran out of cheerful things to say.

Finally traffic noise and the radio station the cabdriver had on were the only sounds inside the car. Morgan wasn't really listening to the radio, but then the DJ said something that made him pay attention.

Okay, guys, tomorrow's the big day. Mother's Day. Time to get your act together for those special women in your lives.

Mother's Day. He'd never put much effort into the holiday before. At an early age he'd learned that his mother hated sentimental displays, so now he ordered flowers and let it go at that. If he missed this year he had a good excuse. But his mother wasn't the only one to be considered. Tomorrow he needed to honor Mary Jane.

She wasn't flying to Austin until the middle of the afternoon, so he'd have the whole morning to celebrate with her. His mood lifted as he started thinking of possibilities. Central Park. A carriage ride. He might be too late to get brunch reservations, but he could put together a picnic they could eat on the grass. Mary Jane would like that better, anyway. They could feed the ducks, maybe even fly a kite. She would love the—

"Morgan, we're here."

He snapped out of his nice little daydream to discover the cab had pulled up in front of his apartment building. His gut tensed. Reality time.

After paying the driver, he climbed out of the cab and gave a hand to Mary Jane. She gripped it as if she never intended to let go. They held on to each other as they walked toward the building.

"I have to keep reminding myself she's not up there," Mary Jane said.

"I know." He felt as if he'd swallowed a chunk of hot asphalt. "This isn't going to be much fun." He hadn't spent more than an hour here during the short time he'd stayed in New York after the accident. One good thing about this city— there were lots of places to hang out if you didn't want to go home.

He opened the front door with his key and went into the hallway. Fortunately at this hour the apartment building was quiet, with most of the tenants hard at work somewhere in the city. They weren't likely to meet anyone. Automatically he glanced at the wall lined with brass window mailboxes. The one labeled *Tate, M and A* was jammed with mail. He took a deep breath. "Maybe I should get the—"

"Later." Mary Jane tugged him toward the elevator. "Let's go upstairs before we lose our nerve."

"All right." His former way of life closed in on him as he went through the familiar motions of punching the elevator button and stepping inside the walnut-paneled unit. He no longer wanted to live in a building that required him to use elevators. He wanted to open a door and walk into his own house, a house with a big fireplace and a shady backyard.

"Maybe we should have a game plan," Mary Jane said.

He glanced at her. "Like what?"

"Define our purpose."

"Okay. I need to pack up some clothes, maybe some books and other personal items. It shouldn't take long. I don't want to take too much. Then we'll haul whatever we have downstairs to the garage and get the car. And go to the hotel." He could hardly wait to escape this place.

"Should we deal with Arielle's things? Her clothes, for example?"

The prospect made him feel queasy. "I guess so. I've been thinking I'd hire a moving company to come in and get the furniture once I have another place to stay. But I don't want them shipping Arielle's clothes over there."

"Then I'll pack up her clothes. What do you want to do with them?"

"I don't know."

"Let's give them to charity."

"Yes." He sighed with relief. "What would I do without you?"

She squeezed his hand. "And you didn't want me to come with you."

"I *always* wanted you to come with me. I just wasn't sure it was a good idea from your standpoint." The elevator stopped and the doors slid open. "I still feel guilty about dragging you up here."

"Don't." Holding his hand, she walked into the hallway. "Like I said before, we're lucky we have each other so neither one of us has to face this alone."

"We sure as hell are lucky." In the beginning he might have thought sharing this tragedy was all that held the two of them together. But now he knew better. If things had turned out differently and Arielle had succeeded in getting Mary Jane to come to New York as the baby's nanny, he would have been thrown into a serious marital crisis. It wouldn't have taken long for him to realize that Mary Jane was everything he wanted in a woman, everything Arielle had not been.

The door to his apartment had three locks and an alarm system because of the art Arielle had hanging on the walls. Morgan was really tired of protecting valuable art, especially considering that he didn't like any of it. Mary Jane's pictures of flowers and happy people suited him much better.

He swung open the door and stepped inside with Mary Jane following close behind. The apartment was cold, but then it always had been. Arielle had liked it that way. She'd used heat sparingly in the winter and air-conditioning liberally in the summer.

The living room smelled of stale air and expensive leather. He shuddered as he looked around at the white calfskin furniture and the black lacquered tables. He wondered why they weren't dusty and then realized the cleaning woman must have come right on schedule.

The only spot of color the room had ever contained was gone. Arielle kept a bloodred rose in a Baccarat vase on the coffee table, but the last one she'd bought would have wilted and the cleaning woman had obviously thrown it away.

He turned to Mary Jane to see how she was doing. She looked pale but resolute. What a little trouper. Even with the lack of color in her cheeks, she was still the most vibrant presence in the room.

Looking at the furniture, he came to a decision. "I'm going to sell it all. I don't want it. I've never liked it."

"Sell it?" Mary Jane's eyes widened. "But this is pricey stuff! I remember Arielle telling me how much she paid for that leather sofa. You'll never get your money out of it, and it looks brand new!''

"That's because we barely used it,'' Morgan said with a trace of bitterness. Once he'd made the mistake of putting his feet up on that pricey sofa, and Arielle had given him a real tongue-lashing. "I'll call around, find out who could come over here and take it off my hands.''

"Now, don't be hasty, Morgan. What are you going to sit on in your new apartment?''

"I don't care. Big pillows. Maybe a beanbag chair. Arielle wouldn't have one of those in the place, but I kind of like them.''

Mary Jane smiled. "Me, too. But I think selling all your furniture is a bit reckless. You'd better at least keep your bed.''

If he knew one thing, he knew he wasn't keeping the bed. "Nope. Everything goes. Even the art.''

Mary Jane gazed at a painting over the fireplace. It was a series of cubes in shades of black and gray and was typical of the lifeless pieces hanging in various places around the apartment. "Now, there I agree with you,'' she said. "And those puppies have probably gone up in value, so maybe you won't come out so bad in the end.'' She paused. "What about the teacup collection in the dining room? That's probably worth something, too.''

"Do you want it?''

She hesitated, then shook her head.

"Then I'm selling that, too.''

"Okay. But I think you should reconsider selling all the furniture. Maybe you should move it to your new place and see how it goes before you decide.''

He had an intense need to hold her. "Come here, you.'' Gathering her into his arms, he pressed her head against his chest and rested his cheek on her glorious hair. "Tell me the truth. Do you like anything about this furniture?'' he asked.

She held him close, as if eager to lend him her warmth. "It's clean, and it doesn't have any nicks and scratches on it.''

"Other than that. Do you think it's pretty?"

"I think…" She hesitated. "I think it's sort of blah, but that's just me. I'm not very sophisticated when it comes to interior decorating. As you noticed when we picked out baby furniture, I wanted rainbows."

"I must not be very sophisticated, either, because I think it's blah. And so damned white. Give me a break. Can you imagine eating pizza on a white sofa?"

"I see your point."

"It goes." He nuzzled his cheek against her hair. "And for the record, I'm crazy about rainbows."

CHAPTER NINETEEN

MARY JANE would have loved to stay safely tucked inside Morgan's arms forever, but that wasn't getting the job done. She gave him an encouraging squeeze. "We need to get to work."

"Yeah." He looked very reluctant as he stepped away from her and glanced down the hallway toward the bedrooms.

She could imagine why he didn't want to continue with the program. The formal living room was one thing. Now they had to face the more personal space of the bedroom he'd shared with Arielle. Mary Jane wasn't looking forward to that, either.

Like a doomed prisoner taking his last walk, he headed down the hallway.

Her mouth was dry as she followed him. "Do you remember if the bed's made?"

"It always is. Arielle insisted on that before we left for the day."

Mary Jane was grateful for Arielle's compulsive neatness. If the sheets had been rumpled, it would have made the bedroom seem even more intimate, the marriage too real.

Morgan walked into the room and straight to the louvered closet doors. "We can get this done in no time," he said briskly, as if trying to convince himself.

Mary Jane wasn't so sure. The bedroom furniture wasn't any cozier-looking than the living room set had been. Black lacquered pieces dominated here, and the comforter was, predictably, snow white.

But on the sleek surface of the dressing table sat Arielle's silver-backed brush and hand mirror, the ones she'd bought herself while she was working as Mary Jane's nanny. The exclusive perfume she'd used was there, too, along with bottles of her favorite brands of lotion and makeup, and a Waterford crystal cotton-ball holder that Mary Jane had given her.

Mary Jane felt the tears coming. She turned away from the dressing table and found herself looking at Morgan and Arielle's framed wedding picture sitting on a desk by the window. They looked so happy, so right together. Guilt slammed into her.

Behind her Morgan was making quite a racket pulling his clothes out of the closet. Eyes blurred with tears, she turned to watch him frantically tossing slacks and shirts, still on their hangers, onto the bed. The closet door was open wide. Morgan's side of the closet was nearly empty, but Arielle's was full of her designer suits and dresses, all in tasteful, neutral colors.

Mary Jane's old insecurities came roaring back. Compared with Arielle she was so lacking in culture and sophistication. Arielle had tried to educate her, but she hadn't been a very good student.

Morgan had. His clothes were the same shades as Arielle's, she noticed. Next to all that subdued elegance the loud Western shirt he wore seemed totally out of place. She'd encouraged him to buy that bright shirt. Arielle would have called it tacky. She would have lectured Mary Jane for destroying whatever fashion sense she'd been able to instill in Morgan.

But the problem went deeper than fashion. Meaning to get his mind off his grief, Mary Jane had started him thinking he didn't want all that he'd worked so hard to have. Now he seemed ready to completely change his life, mostly because of her influence.

A fresh wave of guilt washed over her. A house in Austin would not have been what Arielle would have wanted for her husband and baby. A house in Connecticut was more like it. Yet Mary Jane had aided and abetted his decision to buy the Slattery place. She'd also taken him to the dealership to buy a red truck. He even listened to country music.

But there was a good chance that in a few weeks he'd wake up and realize he didn't want any of those things, that he was a sophisticated New Yorker, not a Texas cowboy. He might wish he'd kept the black and white furniture.

Morgan threw a large suitcase on the bed. Then he pulled another one out of the closet and put it on top of the cedar chest at the end of the bed. He glanced at Mary Jane, his gaze haunted. "I'm going to carry my clothes down and put them in the car. We can use the suitcases for Arielle's stuff. Are you still up to packing her clothes?"

She nodded, not trusting herself to speak. She would help him through this, and then she needed to convince him to sell the Slattery place, trade in his red truck and stay on the path Arielle had mapped out for him. Arielle had known what she was doing, and Mary Jane had no right to upset things.

She moved to the closet, took Arielle's clothes off the hangers and folded them neatly as she put them into the suitcases. Arielle would have wanted her to do it that way. Tears streamed down her cheeks as she thought of how completely she'd messed up the life Arielle had created for Morgan. But she still had time to fix things the way they should be.

Morgan scooped an armload of his clothes from the bed. "I'll be right back," he said.

She nodded again.

"Are you okay?"

She swiped at her eyes and kept packing. "Sure." She felt him hovering, as if he didn't believe her. "Go!" she snapped.

He went.

Once the front door closed after him, she fought the urge to break down. She knew he wouldn't be gone long, and she wanted to be finished by the time he came back.

And then, on a top shelf, she found a notebook tucked between boxes of sweaters. Pulling it down, she discovered it was a journal belonging to Arielle. She flipped to the first page, dated the day after her marriage.

I think Morgan expected more passion out of me, Arielle had written. *Maybe he thought the wedding ring would make a difference. Maybe I did, too. But we'll both have to face the fact that I'm no sex kitten. Morgan probably wouldn't know what to do with one, anyway.* Arielle went on to catalog the expensive gifts they'd received with far too much relish to suit Mary Jane.

She closed the journal and held it against her chest, shaken by what she'd read. Well, that had been the first day of their marriage, after all. She couldn't imagine a woman living with Morgan for six years and not realizing he was an outstanding lover. Opening the journal again, she riffled through the pages. The entries were hit and miss, sometimes skipping several months, but they continued right up to the week before Arielle had died.

The front door opened, and Mary Jane panicked. Reading this journal might be devastating for Morgan, but hiding it from him wasn't right, either. Clutching the journal to her chest, she faced the door as he walked into the bedroom.

Strain showed in his face and his rigid body. He reminded her of a boxer who had already gone ten rounds with a better opponent. "Almost done?" he asked hopefully.

"Almost." She took a deep breath. "I found Arielle's journal."

Anguish showed in his eyes. "Oh."

For one horrible moment she thought he might have read it.

"I knew she kept one," he said. "But I considered it private. I'd forgotten about it, to tell the truth."

She let out her breath in relief. "By rights it's yours. But I was wondering if you'd...if you'd let me have it."

"Of course."

He gave in so quickly that she wondered if he had an idea the journal would contain things he'd rather not read. All these years she'd thought Morgan and Arielle had the perfect marriage. Maybe not.

"Thank you," she said, setting the journal on the bed. She put a few last things in the two suitcases, then closed them. "Did you hear on the radio that tomorrow's Mother's Day?"

His expression lightened. "Yes, and I thought we could do

something special before you leave. A picnic in Central Park, maybe.''

How she would love a picnic in Central Park, but she knew what they had to do instead. ''That's a nice idea, but I think we should have our private memorial service for Arielle tomorrow. Mother's Day seems right, somehow. She is the mother of this baby.''

''So are you.''

Her heart ached. ''That isn't the way it was set up.''

''I know, technically speaking, but—''

''No matter what happens, we owe a debt to Arielle. Tomorrow belongs to her.''

He studied her for a long time. ''All right. What did you have in mind?''

''I'm not exactly sure, but we can work on it today. We could get some flowers, pick out some things to read that she especially liked.''

He nodded. ''Where did you want to do it?'' he asked quietly.

Mary Jane had been thinking about that ever since the ride in from the airport. ''On the spot where she died.''

SOMETHING about Mary Jane's thinking had changed. Morgan wanted to blame it on the strain of planning for the memorial, which put Arielle in the middle of their thoughts. It stirred up his feelings of guilt and sure seemed to be doing the same for Mary Jane. The emotional shift might be natural, and maybe they'd both get over it once they'd completed the service.

In the meantime, life was pretty grim. Mary Jane had brought several books of poetry from the apartment, and she spent hours going through them, picking selections and then rejecting them in favor of others. He heard enough readings of Keats and Shelley to last him a lifetime.

And he could tell there would be no more lovemaking in their hotel room. The lightheartedness of the night before when they'd shared cake in bed was gone. Mary Jane had No Trespassing signs hanging all over her.

As the distance between them grew, he began to wonder if

she'd decided she wanted nothing to do with a guy like him. In Austin she'd seen a different Morgan Tate, but the picture she was getting in New York might have turned her off.

He supposed he was different here. Going back to his apartment, hauling all his boring clothes out of the closet, driving the luxury sedan Arielle had thought a man of his position should own—all of it drew him into the role he'd once played. And he hated it.

He also feared it. Deep down he was afraid this was all he would ever become. The man who had bought a ranch house in Austin, the man who'd picked out a bright red truck and thought he could learn to ride a horse, that man might be an illusion. Arielle would have laughed at his efforts and told him he'd better stick with what he was good at—being a big-city doctor and making money. She would have said he wasn't the type to live a cowboy's life, and a leopard couldn't change his spots.

If any of that was true, he sure as hell didn't want to impose himself on Mary Jane. Normally she was as colorful and buoyant as a helium balloon, and he'd be damned if he'd be the guy to weigh her down.

By noon on Sunday they'd planned the service and were ready to leave for the airport. Mary Jane had rightly pointed out that two trips to the vicinity of the airport would be dumb, so they'd decided to leave early enough to have the memorial before he took Mary Jane to catch her flight. It wasn't exactly the kind of Mother's Day celebration he'd had in mind, but as he'd watched the dedication Mary Jane brought to the planning, he'd completely understood why they had to do things this way.

If only he didn't feel as if he was losing Mary Jane in the process.

The weather, he noticed with some irony, was perfect, a fine spring day in the best New York tradition. As he drove down the road, he thought of Arielle on this same road in the dark and the rain...and in a hurry, as she usually had been. He found himself counting off the distance, the minutes. On this part of the road she'd still been alive. He kept his speed down, and cars whizzed around him.

"I don't think I should move into your house," Mary Jane said.

He wasn't surprised to hear her say it, but pain squeezed his chest as he sensed her trying to cut the ties between them. He should let her go, but he wasn't quite ready to do that. "You'd be doing me a big favor if you would stay there." He came up with the first excuse he could. "It's getting hot, and somebody should monitor the watering system for the plants. I could hire a yard service, but I'd want someone to supervise that, too."

"Oh. I forgot about that."

"Do you think it was a mistake for me to buy that place?"

She hesitated. "Maybe."

He wept inside, but he forced himself to act nonchalant. "Tell you what. If you'll stay there and watch out for the place at least until the baby's born, I'll reevaluate at that point. But when I come down for the birth, I'll need somewhere to stay and get acquainted with the baby. If, after she's born, you're willing to stay at the house yourself for a few days, I think it would make for a smoother transition."

She stared straight ahead and didn't answer, but her fingers tightened over the crystal vase full of rose petals she held.

"I know I have no right to ask it of you," he said softly. "But I'm asking anyway. Just give me a few days after she's born."

Slowly she turned to him, compassion in her eyes. "I can do that."

He wanted to hold her so much that he almost pulled to the side of the road. But he kept driving. "Thank you."

Moments later, they'd reached their destination. He guided the car to the shoulder next to the mangled guardrail that marked the spot where Arielle's car had left the road. Wind stirred up by passing vehicles buffeted the sedan.

He looked at Mary Jane. "Ready?"

She swallowed. "Ready."

He unfastened his seat belt and waited for a break in traffic before he climbed out quickly and slammed the door. By the time he rounded the car, Mary Jane was standing beside the car. She held the vase of rose petals in one hand and the verses she'd copied down in the other.

Taking the vase from her, he helped her over the twisted metal rail and into the shallow gully beyond. He could swear there was still an imprint of the car in the grass and weeds.

But there were also butterflies and chirping birds and some delicate little yellow wildflowers he couldn't name. The scent of the grass reminded him of the hayloft in Garrett's barn. Mary Jane's cotton dress nearly matched the flowers, and with her hair loose and touched by the sun, and her rounded belly pushing gently at the material of the dress, she looked like a picture of spring. He wished they were here for a different reason.

She squinted as she glanced around the area. She'd decided against sunglasses for this occasion, so he wasn't wearing them, either.

Finally she took a deep breath and walked to one side of the faint depression in the grass. "I'll stand here." She handed him a page containing his part of the service and motioned to a spot on the opposite side of the depression. "You can be over there. That way we're surrounding the spot, as much as two people can, anyway."

Standing on the very place Arielle had died, he was starting to shake. He followed Mary Jane's directions with gratitude and once again marveled at her strength.

Clearing her throat, she held her paper out and began to read a poem by Shelley. Her voice trembled a little, but she forged on. He'd heard her practicing the reading under her breath last night in the hotel room. Her earnest attempt to do this right, for Arielle's sake, affected him as much as grief, and tears blurred his vision.

Then it was his turn to read a poem by Keats. He set the vase of rose petals by his feet so he could concentrate on the words. He stumbled over the poetry, but managed to get it read. When he was finished, Mary Jane was supposed to say the personal things she'd written down, and then he would say what he'd decided on.

He looked up, a signal to her that she could begin. She was staring at him, the tears running down her cheeks. Instantly he started around the depression toward her. He couldn't make himself walk through it.

"Stay there." She choked the words out. "I'm okay."

"No, you're not." He reached her and took her into his arms. "Nobody says we have to follow a script," he said hoarsely.

She held on to him and cried softly against his shirt. Not a cowboy one this time. He'd worn a dress shirt, a tie and slacks, as if he needed to dress to please Arielle today.

Sniffing, she pushed gently away from him and wiped her eyes with her free hand. "Sorry."

"No need to be sorry." His throat felt raw.

"I didn't realize how it would affect me, to watch you reading that poem."

His heart lurched. He'd assumed she was crying because of Arielle. Instead she'd been crying because of him. Maybe he hadn't totally lost her, after all.

She drew in a shaky breath. "I'm ready for the next part. You can go back over there."

He laced his hand through hers. "I'm staying here."

She didn't contradict him. Instead she nodded and closed her eyes, obviously concentrating. At last she opened them again and began to speak.

"Arielle, at a time when I had no one else to count on, you were both mother and father to me." Her voice gained strength as she continued. "There are no words rich enough to thank you for the part you played in my life, but now that you're gone, I wish I'd told you more often how much I love you. I love you, Arielle, and I will miss you forever."

Morgan held on to Mary Jane's hand like a lifeline. His heart beat faster as he tried to remember what he'd planned to say. The speech had disappeared from his mind. He'd have to do the best he could.

"Arielle, you were my first real love," he began. Then he

discovered the words came easily. "We made lots of mistakes, but we got some things right. You loved me enough to give me a child, and I will cherish her and be grateful for your generosity every day of my life. Godspeed, Arielle...my wife." His voice broke, and he bowed his head as the tears came.

As he cried, he felt all the hurt and anger wash out of him, and when at last he raised his head and wiped his eyes, when the warm sun dried his tears so that he could once again see the butterflies floating on the breeze, he understood why he and Mary Jane had needed to do this. Arielle's death had been like a nightmare, a wispy event that had no anchor in reality. Standing on this spot, saying goodbye to his wife, he finally accepted the truth of it.

Mary Jane's whisper eased into his thoughts. "Now the rose petals," she said.

Releasing her hand, he walked around the depression and picked up the vase. Returning to her, he tipped the vase. "Hold out your hands." When she did, he sprinkled petals into them. Then he poured the rest into his hand.

"To the memory of my best friend." Mary Jane threw her hands in the air, scattering rose petals everywhere. Some fell in her hair.

"To the memory of my wife." Morgan flung his rose petals into the breeze. Then he looked at Mary Jane and slowly picked a velvet petal from her hair. "We did it."

"Yes." Her gaze was warm and soft. "And it was the right thing."

"Yes, it was." He wanted to take her into his arms again, but he was afraid if he did that he would never let her go.

"Morgan, we haven't talked about this, but have you thought about what to name the baby?"

He gazed at her and knew that on this matter their minds were perfectly in tune. "Arielle."

She smiled. "Yes. Arielle."

CHAPTER TWENTY

FOR THE TRIP to Austin, Mary Jane tucked Arielle's journal deep in her suitcase, not wanting to keep it out to read and possibly remind Morgan of its existence. When he insisted she check the suitcase at the gate, she realized she wouldn't be able to get to the journal until after she returned to Austin. And she was more than a little curious.

"It's only a small suitcase," she told him as they sat waiting for her flight to be called. "I carry trays heavier than that at the diner every day."

"Which reminds me. We had a deal that if you lived in my house for the rest of the pregnancy, you'd ask Shelby about cutting your hours at the diner."

He was getting kind of bossy, but she was so miserable at the idea of leaving him that she didn't mind. "I'll see what she says."

"I swear if you don't cut back, I'll fly in and work your shifts for you."

She knew he was kidding. Right now he still felt connected to her and to Austin, but once he returned to his normal routine the connection would weaken. Still, she smiled at the thought of Morgan waiting tables.

"Laugh all you like. I have experience. I waited tables all through college, and I'm sure it would come back to me."

"Says you." She winked at him. "I'll bet when the lunch crunch is in full swing you'd forget and revert to busy doctor mode. Instead of taking their order you'd whip out a tongue depressor and examine their tonsils."

"What's wrong with that? Where else could you get a burger and a checkup?"

She grinned and started to reply when the first boarding call came. Her grin faded as she gazed at Morgan. "I'm going to miss you."

His voice was husky. "Yeah, that's what they all say."

She wondered how she'd ever turn and walk away from him. He was such a part of her now. His feeling of connection might fade, but she knew hers wouldn't. "Are you going to be okay?"

He nodded. "What we did today…that was the right thing. Thank you for insisting on it."

"I feel a ton better about Arielle, now that we had a chance to say goodbye," she said softly. Morgan was a different story. Leaving him felt like cutting off a piece of herself.

Her row was called to board, but she couldn't seem to make herself stand up. "I'd better go."

"Yeah."

Finally she rose, and he did, too.

She wasn't sure if she moved first or he did, but suddenly they were in each other's arms, kissing as if they would never stop. She tasted salt, and wasn't sure which of them was crying. Both of them, probably.

Then, knowing if she stayed another second she'd never leave, she pushed away from him and ran toward the jetway. She thrust her ticket blindly at the clerk and headed down the ramp toward the plane without ever looking back. Seeing him standing there alone would have destroyed her.

MORGAN WASN'T SURE how he got through his days. Work claimed part of his time, although with the young female doctor Chuck had recruited, Morgan wasn't required to put in a lot of hours. The rest of the time he took care of the mundane details surrounding Arielle's death, and there seemed to be an endless number of them. The amount of paperwork was unreal, but at least it kept his mind occupied during the day.

The nights lasted forever. He told himself that continuing to live in the hotel was ridiculously expensive, but it held memories of Mary Jane so he couldn't make himself check out. Besides, renting an apartment meant admitting that he wasn't moving permanently to Austin. Try as he might, he couldn't give up that dream.

He couldn't give up contact with Mary Jane, either. He rationed himself to calling her every third night. Although he didn't always connect with her, just hearing her voice on the tape was the most vibrant part of his otherwise colorless life.

She'd moved into the house, and he could feel her excitement about that, although she tried hard to be noncommittal. He had the feeling she was sorting some things out in her mind, and some of them had to do with him. That might explain why she spent more time filling him in on local gossip than talking about herself.

He listened happily, grateful for the sound of her voice, as she described the controversy that continued to swirl around little Chase Maitland, the mystery baby. Mary Jane wasn't convinced Janelle Davis was the baby's mother, but nevertheless, plans were nearly finalized for the wedding between Janelle and Connor O'Hara.

Meanwhile Sara, the cook at the diner, had a huge crush on Harrison Smith, a guy who kept coming to Austin Eats, and Mary Jane was irritated because Sara was too shy to pursue the matter. Morgan wondered if Mary Jane was projecting some of her frustration onto Sara. Judging from his state, he wouldn't be surprised.

Mary Jane also brought him up to date on Garrett's "secret" houseguests. Since Christmas Jake Maitland, Ellie and Beth's brother, had been sequestered at a remote cabin on Garrett's property with a pregnant woman who was hiding out from her gangster husband. No one was supposed to know where they were staying, to protect the woman's safety, but thanks to Garrett's sister Shelby, the entire diner staff was aware of the situation. So far no one had seen Jake's mystery woman.

Throughout these conversations Morgan clutched the phone and closed his eyes so he could imagine himself sitting next to Mary Jane on the sofa in the living room of that beautiful house. He knew it was too warm for her to have a fire in the fireplace, but he added that to his fantasy, anyway.

When he had to finally hang up and face his lonely hotel room, he'd have had a moment of insanity when he thought about taking a cab to the airport and hopping on a plane, the way he had once before. This time, though, he'd make a phone call to let Chuck know what was happening.

His hand resting on the telephone receiver, he'd make himself think of what was best for Mary Jane. Flying to Austin would force a decision about their relationship, and he couldn't expect her to make a decision like that until after she'd had the baby. The world might look completely different to her once she was no longer pregnant with his child.

When he could finally make himself let go of the telephone receiver, he'd pull out his desk calendar and mark off another day—another day he'd made it through without adding more chaos to Mary Jane's life. Then he'd count the days left before the baby was due. And wonder if he could survive that long.

MARY JANE discovered she could only read Arielle's journal in short sessions. Reading Arielle's account of her life with Morgan reminded Mary Jane of taking off a bandage. Some people thought a bandage should be ripped off all at once, so the pain was concentrated in one short period of time. Mary Jane had always peeled a bandage off slowly, adjusting to the pain as she went.

Therefore it took her nearly two weeks to finish the journal. The night she read the last page, she left the window seat and paced the house, the journal clutched in both hands. Tears filled her eyes as she mourned the death of her idol.

Only this time it wasn't Arielle's physical death that tore at her insides. Instead it was the death of her illusions about the woman she'd placed on a pedestal.

From the time she was eight years old she'd looked up to Arielle as the essence of elegance and right living. If Arielle said it, it must be true. If Arielle did it that way, then everyone should do it that way, too. Mary Jane had tried to follow in Arielle's footsteps until she began to realize she didn't have what it took. She wasn't as smart as Arielle. She didn't have Arielle's inborn sense of style.

Sometime during her teen years she'd given up on becoming a carbon copy of Arielle, partly because Arielle had found her attempts so amusing. But that hadn't stopped her from wishing, deep in her heart, that she could be more like her.

In the past two weeks she'd picked up the journal each night, hoping to find evidence of that wise, elegant person she'd imagined Arielle to be. But no matter how she tried to twist the entries into a different shape, they continued to paint the same picture. Arielle had grown into a shallow, self-absorbed woman who cared for practically nothing except material possessions and her social status.

And worst of all, the one thing that Mary Jane found so difficult to face—Arielle had never loved Morgan. He'd only been a means to an end.

She didn't want him to ever find that out. She didn't want Arielle's daughter to read this journal. Several entries were long complaints about how a baby was going to louse up Arielle's well-ordered life.

Moving the screen on the huge rock fireplace, Mary Jane opened the flue, found a box of matches and began tearing pages out of the journal. When she had enough to start a small blaze, she lit them and kept feeding more pages into the fire. Eventually she was able to add the journal cover and watch it curl up and burst into flame.

Poor Morgan. No wonder he hadn't thought of himself as desirable or sexy after spending six years with a woman who didn't love him. Now that Mary Jane knew his family background, she had no trouble figuring out why he'd been attracted to Arielle. He'd married someone like his parents, someone who preferred to live on the surface, someone who cared more about how things looked than how people felt.

But Morgan wasn't like his parents. And he especially wasn't like them when he was here in Austin with her. She'd been so afraid she'd be a bad influence on Morgan, when in fact she might be the only one who could save him.

She felt the baby move and laid her hand over her tummy. "We need to get your daddy to come home, sweetheart," she said.

From little things he'd let slip during their phone conversations, she'd become convinced he was staying away for her sake. He didn't think he was right for her, and that made sense, given the beating his ego must have taken over the years of his marriage.

Chances were she couldn't get him to Austin just because she said she wanted him there. She could only think of one sure-fire way to get his attention. She glanced at the telephone, then at the clock. It was late. So much the better.

WHEN THE PHONE RANG Morgan leaped out of bed as if he'd been jabbed with a hot poker. For a moment he forgot where he was. Then he remembered he was in a hotel, not in his apartment. Heart racing, he whirled to the bedside table, where one of the two phones in the room was located. Grabbing the receiver, he offered up a silent prayer that this call wasn't like the one he'd answered after the accident.

His greeting came out a frightened croak. "Hello?"

"Morgan?"

"Mary Jane! Are you okay?"

"I think so. But, Morgan, I've been feeling a little... strange."

His heart pounded painfully. "Like what?"

"It's hard to describe. I just—don't feel right."

"Go to the ER. Now. Do you want me to call Abby? I kept her number. I have it right—"

"No, no. I don't think I really have to go to the ER."

"I don't care! Call an ambulance if you're not up to driving, but go! Or get Garrett out of bed. He could take you."

"Okay. I guess I could call Garrett. I hate to, though. He has his hands full with Jake and that pregnant lady, Camille Eckart." She sounded very quiet, not like Mary Jane usually sounded. "Morgan, I feel scared."

That was all he needed to hear. "I'm flying down. Call an ambulance. Maybe it's nothing, and you'll be home again by the time I get there. I'll check at the house first."

"Okay, but it's probably nothing."

"Probably. But I want to see for myself." Wild horses

couldn't have kept him away. "Now call the ambulance." He was reaching for his pants as he hung up the phone.

Cursing himself for letting her stay alone in Austin, he dressed so quickly he buttoned his shirt wrong. He didn't discover it until he was in the cab on the way to the airport. Once there he threw down his gold card at the first airline ticket desk he came to and told them to do whatever it took to get him to Austin ASAP.

The process of getting booked was interminable, but finally he raced down the jetway of a plane that was in its final boarding. When he sat down, his seatmates looked at him strangely, and he wondered if he'd bothered to comb his hair. Probably not. He didn't give a damn. Several times during the flight he found himself leaning forward as if he could will the plane to go faster.

And all the way, he prayed that Mary Jane would be all right. He gave a passing thought to the baby, but it was Mary Jane who occupied most of his worry time. Finally, somewhere over Kentucky, he thought to question why that was so. The answer wasn't hard to find. He loved Mary Jane with all his heart and soul.

Logically he shouldn't be capable of falling in love with her that fast, but logic had nothing to do with the way he felt about Mary Jane. He'd stay in Austin until the baby was born, just to make sure Mary Jane was okay. Maybe he'd bunk at Garrett's so he wouldn't put any pressure on her by living in the same house. Of course, with Jake and that Camille person still staying at his cabin, Garrett might be getting tired of houseguests.

So he'd stay in a hotel. Except then he wouldn't be very close to Mary Jane if something did go wrong. Damn. There had to be a solution that wouldn't make her feel crowded. He'd come up with something. A motor home. He could rent one and park it...somewhere. At the back of the property, maybe.

Living close by and not getting physically involved with her again would be tough, but he loved her too much to stay away at this critical time of her pregnancy. Once the baby was born, once she could think clearly about her future, he'd be able to let her go, if that was what she wanted. And maybe, if heaven smiled on him, she wouldn't want him to leave.

By the time the plane touched down he'd decided a motor home parked some distance from the main house would be his best bet. But first he had to make sure that Mary Jane was okay.

He was out of his seat the minute the plane taxied into its berth. Pushing his way to the front of the plane, he mumbled apologies while he continued to bull his way forward. Once in the jetway he started running and didn't stop until he was in a cab. He gave the driver the address and told him to step on it.

Dawn was still a good hour away when the cab turned onto the road leading to the Slattery place. Morgan's stomach was in knots, and his pulse raced. If she wasn't there he'd take the truck and head straight for Maitland Maternity. Thank God he had such faith in that clinic. As long as she got herself there, she'd be fine.

Then he heard the siren.

The cab pulled over to let the vehicle sail by.

When Morgan saw it was an ambulance and not a police car, he nearly had a heart attack. "Get going!" he yelled to the driver. "Follow that ambulance!"

Oh, God. This was too much like another night filled with the wail of an ambulance siren. Cold sweat ran down his backbone as he struggled for breath. Mary Jane had to be all right. She had to be.

He had a moment of confusion when the ambulance passed the Slattery place and turned in at Garrett's. Mary Jane must have gone over there to get a ride, he thought. Garrett had decided to call an ambulance instead. Good man.

When the cab stopped, he leaped out and charged toward the front door, which the ambulance crew had left open on their way in. He nearly collided with Mary Jane coming out.

He grabbed her. "What the hell are you doing out here? The paramedics went inside looking for you!" Scooping her up, he started toward the house.

"They're not here for me!" She squirmed in his grip. "Garrett called them for Camille, the lady Jake brought here! She's in labor! Abby's on her way, too."

"The ambulance is for Camille?" He stared at her. "Not you?"

"No. I came over to stay with Camille until the ambulance arrived. Oh, Morgan." She wrapped her arms around his neck. "I didn't mean to scare you like that. I had no idea Camille would go into labor tonight, and it was your bad luck that you showed up right along with the ambulance."

He shook his head, still not understanding. "As long as the ambulance is here, you might as well ride in it to Maitland."

"I don't need to go to Maitland. I'm fine. The baby's fine. I'm just heartsick. I need you here with me, Morgan."

"But...you said you felt strange. Not good."

"I sort of exaggerated." She searched his expression, her gaze worried. "I didn't think this would happen. I thought you'd come straight to the house and find out I was fine and..."

"You made that stuff up about feeling bad?" He could hardly believe it. "Mary Jane, you took ten years off my life!"

"I didn't mean to. And I was telling the truth, in a way." She regarded him earnestly. "I've felt horrible without you, Morgan. For all I know that *does* affect the baby."

"You made up a story just to get me down here." He was still having trouble assimilating the information.

"I knew the only way you'd come to Austin was if you thought something might be wrong with the baby." She stroked his cheek, as if to soothe his agitation.

He took a shaky breath and looked into her eyes. "Wrong. I didn't come because I was worried about the baby. I came because I was frantic about you. I've spent hours in absolute panic, afraid something might happen to you before I could get here."

"I'm sorry." She looked miserable. "I should have been up-front with you. I should have just said, 'Morgan, I love you desperately, madly, passionately, and I can't go on without you. Please come home.'"

He gulped. Words like that had the power to wipe out all traces of anger from his system. "Are you sure?"

"That I should have been honest? Yes. You didn't need another scare like that in the middle of the night. It was irresponsible of me, and I—"

"I mean, are you sure about loving me desperately, madly and passionately?"

She gazed at him, eyes shining. "Oh, yes."

His heart lurched, but he told himself to be cautious. "It could be the effect of being pregnant with my baby, you know."

"I really don't think so." Her expression was serenely happy. "But if you're worried about it, feel free to keep me barefoot and pregnant. Our house has lots of room for a passel of kids. Oh, and speaking of being barefoot, did I ever tell you how much I enjoyed having my toes sucked? And another thing. I love being called pet names. You can call me honey, or sweetheart, or honey bunch. I especially like honey bunch."

He was aware that he was fast losing control of the situation. Visions of carrying her to the house and making love to her had replaced all thoughts of motor homes and abstinence.

"See, I knew I had to tell you these things face-to-face. I could never have communicated this very well over the telephone."

His vocal cords didn't seem fully functional. "What...what exactly are you trying to communicate?"

"I'm proposing to you, Morgan. And if you're as smart as I think you are, you'll accept."

He could barely breathe. Heaven was within reach, but he was afraid to grasp it. "I'll weigh you down," he said. "I love you too much to—"

She slapped a hand over his mouth. "Let's rethink that statement, shall we? The way it needs to go is, 'I love you so much.' That's it. No embellishments. Ready to try again?"

He nodded.

Slowly she removed her hand.

"I love you so much, but I'm—"

Her hand came over his mouth again. "Do you love me?" She lifted her hand to allow a response.

"Yes, but—"

She covered his mouth again. "Spare me the embellishments. I may have to give up on getting the right words out of you. Let's try this. Next time I turn you loose I want you to kiss me." She slid her hand away.

He opened his mouth to tell her that he wasn't right for her, but before he could say a word, she pulled his head down and kissed him in a way that made him forget every word he'd ever learned. All that mattered was holding this woman in his arms forever.

When she finally came up for air, he knew he'd lost the fight to do the decent thing.

"So what's my answer?" she whispered, her voice husky with passion. "Will you give me your hand in marriage?"

Flooded with more happiness than he'd ever thought possible, he gazed at her. "My hand, my heart, my soul."

She outlined his mouth with the tip of her finger. "Can I assume that all your other parts come with that deal?"

"You bet."

"Good. I think the paramedics have this situation under control. Let's go next door and try out some of those other parts." She glanced over his shoulder. "Your cab is still waiting. I'll bet the meter's running, too."

He laughed happily as he carried her to the waiting cab. "I'll bet it is. You're going to cost me a fortune, Mary Jane."

"I know that. At first it worried me, but then I realized that I'm worth it."

He smiled at her. "You certainly are, honey bunch. You most certainly are."

MAITLAND MATERNITY
continues with
GUARDING CAMILLE
by Judy Christenberry

Jake Maitland, FBI agent and black sheep of the Maitland family, was home. Only he didn't come alone—beautiful Camille Eckart, her infant son, Jamie, and a whole lot of trouble followed him. Camille's mobster ex-husband was on their tail, and Jake promised to protect mother and son with his life. Only he never expected to give up his heart, too....

Available in June
Here's a preview!

after they let themselves into the room, someone knocked on

CHAPTER ONE

JAKE TURNED off the highway onto Garrett's ranch, keeping his gaze on his rearview mirror. No cars were in sight, but he wouldn't be safe until he was away from the road.

And the dust had settled.

The dirt road on Garrett's ranch left a plume of dust in the air that would tell anyone where he'd driven.

The long driveway topped a hill, then descended into a valley that had numerous trees. He began to breathe a little easier. Okay, so he hadn't been followed. He wasn't endangering Camille and Jamie.

It was time to face what he'd been trying to avoid all day. Thinking about his departure that morning. Thinking about being alone with Camille.

Thinking about the kiss.

He must have been out of his mind.

But she'd been so sweet, so worried. He'd only wanted to reassure her. The kiss hadn't meant anything sexually. It was a comforting kiss, to soothe her.

Liar!

Damn, damn, damn! He wanted her. In his arms, in his bed, in his life.

He couldn't do that. He wasn't meant to have a family. He'd rejected his own relatives, and in everyone's opinion, they were the best. But he'd abandoned them. He had called his mother every Christmas and on her birthday, but that had been his only contact.

Although he had been wondering lately if he'd made a mistake. He'd been so angry about his fiancée's betrayal and his father's attempts to make decisions for him he'd lost control.

But that didn't mean he should mistake sexual hunger for the nesting instinct. He couldn't be that crazy.

But what about Jamie?

He almost drove the new SUV off the road when he jerked the wheel. Where had that thought come from? He was responsible for Jamie's safety. That was all. He was a defenseless baby. Anyone would have like the little guy. And Jake had been there when he was born, and had even handed him to his mother. Jake was a part of Jamie's life—and the baby was a part of his.

Of course he cared about Jamie. Just like he cared about Camille. But caring about the two of them didn't mean anything.

They'd be leaving as soon as Eckart was arrested.

And that meant they'd be leaving—soon.

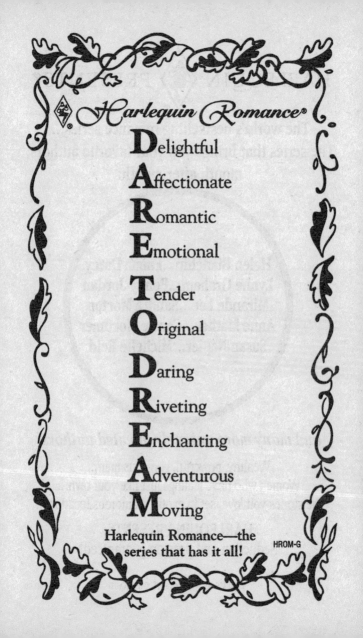

Harlequin Romance®

Delightful

Affectionate

Romantic

Emotional

Tender

Original

Daring

Riveting

Enchanting

Adventurous

Moving

Harlequin Romance—the
series that has it all!

HROM-G

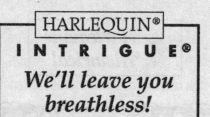

Harlequin® Historical

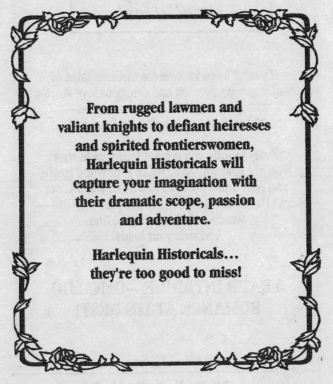

From rugged lawmen and
valiant knights to defiant heiresses
and spirited frontierswomen,
Harlequin Historicals will
capture your imagination with
their dramatic scope, passion
and adventure.

Harlequin Historicals...
they're too good to miss!

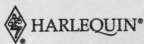

HARLEQUIN®

makes any time special—online...